Drake's Dilemma

A Novel
Barry Deane Stewart

This book is dedicated to everyone who loves history and what it teaches us, especially to those who are willing to challenge the conventional versions of events and to consider new alternatives.

Order this book online at www.trafford.com
or email orders@trafford.com

Most Trafford titles are also available at major online book retailers.

Note for Librarians: A cataloguing record for this book is available from Library and Archives Canada at www.collectionscanada.ca/amicus/index-e.html

Printed in Victoria, BC, Canada.

ISBN: 978-1-4269-1648-9 (sc)

ISBN: 978-1-4269-1649-6 (dj)

Library of Congress Control Number: 2009937558

Our mission is to efficiently provide the world's finest, most comprehensive book publishing service, enabling every author to experience success. To find out how to publish your book, your way, and have it available worldwide, visit us online at www.trafford.com

Trafford rev. 9/08/2010

 www.trafford.com

North America & international
toll-free: 1 888 232 4444 (USA & Canada)
phone: 250 383 6864 ♦ fax: 812 355 4082

Drake's Dilemma

A Novel
Barry Deane Stewart

AUTHOR'S NOTES AND ACKNOWLEDGEMENTS

This is a novel and, as such, is a product of my imagination.

As listed below, I am indebted to many people for their inspiration and assistance in its creation; any errors of fact, language or style, however, are mine alone. To assist the reader, I have generally used modern American spelling, although there are a few obvious places where British and Canadian spelling was required.

I am a collector of antiquarian books and maps related to the exploration of the northern and western reaches of North America and I am an avid reader of that history.

The adventures and exploits of Sir Francis Drake in the time of Queen Elizabeth I, the late 1500s, creates the background for the tale. While I have endeavored to keep faith with the historical record, there are necessarily some simplifications and, critical to the tale, some new, imagined events. I would suggest that historians just relax and go with the story; it will be more fun if you avoid debating details.

The *Secret Voyage of Sir Francis Drake*, written by Samuel Bawlf early this century, makes a compelling case for Francis Drake having sailed to the northern waters of the Pacific coast of America during his around-the-world journey of 1577 – 1580. This conclusion is still disputed by many scholars. The inspiration for this story was simply the thought, "What if Sir Francis Drake did leave behind a document that verified the voyage?"

I have examined dozens of books about Drake and Elizabethan times. As might be expected after four hundred years, there are many contradictory versions, I have relied on John Sugden's biography *Sir Francis Drake* as my primary guide for historical events and timelines. As well, the Hans Kraus publication *Sir Francis Drake: A Pictorial Biography* was an invaluable reference. I am also fortunate to have copies of many of the publications and maps referred to in the book in my own collection.

The main storyline occurs in modern times, in the world of antiquarian book collecting. Again, I ask the experts to accept my generalities and slight adjustments to the descriptions and timing of events such as book fairs.

There are many outstanding dealers in antiquarian books who have guided my learning and the assimilation of my collection over the past few years. They certainly include Cameron Treleaven, Bjarne Tokerud, Bob Gaba, Eric Waschke, Donald Heald, Mike Riley, Sam Hessel, Helen Kahn, Courtland Benson (bookbinder extraordinaire), and many others. I hope they do not spend too much energy trying to identify themselves in the story; all of the characters are imaginary. I know this advice will be hard for them to follow!

My wife Pat was the encouraging, driving force that gave me the courage to try my hand at writing fiction. She also has been the invaluable primary editor and advisor during my early drafts. I thank her so very much.

Many family members and friends have also provided editorial comments, storyline advice, and encouragement. I thank them all, and in particular, my grown children Deron, Deane and Heather.

I have inserted a chronology and a couple of maps in the front of the book which should help the reader follow the many adventures and exploits of Sir Francis Drake, perhaps the greatest seaman, explorer, military leader and pirate of all time; he was certainly a one-of-a-kind combination of all of those dimensions.

Enjoy.

Barry Stewart

Drake's Dilemma

(What really happened in 1579?)

Contents

CHRONOLOGY OF SIR FRANCIS DRAKE'S LIFE AND ADVENTURES

1543	Born
1555	Apprenticed as a seaman
1566 – 67	1st Caribbean Voyage); slaves; rebuffed by Spanish
1567 – 69	2nd Caribbean Voyage); slaves; Spanish treachery
1569	Marries Mary Newman
1570	1st Caribbean Raids; limited success
1571	2nd Caribbean Raids; some treasure
1573	3rd Caribbean Raids; success; sees Pacific
1573 – 75	Leaves England; Irish raids; Plans Pacific Voyage
1576	Permission from Queen Elizabeth for Pacific Voyage
1577 – 80	Voyage around the World; huge Spanish treasure
1581	Knighted by Queen Elizabeth
1581 – 85	Retires to Plymouth (Mayor, MP, business success)
	Mary dies (1583); marries Elizabeth Sydenham(1585)
	Publication of Pacific Voyage forbidden by Queen
1585 – 86	Caribbean Raids (25 ships, 2000 men); failure
1587	Attack Spain); great treasure; delays the Armada
1588	Defeats Spanish Armada
1589	Attack Spain and Portugal; huge fleet, failure
1589 – 95	Plymouth (MP, magistrate, large investments.)
	Writes Sir Francis Drake Revived re 1573 Voyage; presents to Queen in 1592
	Writes The World Encompassed re 1577 – 80 Voyage; keeps it hidden
1595 – 96	Voyage to Caribbean; repelled by Spanish
1596	Dies at sea in Caribbean
1628	Nephew publishes The World Encompassed
1698	Fire destroys all of Drake's journals and charts

Drake's Voyage Around the World: 1577 – 1580

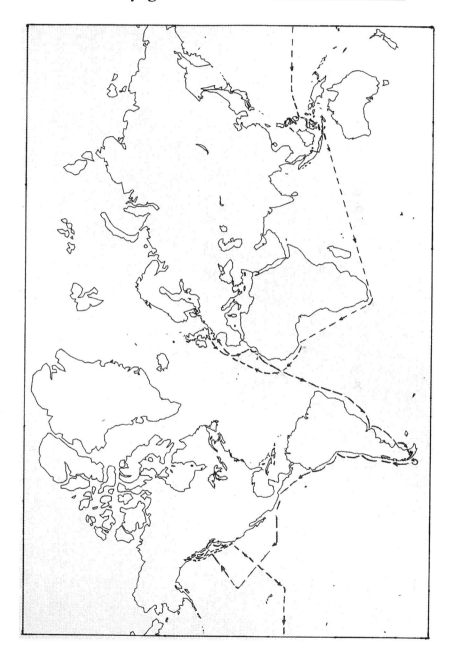

Drake's Voyage: Coast of North America, April – August, 1579

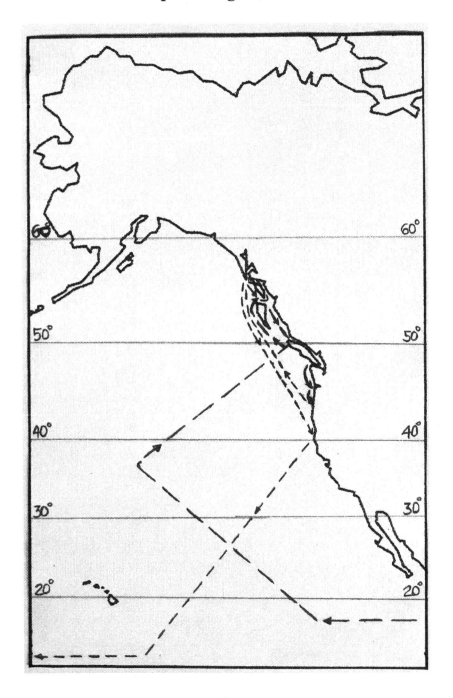

PROLOGUE

(TWO YEARS AGO)

PROLOGUE

It was election night. He was seated at his desk in his small home library watching the televised returns as they were being reported, although there really wasn't much suspense.

President Harris and Vice-President Cartwright were winning by a significant margin, a dramatic contrast from all of the elections over the past two decades, including their first victory four years earlier. He was pleased with this as he believed they were both good people. He raised his glass of wine to them in a silent toast of congratulations.

As the election details continued to come forward he turned his attention to the ledger that was open on his desk, as he often did when he was alone. The numbers never seemed to change very much – he had a decent income, the equity in his home and some modest financial investments. This allowed him to live quite comfortably now and would probably permit him to maintain a similar style in retirement. However, they would certainly not allow him to retire to the better lifestyle of his dreams, in some ocean-side home where he could watch the ocean in the morning mist, walk the beaches in the afternoon sun, and enjoy the evenings at home or in some local pub as the sun set over the horizon. No, the reality of his actual net worth after the overhanging lines of credit that backed his investments left him well short of that possibility. The conclusion was always the same. He needed at least another million, actually more.

As he tuned out the repetitive television coverage, he started to digest the recent newspapers and newsmagazines that cluttered his space. He loved to read them, all the way from the headline stories to the small items of trivial interest.

He picked up the *Economist*, the British weekly with so much in-depth reporting of world news. The cover story showed a photo of President Harris and Vice President Cartwright in the typical political pose with uplifted arms and wide smiles that was taken at their party convention the past summer. The cover banner read, "American Consensus at Last."

After browsing through the background articles that described the history of the American leaders and their remarkable rise to power, he glanced through the rest of the magazine. A minor article near the back caught his eye and, initially, caused him to smile in amusement. Apparently some would-be robbers had attempted to tunnel into the Tower of London from the basement of a shop outside the walls, hoping to steal valuable treasures that were stored there, even, perhaps, some of the Crown Jewels. They had almost pulled the caper off, in spite of all the security and technology that guarded the fortress. Nevertheless, they were apprehended during their escape due to an alert watchman. The Sergeant-of-the-Guard was quoted as saying, "They were an ingenious lot, but in the end we rounded them all up quickly and recovered essentially everything that they took."

He was mulling over that story when the television image changed to show Vice President Cartwright as he was about to start his victory address to his supporters and the nation. The President would follow with his own speech in about half an hour.

The image of the Vice President and the details of the article he had just read came together in his mind in some mysterious juxtaposition that brought a wry smile to his face.

"Maybe there is a way to the beach," he said as he poured himself another glass of wine.

BOOK ONE

LONDON, 1576

The Determined Avenger

1

"Lord Walsingham, I must meet with the Queen.

"The voyage I propose and the devastating impact it will have on the Spanish will most assuredly bring glory to England and riches to those who invest in it. I can organize it, secure the financial support, and lead it, but I must have her blessing. Otherwise, I will just be a common pirate and will not be able to peacefully benefit from the treasure we will secure. It would just be confiscated and I could be jailed upon my return. I don't propose to undertake this huge challenge and end up in exile or worse."

"Captain Drake, be assured that I have briefed the Queen thoroughly and that she does support your voyage, but she can not say so publicly in her court or even in writing, since any disclosure of that would surely enrage the Spanish and could lead to war and their invasion of England. She must be cautious."

"I know that, My Lord, but I must have her personal assurance that I will not be prosecuted upon my return to England."

"Fair enough; I will arrange a meeting but it will need to be very circumspect. And remember, my dear Captain, do not put anything in writing – not about our meetings and plans and certainly not about the intention to attack the Spanish. These are troubled times, and it could very well be that the Spanish supporters will overcome our beloved Queen and attempt to return England to a papist Catholic realm. If that happens, any documents about our undertaking could lead to our torture and death. Tread carefully!"

"I realize that, My Lord. Before I leave you, let us summarize the proposal one more time.

"I will build a flagship and will organize a fleet of four or five other ships for a voyage to the far side of America, around the bottom of South America via the Strait of Magellan. The departure of the voyage will be camouflaged as a trading voyage to Africa and the Mediterranean.

My purposes will be to harass the Spanish towns and ships and to seize treasure from them; to conduct a reconnaissance of the coasts and territories of the Americas, especially the northwest coast in search for the outlet of a passage across the north of America; and to return home via that route, if possible. Otherwise, I will continue across the Pacific Ocean and return via the spice islands, the Indian Ocean and around the Cape of Africa."

"That's all?" replied Lord Walsingham with an uncharacteristic smile on his face. "Other than the fact that only three ships have ever navigated the treacherous Strait of Magellan westward, with its strong winds, tides and currents, and no sheltered havens along its steep-sided, mountainous shores; no one has ever managed to sail through it eastward; the Spanish are entrenched all along the western coast of the Americas; and only one ship has ever sailed around the world – Magellan's ill-fated *Victory* that returned with but a few sickly crew members since Magellan and most of the officers and crew died of exposure, starvation, diseases and encounters with hostile natives; other than those things, it should be an easy journey."

"I can do it," replied Francis Drake without hesitation or even a returning smile. "It is my determination and my destiny to avenge the treacherous and murderous deeds of the papist Spanish upon our ships that have tried to peacefully trade with their settlements in the Caribbean and the eastern coasts of America. We will be successful."

"So be it, Captain Drake. I will summon you when I have arranged an audience with Her Majesty."

2

Francis Drake returned to the house he had leased in London for use during his visits to promote the around-the-world journey. He and his wife, Mary, primarily lived in Plymouth, on the south shore of England near the western entrance to the English Channel from the Atlantic Ocean. He had been born in that area and had spent most of his adult life there. He had learned and plied his trade as a seafarer along the coasts of England and the European side of the channel. He was now in his early 30s, having worked the seas since his teens.

Sitting in his living space, he reminisced about how he had reached this point in his life. For him, it had all started ten years earlier, when he made the first of his five voyages to the Caribbean shores.

That first voyage had been with Captain John Lovell in 1566, serving as an officer on one of the three ships in the small fleet. They had first sailed to the African coast where they attacked Portuguese ships carrying merchandise and slaves. They then proceeded to the Spanish Caribbean where they intended to trade those commodities for gold and spices. However, they were rebuffed by the Spanish since King Philip had forbidden trade with the English. A few tenuous encounters permitted them to secure provisions but the journey was a financial failure. It had given him his first taste of sailing the oceans, attacking ships and towns, and dealing with the deceitful Spanish, albeit as a freelancing pirate.

He returned in 1568 with Captain John Hawkins as leader. Again they picked up slaves in Africa and seized Portuguese ships before proceeding to the Caribbean. And again they had difficulty dealing with the Spanish. They attacked a few towns and secured some valuables, both directly and by ransoming the towns back to their inhabitants who had fled into the hinterland when the attacks occurred. The towns were not well defended; no one had ever attacked the Spanish settlements before. However, the voyage turned into disaster when they were driven into the Gulf of Mexico by violent storms and trapped at the Spanish town of San Juan de Ulua. After first agreeing to allow them to peacefully repair and provision their ships, the Spanish fleet turned on them. In all, 500 Englishmen were killed and captured. Drake managed to escape on his small ship, the *Judith*, and, after many months at sea that saw the loss of many crew members due to starvation and disease, he returned to England in early 1569.

"Yes," he said to himself, almost out loud, "that is when I learned of the treachery and cruelty of the Spanish and became determined to avenge the torture and death of my fellow seamen for the rest of my life."

That also led to the first time he had gone to Queen Elizabeth's court, although he did not see the Queen herself. William Cecil, now Lord Burghley, the Lord Treasurer and chief counsel to the Queen, had conducted an enquiry into the disastrous voyage, to determine what had transpired and whether he had abandoned his comrades in his departure, and to satisfy the investors who had lost money on the venture. It was also designed to provide some political response to the Spanish who were protesting to the Queen about the English voyages. Drake was fully exonerated.

Over the ensuing year, as well as getting married, he organized raiding trips back into the Caribbean. In both 1570 and 1571 he had commanded two-ship voyages. The first one was limited in financial success, but it did provide him with valuable lessons in planning, logistics, provisioning and survival. He also learned Spanish, in order to deal with the people he would encounter in the region. Although he was a pirate to the Spanish, he gained some recognition in England as a hero who had "crossed the line" to hassle the Spanish. The "line" was the longitude in the middle of the Atlantic which King Philip of Spain had declared as off-limits to the English traders.

The voyage in 1571 was much more bold and successful. He had captured some small Spanish ships and raided ships in ports along the coasts of South America and the Caribbean such as Santa Marta, Cartagena and Nombre de Dios. He even went inland on the Isthmus of Panama to Venta Cruces. He established that raiding the Spanish was much more profitable than trying to trade with them for merchandise and slaves. Over the next two years other pirate adventurers had followed his example and hassled the Spanish Main.

It was then that he had decided that the big opportunity was to actually attack the Spanish treasure ships which transported the gold, silver and jewels from America to Spain. The Spanish gathered their treasure at Nombre de Dios on the Atlantic Panama coast for periodic flotillas to Spain. The treasure came from the Atlantic South American, Caribbean and Mexican ports, as well as overland across the Isthmus of Panama from the Pacific coast settlements that ranged from Chile to California. These shipments represented a large portion of the annual income for King Philip of Spain.

His voyage of 1573 was the most successful yet in terms of treasure that was seized from the various ports, although they did not encounter the actual treasure ships. It also emphasized the danger of these ventures:

3

Two days later, he met up with Lord Walsingham and was escorted to Windsor Castle, west of London, which had been home to English monarchs for hundreds of years.

As they moved through the castle to the elaborate sitting room where the meeting was to occur, Francis noted that, although there was a lot of staff around, there were few Lords and officials. Walsingham told him that the Queen wanted to meet him in private, but he also said that he could be sure that the visit would be noticed and reported to everyone that mattered in the Queen's court. It was difficult to keep secrets.

After a few minutes the Queen entered the room. Francis Drake immediately dropped to one knee and bowed his head in greeting, "Your Majesty."

"Welcome to Windsor, Captain Drake," she said with a light tone. "Please join me here in the sitting area. Lord Walsingham, how good to see you; I am sure you will leave us to our discussions as I know you are busy with affairs of state."

Somewhat taken aback, Walsingham simply said, "Thank you, Your Majesty," and left the room.

"Well, Captain Drake, do tell me about your last voyage to the Spanish Caribbean."

Drake sat on the chair with a slight tightness in his chest, although that quickly passed. The Queen, some ten years older than him, dressed in an expensive gown, her red hair standing out against the dark colour, projected a regal authority and confidence that somehow also put him at ease.

Although he was anxious to get to the subject of his new proposal, he described the adventure of 1573. Prompted by questions from the Queen, he shared details of the sailing, the attacks on the Spanish, and the hardships for his crew for more than an hour. He made sure that he described his sighting of the Pacific in detail and with enthusiasm.

"That was an amazing undertaking; well done. I am sorry that you were required to disappear from our realm for a few years but the affairs of state and our diplomatic relations with Spain necessitated it. They were naturally upset with your activities and we needed to be able to disavow any involvement as we are not likely to withstand an invasion right now.

Thankfully, with their current problems in the Netherlands and with France, we have established a quiet truce."

"Your Majesty, I recognize that my proposed voyage to the Pacific Ocean side of America will certainly upset the Spanish, but it will also bring great glory to England and will reap great riches."

"Do not mistake me, Captain Drake. I certainly want to cause problems for the Spanish, who have caused me, the English merchants and investors, and England itself, so much difficulty and hardships. I wish you well in your venture.

"However, I can not give you a commission in writing, and can not provide you with one of my ships for your fleet. I must be able to deny knowledge and involvement should you succeed or fail. If you succeed, the Spanish will be outraged and I must keep my diplomatic flexibility. Should you fail in your attacks, I can not have the Spanish discover any documents from me that authorized your voyage. Nevertheless, I will invest one thousand pounds in your venture, certain that you will provide a handsome return for me."

"Thank you. I understand and accept your conditions, Your Majesty. With your assurance that if I do return successfully I will not be jailed as a pirate nor stripped of my portion of the bounty we will have taken, I will proceed."

"Do so, Captain Drake. Be my secret privateer, although a public pirate, at least for now. And do take care how you share this information. Lord Walsingham and the Earl of Leister have my confidence, but beware of Lord Burghley. He fears antagonizing the Spanish to the point that he could seek to jeopardize your mission."

"I will certainly be careful. We will represent the whole voyage as one of trade to Africa and the Mediterranean."

"I know the plan, but it will look strange to see a large fleet, heavily armed and manned with marines as well as sailors head out on a trading mission."

"I will marshal everything at Plymouth. Once we are at sea, there will be no turning back."

"Also, Captain Drake, never forget that there is more to your mission than just attacking the Spanish and seizing their treasure, although I know that your investors will only care about the latter.

"Once you have entered the waters of the Pacific and have carried out your actions all the way to Mexico, you must proceed farther to the north and search out the entrance to the passage across the top of America.

"The discovery of such a northwest passage will give England the ability to access the riches and trade opportunities of the Far East and the Spice Islands without the threats and hostilities from the Spanish and the Portuguese who control the passages around southern America and Africa.

"You know we are searching for the passage from the North Atlantic; Captain Martin Frobisher is attempting such a journey this year. However, many of my advisors believe that it will be easier to discover the passage from the Pacific end. They expect it will start further south and therefore will be more amenable to navigate in the short ice-free season for the discovery of the Atlantic outlet..

"Of course, if you were to discover that there is no eastern entrance or that America is actually joined to Asia along the north that would be invaluable to us. We would avoid the needless large expense of attempting to sail across the Arctic waters from the Atlantic.

"This must be a priority for you, Captain Drake. It must also be your secret, even more than your plan to go to the Pacific at all. The knowledge you obtain could change the future of England."

"I will follow your instructions, Your Majesty."

4

The next year-and-a-half was consumed with the preparations for the voyage.

The construction of the flagship *Pelican*, almost 100 feet in length with a displacement of 100 tons, was the centerpiece of the activities.

There were four other smaller ships, plus four disassembled pinnaces in the holds that could be used for shallow water excursions, approaches to ports and other ships, and even as towboats under oar power in calm or grounding conditions.

A total complement of 168 men and boys was recruited. As well as sailors and marines, it included tradesmen such as carpenters, blacksmiths and barrel makers. It even included musical instruments for entertainment on the long journey.

Provisions for eighteen months were stowed, not an insignificant amount for so many people. That included rice, biscuits, dried meat and fish, oatmeal, honey, salt, and cheese. Beer and wine were necessities.

Tools and building supplies such as spades, axes, buckets, rope and twine, nets and hooks were all loaded. This was in addition to the tradesmen tools and equipment such as a forge. There would be no merchants available for restocking during the long voyage.

They also assembled fabrics, buttons and beads, small tools, and decorative items to be used as gifts and trade items with the natives that they expected to encounter.

Of course, there were arms: muskets, pikes, crossbows and swords, as well as powder, cannonballs and iron pieces for the cannons, along with grenades and incendiary projectiles.

In addition to the ships' crew and officers there were a number of gentlemen and merchants in the contingent, among them a botanist, a naturalist, an artist and a preacher.

On the day before the fleet was scheduled to depart, Francis Drake was in his cabin aboard the *Pelican* looking at his collection of books and documents. Along with the Bible and various psalm books were his collection of navigation manuals, a journal of Magellan's voyage, and some world maps.

He mused that the maps were of little real use for navigation as they were drawn to a scale that showed the whole world on one page. They were also totally inconsistent in their depiction of the coastlines of America and the sea routes across the Pacific, often based on seafaring rumors or just the imagination of the mapmaker. In fact, much of the area he planned to visit was uncharted territory. What had been explored and settled by the Spanish and Portuguese was kept secret by them; it was a treasonable offence to publicly share such information.

"No," he thought, "we will be sailing blind once we enter the Pacific. It will take all of our wits and guile, and some good fortune. May God be with us."

On November 17, 1577 the small fleet of ships sailed out of Plymouth harbor.

Francis Drake was about to change the course of history.

BOOK TWO

SEATTLE, MID-NOVEMBER

The Customer

5

Ray Cartwright was having a good day. The Vice President was in Seattle, his home, after the grueling political rounds of speeches and appearances with candidates across the country. Their party had made notable gains in the recent mid-term elections, a satisfying achievement on top of their successful re-election two years ago. Yes, he was elated that his personal popularity was riding high and it seemed that he could take a bit of a breather before the campaigning started in earnest again next summer. That would lead up to the primary rounds and the fall election in two years, which he was sure would see him become President.

But for now, it was time to relax. For him there was nothing better to divert his mind away from politics than spending time with old books. Here he was at the Seattle Antiquarian Book Fair having a great time.

The book fair was held in a convention display building that was part of the large complex known as Seattle Center. Slightly north of downtown, the area hosted the city's famous Space Needle, an amusement park, the ballet, opera and theater facilities, and some wide open spaces. It was an exciting gathering place for many of Seattle's community and arts activities.

The convention hall itself was rather plain, with moderately high ceilings, bare white walls, and functional fluorescent lighting. About one-third of the total space was cordoned off with ten-foot high, cloth-draped metal frames as the book fair didn't need all of the area and this gave it a modest sense of confinement and coziness.

The space was laid out with four aisles between small display booth areas for each of the one hundred dealers who gathered from far and wide. Each booth was about a dozen feet square, usually lined with bookcases along the sides and back, and often with a glass-encased display case in front. Each dealer had their own specific layout, designed to catch a potential customer's attention.

Ray's routine had changed over the years since he became Vice President. In the old days he would wander through the fair over two days, browsing through the many booths and chatting to all of the vendors, whether they were the small local dealers who came every year or the representatives of some of the big dealers from New York.

He loved watching the dynamics between the dealers as much as savoring the books. As one of the local dealers, Murray Richards, liked to say, "We all have our roles. There is a hierarchy. The big dogs come out here to feed on us little guys and then move on to resell the books at much higher prices at the big international fairs or to their network of affluent collectors. This works out just fine for us too; we accumulate books from our local and regional sources over the year and get to sell a lot of books at a good profit without all of the high costs and elaborate systems that they need to survive in that high-flying world."

Now, with all of the security issues associated with being Vice President, he couldn't just wander through the crowded aisles of the convention center during the fair – his secret service guardians would never allow that. He smiled every time he noticed that they used the code name "Shakespeare" for him, reflecting his love of books.

Instead he was able to get special access in the morning on the opening day of the fair when the dealers were still in the final stages of their set-up before the early afternoon opening to the public. In fact, most of them had laid out their booths the evening before or very early in the morning. Their highest priority in the few hours before the doors opened to the public was to scout out all of the other dealers and look for opportunities to get a bargain. Everyone's mantra was the same, "Nobody can know everything about all of the different genres of books and so there must be books out there that are priced too low. The secret is to find them first."

As the Vice President wandered along the relatively quiet aisles, he naturally attracted a lot of attention and many glances if not stares from everyone there. He stopped to chat along the way. He knew many of the dealers by name as he had dealt with them over the years and they knew him. He could easily say, "Hi, Alan," "Hello, Herb," or "How are you, Jeremy" and get a relaxed reply from those that knew him although now it was always something like "Fine, Mr. Vice President," rather than the old day's response of "Hi, Ray."

He loved to start a conversation with the dealers, especially the ones that didn't know him as well, with "What's new?" This always caused them to hesitate. In the normal world such a greeting would elicit comments about their lives, their businesses, the weather, politics, whatever. In the book world such a question invariably led to a direct response about what new books were in their inventory.

He spent a couple of hours at the fair, making a few purchases. From Alan Page he obtained a bound report by a Hudson's Bay trader working out of Fort Victoria in the mid-1800s that described early dealings with native tribes in the Puget Sound area. It only cost $200. From Herb Trawets he bought an original publication of a Spanish explorer who had been one of the first to define the details of the upper Oregon coast in the late 1700s. He wasn't famous and this was after the initial grand discoveries of people like James Cook and George Vancouver. It cost $350. From Jeremy Boucher he secured a pristine copy of a publication by an early explorer who had followed after Lewis and Clark in the 1820s and who had more fully defined many of the tributaries that fed into the Columbia River. It cost $800 due to its fine condition and general collector demand for anything related to early American adventures. In the grand scheme of his collection of books related to the discovery and development of the northwest regions of America these were minor purchases, but they filled in gaps.

Pricing was always an issue for him now. Unlike the past, it now seemed unbecoming to haggle with dealers, even in a friendly bantering way. Thus he just avoided books that he felt were noticeably overpriced, even if he wanted them, although he might follow up with general enquiries later on. The dealers that he knew and did business with on a more regular basis generally gave him a standard "dealer-serious collector" discount of ten to twenty percent depending on the price level of the book. Today's books just qualified for ten percent, which tended to offset the sales tax.

That evening, at his personal home in the hills surrounding Seattle, he settled into his wood-paneled library and perused his extensive collection. He cherished his books and kept them here rather than in his official residence in Washington. He considered this to be a private dimension of his life that provided him with some relief from the hectic pace and fishbowl existence of politics. Although people generally knew that he collected books, it had not become a point of much interest or attention by others, including the press. He liked that and did nothing to change it.

He had the evening to himself. His wife was taking a side trip back to Denver to visit their son and his wife and their new grandson before meeting him back in Washington. He had stayed on here in Seattle to work a few local connections over the next couple of days as he contemplated the fund-raising necessity of his run for the Presidency. Although he was now personally very wealthy, it was politically unseemly to finance a campaign yourself. You needed to demonstrate outside support.

As he spent that quiet evening he couldn't help but reflect back on how he had arrived at this point in his life. "It has been a great ride," he mused to himself.

It had all started fifty years ago in Denver where he was born, grew up to finish high school, met his future wife and attended the engineering school at the fabled Colorado School of Mines on its western outskirts in Golden, Colorado, "Where the West Lives." All of his early life was within sight of the Rocky Mountains and easy access to the hiking and skiing that he came to love.

He studied engineering and geophysics at CSM, graduating top in his class, which gave him many choices for employment. He joined the Colorado Oklahoma Louisiana Texas Oil Company, or COLT Oil as it was then labeled, complete with a bucking bronco logo that reminded him of his favorite home town team the Denver Broncos. He never did quite get used to cheering for the CSM Orediggers.

COLT Oil was a large regional company that specialized in finding and developing new oil fields in established producing areas by applying advanced technological methods, primary among them being sophisticated geophysical seismic programs that became a specialty of Ray's.

As he grew in experience and maturity over the next few years, working first in New Orleans and then in Houston, he came to realize that, although the technical specialists provided the core skills for the company's activities, the business development specialists who identified acquisition and merger opportunities for the company, and who negotiated the financial and legal arrangements, were the real movers and shakers and, more importantly, the ones who earned the big bonuses. Therefore, after four years of engineering employment he headed back to school, this time to Harvard Law School. Again he excelled at the studies and, as an aside that he didn't fully appreciate at the time, made many personal contacts that would surface in his political life two decades later.

Again he was faced with many employment opportunities when he graduated. Not being interested in criminal law and unwilling to start at the bottom in one of the large corporate law firms, or factories, as the lawyers liked to call them, he decided that he wanted to join a large commercial company. Although COLT Oil wanted him to return, he decided to join a true technology company by hiring on with Systems Inc. in Seattle. Their name was simple but their business was complex as they identified and introduced advanced new technologies to industries and the internet.

He found the west coast in general and Seattle in particular to be extremely stimulating. It seemed that everyone he met had new ideas and unbounded energy and enthusiasm for pursuing them. What they didn't usually have was the money necessary to pursue these ideas or the business discipline to take them forward into the real world. That's where Systems Inc. came in with all of the financing, planning and marketing skills to make it happen. Ray fit right in with his technology background, operating experience and newly gained legal training. He quickly became a star employee and steadily rose up the corporate ranks.

Those years were good ones for Ray. He and his wife, Anne, settled into the twenty-something group in a new residential community, complete with an active district recreation center, where over time they became involved in community affairs and social issues. They started their family there, first with a son, Christopher, and then a daughter, Carolyn, two years later.

Everything progressed smoothly along this path for more than six years. Ray was earning a good salary, receiving very good annual bonuses, and was assuming more and more responsibility in the firm. However, something started to both bother him and intrigue him.

Over the years he would see many creative young people who would come to Systems Inc. for support and who would receive significant up-front payments for their ideas, would be paid handsomely for working on them in the company and would also receive some residual royalty or profit sharing in the final product. This all seemed fair; the young inventors could often end up with a million dollars. The company made many times that amount in profit on the idea, let alone on the inevitable follow-up enhancements, spin-offs and integration with other systems. Of course, that only applied to the successful projects; in effect the company was just averaging out individual project risks.

It wasn't that the young inventors were being cheated; it was more that they had limited leverage to extract more value from their ideas when they had few alternatives for proceeding. For every billionaire that the public heard about over the years who was involved with new enterprises such as Microsoft, Cisco, Dell or Google, there were hundreds of people who sold their ideas for much less to those companies and others like Systems Inc.

Ray knew that, in spite of his exceptional technical and business skills, he wasn't an inventor. Those people were just wired differently he decided; they could see things that no one else could. However, he also came to believe that if he could find a few independent inventors and work with them directly, using his talents and his saved funds, they could all do much better. In other words, he could become a personal version of Systems Inc.

Of course he couldn't do that while he worked at Systems Inc.; that would be an enormous conflict of interest. But, to launch out on his own entailed a big risk. What if the systems he chose didn't work? The big companies had the security in numbers; the successes paid for the failures. He wouldn't be able to stand many failures.

He and Anne talked out the concept many times over a year or more. Life was good and secure. The kids were growing and would be off to university and their own lives within a decade. "Why take such a risk?" they asked themselves over and over again, although the idea would just not go away. Deep down they trusted Ray's instincts and his ability to be successful; they just needed a catalyst to get them started.

Then, one day it happened. An independent systems programmer named Brian Butler approached Systems Inc. for support. He proposed that they develop a large program that would enable investors to track and manage their portfolios directly and quickly. They would have immediate internet access to market information, research reports, and current news. They could generate performance reports and get comparisons to other benchmark portfolios. They could generate charts and tables. They could run out long-term projections and test them for various sensitivities. It would even generate their income tax returns.

The Review Committee at Systems Inc. looked at the proposal and turned it down almost immediately. It was a bad idea, they said: "It is just an accounting program." "Most financial institutions already have programs like that." "Most serious investors get that type of information from their advisors now." "There is no real value added." "There is no competitive advantage." "There is no upside."

As they left the Review Committee meeting, Ray walked along the corridor to the elevator with Brian Butler. "Sorry, Brian," he said.

Brian turned to him and looked him straight in the eye. "You just don't get it," he said, quietly but determinedly. "Of course those comments were true. But this system would replace all of those other ones. All the big financial and investment firms would convert to this. It would become the standard for everyone, big and small. They would not need to spend their millions every year on developing and maintaining their own programs; they could concentrate on their real purpose of making investments and advising customers based on the information. No one would be information-limited. Everyone would win."

"Do you really believe that all of those big firms with their proprietary programs and data bases, maintained by their large in-house staffs of experts and analysts, would convert to a common system?" asked Ray.

"Yes, because it will be a better system and they will make more money," replied Brian.

Then the elevator came and Brian was gone. Ray walked back to his office ready to move on to the next project but the image of Brian's confident determination would not go away. "Now what?" he pondered.

That evening he told Anne about the experience. "Although it's irrational, I just believe what he said," concluded Ray.

"It sure seems like a huge risk," replied Anne. "An accounting system? I always assumed that if you did launch out to do something like this that it would be high technology. How could he possibly break into the world of the major financial institutions?"

"That's the conundrum alright. It doesn't make sense, but…" he trailed off.

Late into the night they discussed it, going around and around the same issues time and again. Finally they reached a consensus, maybe out of exhaustion. As Anne summarized it, "We have always done well by following your instincts. OK, go for it. Of course, you have to do it right."

The next day Ray met with the President of his Division, who was also the chairman of the Review Committee. Ray explained that he had second thoughts about the proposal and believed it was worth pursuing. He suggested that the committee give it another look. However, the President disagreed; he said the issue was closed; the idea was not a fit for Systems Inc.

Then Ray surfaced the idea that he would be willing to support the proposal with his own resources and on his own time, provided that the company would give him a waiver that it was not a conflict of interest. That caused a lot of angst for the company. They did not want to lose such a valuable resource as Ray but they could not see how he could get involved with such an undertaking without compromising his work at Systems Inc. Also, the precedent of such an arrangement would be debilitating if others wanted to do the same type of thing. It was always a fragile relationship between the company and its inventor clients, and these types of off-line arrangements would make it impossible to manage. Ray would need to give up the idea or give up his job.

"Well," Ray murmured to himself as he continued his reminiscences, "as they say, the rest is history. I should write a book about what happened next."

After meeting with Brian a couple more times, Ray left Systems Inc. and joined up with him. He was surprised as to how far Brian had actually progressed with the development of the programs. That was the good news. The bad news was that there was no coherent business plan for developing the markets. Over the next two years they enhanced the programs and they pitched the ideas far and wide to every financial group they could get in to see. They seemed to stimulate a lot of interest and admiration for the system but they just couldn't seem to get any traction for making a deal.

The only truly light moment Ray recalled during this period was when they decided they needed a catchy name for their system. They were at Ray's home bandying about the obvious such as Financial Systems and Analytical Solutions; which they decided had no pizzazz and were boring. Then they played with cuter phrases like MoneyMan, InvesterYou and even Finangle. Finally they started playing with the word ticker, as in stock ticker but also with a connotation of time passing with the ticking of a clock; after all, Time is Money, as the old homily says. Ticker Time, Ticker You, Ticker My Fancy and Ticker Yourself were all tossed about. At that point Anne, who had been listening to all this in a somewhat distracted way, looked up at the wall calendar and seeing the October image said, "Ticker Treat." That was it, they agreed.

Finally a legitimate opportunity surfaced. One of the big investment firms, Douglas, O'Brien, Long, Langcroft and Richardson, known to investors as DOLLAR Financial, was in a bind. As an aside, Ray heard from some insiders that Albert Long was a weak link, but they had needed him to complete the name originally. Although DOLLAR was large, it was being outperformed by the giant firms that had been formed in recent years through various mergers. DOLLAR's systems were becoming obsolete and uncompetitive. They approached Ray and Brian, having heard their proposals earlier, for an exclusive right to their package.

This precipitated a minor crisis. Their whole concept had been to develop a universal system; it couldn't become the exclusive tool of one group. However, they had made little progress after a lot of effort and the payment from DOLLAR would be substantial. How could they say no? But they did.

More importantly, Ray went back to them with a counter-proposal. DOLLAR could use their system for a modest royalty fee if they would give the system visible credit in their dealings with customers. He used the personal computer history as an example. When companies sold their PCs, they labeled them with the decal *Intel Inside*. As a result Intel assumed an identity all of its own, although it never sold anything directly to a consumer. Now, all DOLLAR had to do was include the logo *TickerTreat Generated* on their reports to clients and analysts. DOLLAR agreed; it seemed like a small concession for a big financial saving.

The results were truly amazing. The new system allowed DOLLAR to compete with renewed energy and they were soon growing faster than ever as customers were drawn to their easily accessible analyses and reports.

Then other institutions started to sign on for the service, albeit smaller ones at first, but over a couple of years the growth was huge. As more and more people received their information with *TickerTreat Generated* labels attached, more people started looking for it and then asking for it. The market multiplier effect was fully engaged. Within those few years TickerTreat was becoming the standard for the whole industry; Brian's dream was coming true.

Naturally this growth required them to hire staff, set up offices, undertake much more extensive marketing initiatives, and to develop their own internal systems. Ray led all of those activities while Brian concentrated on leading the technical teams to constantly improve the product. This was critical as there was no other way they were going to fend off any competition that tried to encroach on their market. They never forgot those comments from the Systems Inc. Review Committee years earlier, "It's just an accounting system. There is no value added. There is no competitive advantage." Thus TickerTreat's internal mantra became, "Tick, tick, tick… the clock never stops ticking."

As Ray recalled, the final step in that story was taking the company public. It was a blockbuster happening. Brian and Ray, along with other key employees that had joined them in the early years reaped large payouts for the share they sold out. For the two key players it was over one hundred million dollars. On top of that, the shares they kept had a similar value and would continue to grow with the company.

After all of that, Ray and Anne moved to a larger home in the hills above Seattle with a view of the surrounding mountains and Puget Sound. They continued to be involved in community affairs; in fact they increased their involvement. They became engaged at the city level and then the state level, as they supported interest groups and lobbied politicians to reduce the political rhetoric and to focus on tangible programs to improve the economy and the lives of all its citizens in harmony with the environment.

Then the call came. It was the Governor of Washington State and he wanted a meeting with Ray. The Governor laid it out, straight and clear: Ray was a smart, business savvy, caring individual who had a passion for the community at large and the independence for action that his relatively new-found wealth provided. He should join the political process directly. He should run for the position of Lieutenant Governor in the next election. The Governor and the party would fully back him. This could lead to bigger things in the future.

Ray was taken aback. Approaching the meeting, he had been expecting to be asked for a donation or to participate in some government study or task force on the economy. He asked for time to respond and again he and Anne had a conversation far into the night. This time she was more direct. "Ray, you can do so much good. You have achieved all that you need to in the business world and you know that you will soon get bored with the routine of managing the company. Go for it." He knew she was right about the business dimensions. It was just that he wasn't sure he wanted to live in the never-ending spotlight that always seemed to be on politicians and public figures. Her response was simply, "Ray, you can do whatever you put your mind to and your natural common sense and independence will keep your public exposure in perspective."

Thus, in what seemed like a whirlwind of events, he retired from the company and in the ensuing election became the state Lieutenant Governor. His campaign message had been one of economic prudence balanced with social responsibility, a message that almost every politician starts with. However, his delivery of the message and obvious commitment to the concepts, coupled with his direct challenge to simplistic biases and positions of special interest groups, whether they be conservative fundamentalists or tree-hugging environmentalists, also came across as just being the common sense belief of what's right. He won easily.

A year later, there was another surprise. His national party was in the midst of a major tug-of-war among the various factions and they could not agree on much at all. When the next State of The Union Speech was due from the President of the United States, a member of the other party, they could not agree on who should deliver the rebuttal immediately afterwards. In reality, it was a thankless role, as almost no one paid any attention to the television after the President's speech, which usually lasted more than an hour. Then there would be prolonged commercials to make up for the lost revenue-generating time, followed by the network political commentators, who were anxious to get on with talking about the Presidential messages. So, in a strange set of circumstances, the Lieutenant Governor of Washington State was asked to give the response. Sure, the party was attempting to show a younger image and Washington had become a key electoral state, but it was still unusual. Ray gave the address, basically a simplified version of his campaign message. It was well done and those that did pay attention were impressed by his sincerity and political civility in a setting that was usually seriously partisan. Nevertheless, not much happened for a while after that.

The contest for the Presidential nomination for his Party consumed most of the next year and a half at the national level. The factions were still deeply divided and no one emerged as the immediate consensus candidate. In fact, the decision was not going to be reached before the convention.

The convention organizers charged with organizing the program were well aware that they did not know who the nominee would be. As they slotted in the various events and speeches, they considered who to include as the keynote speakers each evening. Those speakers filled time and gave the delegates in the convention hall something to focus on while all of the private meetings and lobbying efforts occurred. There were usually three or so such speeches each evening and they generally received limited television coverage unless it was a celebrity talking, things were slow, or the commentators had just run out of something to say, an unlikely event. Based on his performance in the State of the Union response, and the fact that he was not likely to offend any faction too much, Ray was asked to give one of the speeches.

His speech was on the second night of the convention, the day before the balloting would begin for the Presidential nomination. The outcome was still up in the air and so there was more than the usual activity in the hall and an extra-large television audience tuned in. The timing of Ray's speech was in the midst of prime time. Many people were milling and chatting on the convention floor. As his speech began the television coverage tuned it in, expecting to give it token early coverage before returning to their analysts.

After the briefest of introductory remarks, Ray launched into his message:

"Tonight we are a party divided while a nation waits for us to show leadership. If we can not agree with each other, how can we ever get the half of the population that doesn't vote for us to join in our cause? Is it our destiny to seek office by ensuring that our supporters outnumber the others by a tiny margin?

"Where is it written that we are the good guys and the other party has the bad guys? .... We must earn that distinction.

"Where is it written that the nation be divided into two equal segments that can not agree on anything? .... We have always had differences but this nation was built on the goodwill to find compromises and solutions.

"Where is it written that conservatives are right and liberals are wrong? .... We must focus our debates on specific issues not generalities.

"Where is it written that fiscal responsibility must entail social neglect? .... We must do better than that.

"Where is it written that we must choose between free trade with the world community of nations and subsidized protection of our economy? .... We must move forward to be productive and competitive, not isolated and regressive.

"Where is it written that special interests should get their special attention rather than doing what is right for our nation as a whole? .... We must recognize that everyone is part of a special group – corn growers, fishermen, forestry workers, ranchers, miners, factory workers, teachers, nurses, retirees, industrialists, environmentalists, the poor, the rich... everyone. Our decisions must be taken for the long-term national good, not just to cover over problems with short-term bandages .... Otherwise we end up as a crippled nation with too many wounds to heal.

"Those things are certainly not written in the constitution. They are not found in scripture. They are not carved into some tablet of stone. And certainly they are not written in the hearts of our citizens.

"Our nation calls out for leadership and responsible actions. The people of this nation know what is right and wrong. Why don't we politicians? Why can't this party be the one to rise above the divisive partisan bickering and deliver some real honest messages and policies? Hard truths are still truths; the people of this nation are not fooled by sugar-coated messages or half-truths, but we force them to decipher the real situations and our real intentions from the garbled messages that both parties send out as we overly simplify the problems and polarize the options.

"We can do better….We must do better….Our nation demands that we do better."

It was a special moment. The delegates in the hall had stopped talking and listened to the message. The television focus did not move on. One of the shortest speeches ever given at a political convention had caught everyone's attention. The hall broke out in thunderous applause; after all, most delegates were just representative people from their home states, not politicians, and they believed the message.

The next day, the convention got down to its real business. After the requisite elaborate nomination speeches and amid the sonorous tones of each state's spokesperson as they ceremoniously announced their votes: "The Great State of ----, home of the largest----, the best---, and the brightest ----, proudly casts its votes as follows: --- votes for candidate A, --- votes for candidate B and --- votes for candidate C," (Just fill in the blanks) a decision did emerge. Stanley Harris, the relatively moderate senior senator from Ohio, would be their nominee.

Then there was the issue of choosing a Vice Presidential candidate. Because the outcome was so uncertain right to the end, Harris had not announced, or even chosen, a running mate beforehand. He caucused with his key advisers immediately after the vote was confirmed and they considered their options. One choice was to choose the losing candidate or a politician closely tied to him in an attempt to heal the wounds of the campaign and to present a more united front in the fall election. This might have made sense politically, but the campaign had been so bitterly fought that no one had the stomach for it.

There were a number of candidates who were very similar to Senator Harris in their political positions, but none of them had any exceptional stature nor would they provide any diversity for the ticket.

Then someone brought up Ray Cartwright's name. After a moment of quiet uncertainty, someone else rhymed off his attributes – engineer, lawyer, successful businessman, a relatively new politician with no baggage and some newly minted celebrity based on his speech. He was from Colorado, had worked in Louisiana and Texas, went to law school at an establishment northeast school, and now was firmly associated with the west coast. He covered all the right bases and the party could surely benefit from a fresh face to offer the electorate.

Ray was somewhat perplexed when he received a call to come up to the Harris suite in the convention hotel and absolutely flabbergasted when he heard the offer. He still shakes his head at the memory of it all.

On they went to campaign across the nation and to win a narrow victory in November.

"That was six years ago," Ray thought. "How my life has changed!"

6

Alan Page sat at the small desk in his hotel room down the street from the convention center where the Seattle Book Fair was being held, taking stock of his day. It had been reasonably productive. He had sold ten books, bought four from other dealers, and had made contact with a number of collectors who were new to him.

For him, this latter dimension was the most important in many ways. Getting to know people who were serious collectors and finding out what they were interested in was the core reason he attended book fairs. They became his future customers and suppliers; people were always turning over their collections as better copies became available, or they had more money, or their priorities changed.

Alan knew that many of the other dealers considered him to be just a glorified book scout. Alan didn't mind that; he even agreed with it, but he considered himself to be the Eagle Scout in the business.

Book scouts historically have been the lowest level of the business. Their image is one of tediously visiting used book stores, which typically buy books from individuals for ten cents on the dollar of original retail price and resell them for fifty cents on the dollar. Almost every community in the country has such stores. The scout's mission in life is to find missed gems of books, usually first editions of early books by authors who later became famous or older books that have some newly determined collecting value. Their hope is to find books that they can buy for less than five dollars and sell to an established bookseller for twenty dollars or more, knowing they will resell them to collectors for at least twice that.

The appeal for a traditional book scout is that he does not have to carry any inventory, he does not need to borrow or tie up any capital, and he generates a quick turnover. Of course, the downside is that he does not make very much money.

Alan was a book scout only in spirit. He dealt in expensive books. He did accumulate a limited book inventory, but only in his specialty area of historical world explorers. There, he could be an expert in a book's value. He only purchased items that he knew had real market appeal and that would sell relatively quickly. At any time he might have a few hundred books in hand, not the many thousands of a typical dealer, and thus he only needed to finance hundreds of thousands of dollars, not millions. It was a business where total sales values could be very large but where profit margins could be small, especially if a dealer ended up with a costly inventory that was stagnant.

His main avenue of profit was in cultivating a vast network of book collectors and book sellers and in getting to know what was available and who might want it. In this way, when a book appeared in a seller's inventory for the first time, Alan would often be in a position to approach a potential buyer and secure a resale even before he bought it in the first place. He had to be nimble to make this work, meaning he had to be in constant contact with everyone to keep current.

He made a decent living doing this type of business but it was always a fragile existence. Making a significant margin on the buy-and-sell activities was becoming more difficult. In times past he might clear as much as fifty percent on a sale; now he was lucky to get twenty-five percent, often less. The reason was that everyone seemed to be plugged into the internet listings of books on sites such as bookfinder.com. There everyone could see what was being offered.

The price listings on the web sites for a given book title would usually vary greatly, generally reflecting the condition and rarity of a specific edition, but often reflecting the degree of optimism or greed of the seller. A book's condition was always described, but, in spite of the industry's attempt to establish standards for describing this critical factor, it was always subjective and often suspect. Similarly a book's completeness was sometimes not fully disclosed – major missing illustrations or maps would be obvious but details like front half titles or secondary appendices might not be. All of these things greatly impacted the value of books for collectors.

As is human nature when establishing a price, sellers tended to focus on the highest priced offerings and buyers looked at lower offers that seemed to be linked to good copies. They also expected a discount for being a serious collector and long term customer. This wealth of easily accessible information made Alan's job more difficult and definitely squeezed his margins.

Alan managed this by keeping his overhead low, using his home in Phoenix as his base and doing most of his paperwork himself. Travel was his biggest cost as he constantly visited dealers, private collectors and book fairs across North America and Europe. His focus on world explorers from the sixteenth to nineteenth century meant that a lot of his activity took place in Europe, especially the sourcing of books for resale in America.

He didn't mind the traveling life; in fact he had been a loner and a drifter of sorts all his life. However, there were days when he contemplated the time when he could retire from the rat race and maybe just dabble part-time. Sixty wasn't that far into the future.

He had grown up in Chicago, but in his early twenties he tired of the inner city life and the terrible winter weather and headed out to follow the old Route 66 south. He ended up in the open spaces of Arizona. Being a salesman by nature, some would say a wheeler-dealer, he found work in various lines, moving up from furniture to household electronics to automobiles. Within a few years he was doing fairly well selling upscale import cars at the Phoenix Porsche dealer.

His experience there expanded his personal horizons. He observed how business could be conducted on a international scale and he lost any inhibitions about thinking and working outside the American boundaries. He also encountered customers who were rich and who would willingly spend a hundred thousand dollars on a car. He saw that, although they were quite willing to spend such large sums of money, they always demanded quality and value for it. He just needed to figure out how to apply all that knowledge to a business of his own.

A reality of many businesses in Phoenix is that they are very seasonal. From June to September the temperatures are unreasonably hot, the snowbirds from the northern states who come down to escape winter and enjoy the sun have gone back for the summer and the permanent residents are hibernating in their air conditioned homes, offices and clubs or they have fled to the high country of Sedona and Flagstaff or the northern lakes and woods of their earlier lives. In any case, sales drop to miniscule levels in the summer and sales staff have lots of time on their hands.

Alan had always been a reader, perhaps because he was a loner or perhaps it was the other way around. In any case, in the slow times he found himself wandering into bookstores, browsing the various racks, and picking up whatever books caught his fancy. At first he frequented the regular used book stores that generally recycled recent paperbacks and best sellers but that also always had shelves full of older books of every genre. Because he would often spend long periods in the stores, he also observed the people who would come in to sell books, not buy them. Many of those people were regular family folk who just wanted to recover some of their original purchase price so they could buy some more books – they seemed to be happy to get ten or twenty percent of the original price, even for essentially new books.

He also noticed some purchasers who seemed to scan the racks and finger the books in an oddly intense manner, covering a wide range of topics, and then perhaps buy one or two almost randomly. Alan often chatted to other customers in the stores; he was a salesman after all; but he found those people quite reticent to talk in general. After a while, he was able to piece together what they were doing and he had his first awareness of the world of the book scout.

As he had time, Alan traveled farther distances in the city to seek out other bookstores. In Scottsdale he found a few stores that labeled themselves as sellers of rare books, fine books or even antiquarian books. He quickly noted that they tended to stock much older books, almost all hardcover not paperback, and they were often displayed on spacious solid wood shelves or behind glass fronts that were locked.

The biggest difference that took his breath away was the prices. Plain-looking books without outer dust jackets on obscure topics had prices ranging from fifty dollars to five hundred. Some of the books in the special cases were worth thousands, sometimes tens of thousands…he couldn't believe it. He was particularly astonished when he saw copies of the old Hardy Boys series with prices of fifty dollars or more. Oh, to get back all those garage sale items when he was a teenager at home!

Again he observed the customers. They were very different from the people at the general used book stores. There were never many of them in the store at any time; this was not a high-volume business. They almost always talked to the dealer when they entered, even when they seemed to be there for the first time. They tended to totally focus on a certain subject area and seldom even looked at books in the other sections of the store. They knew their business and when they addressed price with the dealer it was in the nature of a mutual discussion of a book's condition, completeness and value, not in any way the general haggling of a flea market.

Similarly, when someone came in to sell books, it was approached in the same business-like manner. It also became apparent that most people who came in to sell their books also left with them. A lot of people seemed to assume that because a book was old, even if it had just sat on grandma's bookshelf for years, it was valuable. The dealer was always very selective. He spent much more time explaining to people why their books were not valuable than he did actually negotiating the purchase of one. Conversations with the dealers quickly taught him that their biggest business concern was buying books that would never sell, thus turning their scarce capital into dust-collecting dead inventory.

Alan became intrigued with the whole business. He knew that he would never have the patience or the discipline to set up a retail storefront as the dealers he had met had done. He also realized that there was no upside to skimming small margins off relatively cheap books as the regular book scouts did. So he invented his own new persona, the one he privately called Eagle Scout, after his youthful experiences in the Boy Scouts.

All of that was more than twenty-five years ago. At first he did it part time, slowly and carefully, continuing to sell cars for another six years. He searched out books and magazines about the book business itself. He talked to anyone and everyone who would give him the time. He started to travel to local and regional book fairs and to see the whole process in action. He was a fast learner and seemed to have the instincts necessary to size up a book or a customer quickly and accurately.

Most importantly, right from the beginning he meticulously developed and maintained his network of contacts, even as he expanded across the country and then internationally when he devoted his full time to the business. It was not much of an exaggeration to say that, today, everyone of note in the business knew or knew about Alan, although he was always treated a little bit like an outsider; that is, like a book scout.

Alan was a bit of a loner. He had many acquaintances, and had enjoyed a number of extended good relationships, but he had never married or even settled into much of a home routine. He knew that he would need to set some deeper roots someday, if only in retirement.

As Alan finished tallying up the day in his ledger, he thought about his sale to Vice President Cartwright that morning. It was always special to deal with him. In the high-end bookselling world it was not uncommon to encounter famous celebrities, but the Vice President was different in many ways. Of course, there was the aura of his office, but Alan had encountered him before he reached that position, when he was "just one of those rich technology guys on the west coast." Ray Cartwright was always friendly and interested in conversations with others, a far cry from many of the others. They had developed a cordial relationship, although their conversations were pretty well limited to book talk.

Alan's biggest deal with Ray Cartwright had happened almost ten years ago. By then Alan was finally plugged into the European network and was beginning to handle higher-priced items. He had narrowed down his specialty to early explorers and managed to get a lead on an elaborate collection that was coming available from an established French family. Although he certainly couldn't compete to purchase the major collection, he did manage to get involved with a small group of dealers who combined to make the successful offer. He chose the books that related to the early exploration of America.

Among those books was an extremely high quality first edition of the journal of La Perouse, the French navigator who explored the west coast of North America during his voyage around the world in the late 1700s. This was after James Cook's famous voyage, but the French always considered it to be more significant since La Perouse determined many more details of the Pacific Ocean in general and the American Northwest in particular. The journal was in great shape, but, more importantly, the accompanying folio of maps and illustrations of the people and scenery from the voyage were immaculate. It was as much a work of art as it was a historical document.

Alan took the La Perouse to the next International Antiquarian Book Fair in Los Angeles. He priced the set at fifty thousand dollars, an aggressive but possible value to a keen collector. As circumstances would have it, the first reasonably serious person to consider it was Ray Cartwright, then the high-flying leader of TickerTreat and a relatively new, but serious, collector of northwest American books.

After the normal routine and posturing of studying the documents, Ray simply said, "Great book…tough price."

Alan, of course, responded with the expected litany of attributes: quality, rarity, completeness.

Then, with the pause that always seems to happen, Ray simply said, "Forty."

Alan, knowing that it was a good offer and that it represented a good profit for him, his best ever at that point in fact, almost said yes but his salesman instincts wouldn't let him do that. Instead, drawing on some obscure piece of information that he had picked up in his earlier travels, he said, "Let's split the difference at forty-five and I will locate an early edition of the English translation of the journal and throw that in. That way you will have another collectible item and you will be able to read what you have bought."

"Agreed," said Ray, which started a relationship that was professional and mutually respectful.

Alan was pleased with the deal. It established a strong bond with a new customer and the extra book would add a few more dollars to his profit. He knew that in the world of antiquarian books, especially those related to voyages of exploration, there was nothing more difficult to sell than a journal that did not have the appendices of maps and illustrations attached. For a serious collector, the missing pieces destroyed their interest in it and thus its value. However, these orphan documents did exist, either because the parts were separated over the centuries or, more often, because they were broken up and sold as separate items for more value that the intact set. In any case, Alan did find an early English translation of the journal, without the attached folio of maps and drawings, for a reasonable price and he sent it on to Ray.

Today's sale had been a trivial thing. Alan had picked up the book by the Hudson's Bay trader as part of a bigger purchase and had brought it to Seattle only because it related to relatively local history. Worth only $200, he wanted to just give it to the Vice President, but that wasn't appropriate in the protocol of things unless he bought something else, which didn't happen. Still, it was important to maintain some form of contact with the V.P.; after all he was always going to be a potential customer for valuable books, as he had been over the past ten years.

7

Jeremy Boucher was in his hotel room a couple of floors above Alan. He had also been taking stock of his day.

He wasn't sure it had been worth his while to come to the Seattle fair; he preferred the larger international events such as those in Los Angeles, New York and across Europe. However, he did come here every few years, partly to check out the regional dealers and to determine if there were any new players of note and partly to make face to face contact with some of his customers who lived in the area. He had done that today.

He had sold a couple of minor books, including the one to the Vice President, and he had bought one, a pristine copy of the 1916 Champlain Society publication of the journals of David Thompson. Thompson was the most accomplished of the explorers in the Northwest during the early 1800s. He defined huge areas of what are now western Canada and the Rocky Mountains. He was overshadowed in history by Lewis and Clarke, the first explorers to trace the lower reaches of the Columbia River to its mouth, now the border between Washington and Oregon. Thompson arrived at the outlet just a couple of years later, having explored much more territory and having actually discovered the source of the Columbia. His relative obscurity was partly because he never published his journals. Thus the Champlain issue of more than a hundred years later was the best reference. Jeremy had found the book in the rack of a regional dealer from Idaho; he paid three thousand dollars for it.

Jeremy was a perfectionist. Everyone in the book business agreed that the condition of a book was paramount to its value. Wear, staining, fading, and certainly rips and tears, were all flaws to be noted and considered in pricing a book. Jeremy only dealt in high quality items, but he also priced them accordingly. Other dealers felt he often overpriced things, but that was OK with them, as it just helped to establish the market upside and provided a useful reference for their offerings to customers. Nevertheless, he seemed to do well as there were always people who wanted only the best.

When Jeremy considered a book he would inspect it meticulously. Of course, as every respectable book dealer would, he had to be sure that all of the pages, including title pages and appendices, were present. Most importantly, he made sure that all of the maps, charts and illustrations were present and were original. It was this issue that sometimes caused him to get into disagreements with other dealers.

The word *complete* had come to take on a somewhat ambiguous and, for Jeremy, a misleading meaning in the booksellers' lexicon. Technically, everyone would agree that it simply meant that everything was present. The phrase *Complete First Edition with all maps and plates* appeared in many book descriptions. What irritated Jeremy, and what lead to some heated arguments, was that many dealers implicitly, if not explicitly, represented this to also mean *original*.

Antiquarian books, by definition, have been around for more than a hundred years, in some cases over five hundred years. They have been handled, read, left sitting on bookshelves, passed on to new generations, bought and sold, and who knows what. Thus they get soiled and damaged and sometimes lose pages. This loss can be accidental or it can be overt as someone might have wanted to frame or sell a portrait or a map. To be sure, the world's inventory of any given publication deteriorates over time.

To have an original, complete, high quality old book is special. The reality, however, is that many complete books are not original. They have been cobbled together from pieces of books that have lost something over time, again usually a key illustration. These reconstructions can be done with extreme care such that most people would not detect them. If the substitution is from a similar original, partial edition, then the book can be legitimately called *complete*. Buyers beware if they also believe it is original. Jeremy was never fooled. Of course, if the substitution is from a later edition or is a more modern facsimile, then it is fraud.

Jeremy did repair books, as required, but he always disclosed the work that had been done and limited his description to *complete*. As with most dealers, he did purchase soiled or incomplete copies of valuable books, at a big discount, to provide a source of repair material. Dealers used quaint names to label their inventory of such items: the warehouse; the stockpile; the infirmary; the surgical supplies; or even, the MASH unit.

Although the book he had sold the Vice President that morning was a relatively obscure publication, it was a nice complement to the most important books he had ever sold him. Some seven years earlier he had an outstanding set of the first publication of the journals from the Meriwether Lewis and William Clark expedition to the Pacific, published in 1814. It was worth $150,000. Ray Cartwright, then Lieutenant Governor of Washington and a very committed book collector, saw it in Jeremy's display at the New York Book Fair. He was in the city making political connections as part of the follow-up to the State of the Union response.

A copy of the Lewis and Clark journals were a "must have" item for any serious collector of northwest America history.

"Beautiful books," Ray said. "Too bad I already have a set."

Jeremy, quickly sizing up the then-unknown customer as a serious collector, worked his spiel about quality as only he could. Within minutes he had determined the nature of Ray's holding and had persuaded him that an upgrade was definitely the right thing to do to enhance his collection. He even agreed to take Ray's current copies as a trade-in for $30,000 credit, a small profit to Ray on what he had paid a couple of years earlier, but a safe venture for Jeremy who knew he could easily resell the books to another dealer for almost that amount and who had a comfortable margin built into the set he was selling.

He had sold a few other books to the now Vice President over the past couple of years, but nothing in value compared to that time.

Jeremy checked his watch and saw that it was much too late to call home, back east in Ohio. He would call in the morning, before the second day of the weekend Seattle fair opened.

Jeremy had always lived in Ohio. His father emigrated from England to the United States just before the Second World War, with a recent doctorate in English history as his credentials. He joined the faculty of Ohio State University.

As Jeremy grew up, he was always surrounded by books related to English history, which included the stories of the settlement of the American east coast. He was fascinated by them. He did attend Ohio State to obtain a Bachelor of Arts degree in history, but he did not have the passion for research and teaching that his father had and, so, he did not pursue any advanced degrees. Instead, he decided that he could make his living by using his acquired knowledge in the buying and selling of antiquarian books.

His business was called Antiquarian Americana, reflecting his specialty in early American publications. It consisted of three rooms in an old brick building on the outskirts of downtown Columbus. One room was a shared space where he and his two office workers had their desks, computers and phones that were integral to their business; another room housed the layout tables where he checked over the books, made any repairs, and wrapped them for shipping. The third room was set up as a library, with the walls covered in book shelves and a couple of easy chairs and small tables for people to sit. This created a retail presence for customers but, in fact, it was by appointment only. This was not a place for casual buyers looking for cheap used books. When people who had located them in the Directory of Booksellers or in the phone book did phone to enquire about coming to see the books, it took all of their tact to subtly inquire into the nature of the caller's interest and to convey the nature of their stock. Whenever someone who was not really into the collecting of costly antiquarian books did come, it could be awkward, although they always made them feel welcome and usually spent a bit of time describing the nature of their books. You never knew when someone might become a serious collector.

His wife, Marian, had been a librarian in the local school system for many years. She was now retired, but she spent a fair amount of time supporting Jeremy's enterprise by conducting on-line searches of the websites of other dealers and the auction activities in the United States and across Europe. The business often changed quickly and it paid to have early-warning systems in place. For example, at one high profile auction in New York new levels of prices were established for many rare books. By monitoring the results real time, they were able to immediately re-price their inventory of key items; the contacts from other dealers had started within hours, trying to buy the books at their previous listed prices.

Most of Jeremy's business was done in books about the history of the eastern United States, whether it related to the early settlers and explorers or the high-demand works about the American Revolution and the Civil War. His involvement in books related to the west was somewhat limited, but it helped to connect with western collectors.

Jeremy enjoyed his periodic trips to the northwest as the weather was generally much better than the dreary, rainy days that dominated central Ohio at this time of year. But Jeremy also knew from experience that the weather could become cold and wet here when winter set in.

8

Herb Trawets was at home, doing the same thing as Alan and Jeremy.

Since he lived in Seattle, he always participated in the local book fair; it was a home game for him. He had a generally good relationship with most of the dealers from the region and thus he often got a first look at any new stock they had. They would contact him any time of the year, knowing he was particularly interested in books related to the early exploration of the Pacific Northwest and that he would pay reasonable prices. The fair allowed him to visit with dealers from out of town face to face, which helped maintain the flow.

Herb lived in a modest neighborhood, not far from downtown and the location of his bookstore, which was simply called Herb's Books. He had been in the book business all of his adult life, having started out as a simple reseller of cheap paperbacks. As his business grew over the years and he became involved with the fine old books of the antiquarian world, he never considered changing the store's name to something more upscale; that wasn't his nature and he preferred to be reminded of his humble beginnings.

Herb had been born in Seattle, the son of immigrants who came to America following the Second World War. He was part of the baby boomer generation, although his family lifestyle was certainly at the modest end of that group.

His heritage was Iranian, or Persian as his father always described it. His father, who had been educated in the English schools of the British colonial system, did work in an imported-rug store, true to the stereotype of the day, but always as an employee, earning basic wages and limited commissions. However, this gave Herb some exposure to retail sales as a youth and influenced his decision to set up his own store, albeit as a small-scale owner to start with.

His true name reflected his heritage, Yrrab Enaed Trawets. However, it caused him anguish as a youngster in school. The other kids became prone to call him "E-rab," a not too subtle variation of the "A-rab," which was often used to describe people from the Middle East in those days. His middle name didn't offer much relief from the problem either. Since the correct pronunciation of his first name was close to "Urb," he simply adopted the English name Herb as his own. Over time everyone followed suit.

Herb had married a high school sweetheart, Tala Samani, also of Persian heritage. They had enjoyed many years of quiet happiness before her untimely death from cancer five years ago. Due to medical complications, they had not had a family, which they both had regretted.

Herb had experienced a good day at the book fair, selling quite a few books to visiting collectors and purchasing a number of books from some regional dealers. His only regret was missing the David Thompson book that he saw Jeremy Boucher buy from a relatively new dealer out of Boise. He should have caught it first, he thought. He knew that he would have to develop a closer link with that dealer.

He was pleased that he had seen Ray Cartwright again. It always amazed Herb, and made him feel so good about his life, that coming from such a low status background he could interact easily with the Vice President of the United States.

Actually his relationship with the V.P. went back more than ten years. One day, out of the blue, Ray Cartwright came into his bookstore and started to browse in the section dedicated to books about the local area. Herb introduced himself and struck up a casual conversation. He quickly learned that Ray was a local businessman who was getting involved in the community and who had developed an interest in its history. It also became clear that Ray had no knowledge about old books.

Once he gleaned some of the basic concepts from Herb, Ray Cartwright became very intrigued and decided he wanted to start a collection. He visited Herb's shop often over the next few months, usually coming during quiet periods when Herb would have time to talk. Then came the questions: "What makes a book so special?" "Where do all the very old books come from?" "How do you know if a book is authentic?" "How can you know if a book is all there?" "How are prices determined?"

Herb educated him about the history of books and book collecting and guided him to many reference books, including those bibliographies that would document books on a given topic and describe what their contents should be. He explained what made a given book valuable: rarity of course, but dominantly condition and completeness. For collectors, there was also the special status of first editions, even if later issues had the same content. The concepts came easily to Ray; basically it was simply a case of supply and demand. Who had something and who wanted it? The beauty of the system from an economic perspective, as Ray saw it, was that the supply was limited and its collective condition inevitably degenerated and so a collection of high quality books should certainly appreciate over time. But that was just part of his rationale; he fell in love with the books and the history they represented.

Drake's Dilemma

Looking at a journal by an early explorer that was complete with maps and illustrations of people and landscapes, he could visualize an English book buyer in his library, holding that same volume some three hundred years earlier, seeing images from the other side of the world for the very first time. It made him feel connected with history.

Ray bought carefully to start with until, one day, he asked Herb straight-out, "What books should I have to form the core of a truly good collection related to the Northwest?"

Herb replied with a brief history summary: The earliest Europeans to explore the northwest coast of North America in the late 1700s were the English captains such as James Cook and George Vancouver, the Spaniards such as Quadra, and the French such as La Perouse, all of whom sailed up to the current Canadian and even the Alaskan shores. The overland route was first defined by Lewis and Clark in the early 1800s. These were all followed by many explorers throughout the 1800s, mostly American, as settlements were established. Of course, if he wanted to expand the geographic area of interest, there were many earlier Spanish explorers who reached at least northern California, and many British explorers who defined the inland areas and coastlines of western Canada. Also, various Russian explorers had visited the Alaskan coast in the 1700s.

Based on the details that followed those general comments, Ray built his collection. He bought many of the books from Herb, starting with a very good set of the journals from the three voyages of James Cook for $50,000. This was followed by a first edition of the Vancouver journals that cost over $70,000. The difference surprised Ray as Cook was so much more famous, again a lesson in supply and demand as fewer Vancouver volumes had been published and had survived.

After finishing with his stocktaking for the day, Herb browsed through his calendar and started to plan his schedule for the New Year. He made at least two trips to London each year; it was truly the book-collecting center of the world with its dozens of high profile dealers. He also conducted extensive trips to the larger cities in the U.S. Once in a while he would visit the European continent and once he traveled to Australia and Japan. Almost all of his trips were planned around book fairs, whether they were the large International Antiquarian Fairs or the more modest regional ones.

He decided that he would start the year with a trip to London in January and then go on to the San Francisco Fair in February. That usually gave his annual business a good kick start.

Although his trip to London would be a few months in the future, he also made some notes to himself, a reminder to soon start phoning the main dealers in London to arrange meetings and to ensure his contacts were still current. As well, he might uncover some new leads from those conversations. It is a small world that the leading sellers live in, somehow competing and cooperating all at the same time.

9

A couple of weeks later Ray Cartwright was back in Washington, D.C. He decided it was time to flesh out his calendar for the coming year; one that would steadily show an increase in political appearances across the country in anticipation of the party primaries that would kick off the following year as it all built up to the Presidential nominating convention and finally the November election. Yes, he realized for the umpteenth time, American political campaigning was a full time job. With his business background, he sometimes envied the leaders of other countries such as Britain and France that had much simpler systems; although that stopped well short of admiring the very efficient one-party systems of Russia and China, heaven forbid.

Ray asked his executive assistant, Elsie Browning, to schedule a joint meeting with his key administration and political staff leaders. Usually he tried to keep those two functions separated as much as possible but now his administrative actions and his political activities would need to become closely linked; that was the reality.

The meeting involved Calvin Begg, his Chief of Staff; Ralph King, his chief political advisor; Vincent Larch, his general counsel; and Elsie, who kept track of all the plans and logistics.

It was an unusual group in that none of them had a long relationship with the Vice President. As a latecomer to politics, Ray had not developed close advisors and confidants who had the requisite knowledge and connections in the political world. Most politicians brought their own entourage to Washington.

Calvin Begg had been a long-time political activist who had worked diligently on the campaigns of Stanley Harris. When Harris had chosen Ray as his Vice Presidential running mate late in the electoral cycle, Calvin Begg had been assigned as his chief coordinator. Although they had no previous personal history, they immediately hit it off and during the arduous campaign became quite close. Ray learned to lean on Calvin's experience and to trust his instincts. When he was elected, he appointed Calvin as his Chief of Staff.

Ralph King had been recruited in a similar manner, although earlier in the process. He had been part of the Governor's staff in Washington State when Ray ran for Lieutenant Governor.

Vince Larch was hired on Calvin Begg's recommendation; he had extensive experience in dealing with the government processes and bureaucracy. Elsie Browning just seemed to appear out of the system as they transformed from campaign mode to establishing an administration. They all worked together very well. The team had been together for six years now and they were all very loyal to Ray. Of course, loyalty and longevity in Washington were a direct function of being attached to a winner and Ray was certainly showing himself to be that.

They all knew that the schedule would need to be flexible and that there would be many changes as time passed due to the vagaries of politics, national and international events, and the availability of others, but they did want to have a framework to guide their planning.

There were four different dimensions to the Vice President's activities. There were the known schedules of Congress and major political events in Washington, as well as the integration with the President's schedule. There were certain international conferences where the Vice President would represent the country. There was the need to schedule trips around the country on a steady and regular basis, early in the year to generate funds and, later in the year, to generate direct political support for his candidacy as the next President. And there was Ray's personal list of major book fairs that he always tried to work into the other schedules; the staff had come to understand that they were important to him and that they provided some needed relief from the never-ending political focus of everything else.

Once they had a rough outline set, Ray turned the conversation to the political logistics.

"I'll need a new set of speeches developed to help me in the transition from Vice President to Presidential candidate and to start differentiating my own position going forward from the current administration, even if it is subtle," he said.

"For sure," responded Ralph. "I'll get the research and writing staff to start working up some outlines for your review."

"Just remember to keep our message simple," said Calvin. "We have a strong starting position and we don't want to muddy the waters. The past six years have been good ones and we must start by conveying a message of continuing to build on the positive momentum. We don't want to negate our association with that success and find ourselves running against ourselves. That has happened before; remember Al Gore."

"Still, I need my own identity and programs," insisted Ray.

"Wow," laughed Vince, "you must be the only person who doesn't believe that you have staked out your own identity. You have been the catalyst for renewed civility and bipartisan collaboration over the last six years, at least compared to the previous twenty. Sure, the President was receptive to the idea, aren't they all in theory, but you made it happen."

"Right," said Calvin. "It all came together with The Vote."

He was referring to the dramatic events that unfolded in the U.S. Senate in the midst of President Harris's first term. They had won the close election two years earlier and had been advancing their agenda forward reasonably well, with some support from the opposition party. In fact, the major grumbling that bubbled below the surface was from the more conservative faction in their own party, still simmering from losing the nomination to Stanley Harris in the first place.

With the mid-term elections approaching, the conservatives decided to capitalize on a number of issues that had all come together that year. There had been violent confrontations between Mexican immigrants and border patrol volunteers in a number of Texas towns. The Supreme Court had ruled against state laws that would not recognize same-sex marriages from other states. It had also refused to hear an appeal of a lower court opinion that negated a Kansas law to limit abortion medical coverage. The administration had negotiated a controversial free trade agreement with the Southeast Asia Economic Alliance nations.

Although these issues all rallied support from conservatives, each one also had some degree of support from more moderate factions, either for economic, religious or purely political reasons. The conservatives introduced a resolution in the Senate that demanded that the President and the Supreme Court adhere to the laws as passed by state legislatures, and that they stop interpreting them so freely. In reality, the resolution, even if passed, would have no actual impact due to its generalities, and it was unlikely that such a resolution could also pass in the more populist House of Representatives.

Nevertheless, fueled by a strong public relations push and the general discontent of many people, the bill became a national cause. The supporters labeled it variously as "Send them a message," "Enough is enough," "Give us our country back," and then simply as "Draw a line in the sand." Politicians who normally would have avoided such a resolution were being swayed by the argument that it was a politically safe and prudent way to take a stand on these diverse issues, even if they were only concerned about one or two of them.

The public rhetoric built to a frenzy. The newspapers and television talk shows seemed to cover nothing else. The mood of the nation became angry, even mean.

Ray had met with the President on the issue for one last time the day before the resolution was to come to a vote in the Senate. They did not like the bill, which people intuitively knew, but they were uncertain how to proceed politically. The President was reluctant to come out and declare that he would veto the law if it came to his desk for signature; everyone knew that was not going to be the outcome of a symbolic Senate vote that would never reach the House. No, it was pure politics, and the emotions involved dictated that the outcome would impact how business would be done in Washington for some time.

The time for the vote came. As the tally was registered on the electronic screens it was obvious that it was going to be as close as everyone predicted. Then the result: a 50 – 50 tie. The tie-breaking vote belonged to the Vice President, the President of the Senate.

The tension was high, but the proponents were confident, even though Ray had been silent on the issue, in concert with the president's position. After all, it was being proposed and supported by his own party and by some members of the other party who had worked with the administration on specific issues over the past year. Their ability to get things done with Congress was still fragile.

The Vice President took a deep breath and spoke slowly and quietly. "We are a nation at a crossroads. We have economic difficulties and philosophical differences that are paralyzing us. We have concerns for ourselves now and for the future that we leave for our children. This bill, although far from perfect, has emerged out of our sense of fragility and frustration; it has been supported by people of good will who do want to "send a message." The motivations are understood by everyone even when the message is not.

"I call myself a conservative, but my definition is very different from the one that has become attached to that label over the last few decades. I believe in limited government – government that provides a framework of peace, order and fair laws for everyone to pursue their personal destinies. This also means a government that allows its citizens the freedom to make their own decisions as long as they do not harm others. It means a government that allows a woman to decide about an abortion, a gay couple to decide if they want to marry, a company or a country to develop economic relationships. Above all it means that we do not deny others their rights just because we do not agree with them.

"I know that similar basic beliefs by others often cause them to support laws to regulate them. Some people might confuse my set of beliefs with the liberal demands for actions by government to intervene and to impose those beliefs. I reject that as well.

"Therefore, based on a belief in tolerance, not regulation; a belief we can solve problems by inclusion, not exclusion; I declare that the resolution before the Senate has failed to pass since it did not obtain a majority of the votes."

The uproar was immense, from every quarter. But, in a few weeks, after the noise abated a bit, there was a change in tone. It was as if the long, emotional debate that had preceded the Senate vote had blown itself out like a land-bound hurricane. It had provided a national catharsis and led to real progress over the next two years.

That transition was aided by the President's unwavering support of his Vice President and Ray's determined and unrelenting effort to meet with leaders on all sides of the political issues, unflinching in his position on the resolution but totally engaged in finding solutions to the underlying problems. He rejected all of the grand schemes of the past; there were no sweeping bills to reinvent Medicare, to subsidize struggling industries or to fortify the borders physically or commercially. Instead there were proposals to chip away at the problems with pragmatic actions, stripped of their political rhetoric. Financial support to states' medical and educational programs emerged. Subsidies and grants for the reeducation of workers and the retooling of factories were approved, always with a need to fight back against funds that just propped up uneconomic enterprises. Budgets were balanced, with a lot of arm twisting and trade-offs between the tax and spending sides of the ledger. By focusing on specifics and not the sweeping generalities that politicians are fond of using, the issues came out into open public debate more easily and agreement could be reached based on a common goodwill and reduced polarized positioning.

It was far from perfect to say the least, but it was such a big difference from the antagonistic behaviour that had permeated everything for so long, right up to that critical vote. President Harris and Vice President Cartwright rode that wave of goodwill all the way to an easy victory in the next election. Ray had continued to work the same process since then, in Washington and in every region of the country.

Calvin continued, "Now, people are going to vote based on your past actions and your ability to deliver more in the future. As a virtual incumbent, it is not what you say and promise, it's your credibility from the past. It's only a newcomer or outsider who can campaign on words and promises, as you and President Harris did six years ago. Now it's time to consolidate the actions of that time into your agenda forward; that's your strength."

"OK," said Ray, "but I still need some new speeches, at least some new jokes. Even I am getting tired of my stories."

With that, the meeting broke up and everyone headed back to work. "Oh, Elsie," said Ray, "would you find Maria for me? I have a few things to cover with her."

"Sure, she's in the office this afternoon."

A few minutes later Maria Rodriguez, his personal administrator, entered his office.

"Hi, you wanted to see me, Mr. Vice President?"

Grimacing a little at the formality, but with a smile on his face, Ray replied, "Hi, Maria. I have a few things to give you."

Maria Rodriguez managed Ray Cartwright's personal affairs, trying hard to keep them separate from the activities linked to his office and position. When traveling and socializing in particular, it was important, politically and legally, to keep good records.

Ray's large financial assets had been placed in a blind trust when he took office so as to avoid any conflicts of interest. He had left a portfolio that was balanced in high quality American equities, corporate bonds and broad-based mutual funds that invested domestically and globally. Although he couldn't know what specific investment decisions the trust administrators made, he was sure the general balance was unchanged. Of course, the largest holding was his residual interest in TickerTreat which he had clearly publicly disclosed and which had not caused any issues to date. Maria interfaced with the trust administrators and the accountants to keep everything clean and above board.

Maria also arranged for the funds Ray needed for personal spending. Normally that didn't amount to a lot, some family activities and gifts were the most common things. However, on top of that were his books, and he never knew when he would spend significant amounts. She handled those payments as well.

"Just a few small things this time," he said as he passed her the invoices. "Back in Seattle, I bought some books at the fair for $1350 and an old map of the west coast in a local shop for $1000."

"I'll take care of it. By the way, that reminds me. I heard from the insurance company and they want to take an inventory of your old books and maps to update their records."

"Alright, but that does seem repetitive. They have photos of everything and copies of the purchase receipts. Set it up for the next time I am back home; I don't like people rummaging through the old books. I know they are careful but some of them are very fragile."

After he signed a few other documents that Maria had brought with her, she left the office.

Having a moment to himself for a bit, he thought, "Well here we go. Everything else has been preamble. It's time to play in the big game."

BOOK THREE

LONDON, 1581

The Knighted Pirate

10

Sir Francis Drake had a huge hangover but a large smile on his face.

"Yes," he smiled. *"Sir Francis Drake."* Yesterday morning, April 1, he was simply *Mister Francis Drake.* Now he was a knight.

The Queen and her royal entourage had marched down to his ship, *The Golden Hind,* at the London docks on the Thames River and in front of a huge crowd of cheering onlookers had declared him *Sir Francis* as the French ambassador administered the traditional touching of his bowed shoulders with a ceremonial sword. The Queen had delegated the actual anointment to the ambassador as a message to the Spanish. Here was an English hero, albeit a hated pirate and plunderer in the eyes of the Spanish, being honored by the Queen and her French allies. International politics and messaging were always a factors in the Queen's actions.

The ceremony was accompanied by the grandest party that had been seen in London for decades. Sir Francis had spared no expense; after all he was now a very wealthy man. People were saying that there had not been such a spectacle since the times of King Henry VIII, Elizabeth's father. But those were royal events, not a private party by someone who had grown up as the son of a yeoman tenant farmer and, until yesterday, had been a commoner.

The Lords and Ladies, the court officials, the affluent merchants, the trade guild leaders, the politicians and the clergy – they had all attended the sumptuous banquet. Many of them fawned over Drake, hoping to court his favor in business or philanthropy. Of course, there were some members of the establishment and aristocracy who disdained the vulgar show, but they kept those thoughts quiet. Jealousy was their real emotion.

Drake's personal demeanor did not help the situation.

He was an average sized man, about 5' 8" in height, but with a strong, stocky body that reflected his years at sea. He had a ruddy complexion, reddish hair, and a striking pointed beard and curved moustache. He did not look like most of the aristocrats.

The feature that most people noticed and remembered was the fixed focus of his eyes when he talked to anyone. He conveyed a stern image, with an uneasy image of challenging everyone. Perhaps this reflected some underlying insecurity from his common-man heritage.

His words and body language certainly didn't convey any insecurity; quite the opposite. To many people he seemed arrogant and abrasive. He didn't wear his new wealth and new social status with the easy grace, as did most people who had been born into that situation.

Drake had been bestowing large gifts widely since his return, especially during the New Year's period when that was the traditional custom. He had given the Queen an emerald-laden crown and a diamond-embedded cross, and had given bars of gold, silver plates, and jeweled chalices to almost everyone in the Queen's court. It was noteworthy that Lord Burghley had refused any gift, still concerned about offending the Spanish.

At yesterday's banquet he had been similarly generous to everyone, presenting the Queen with a large silver tray and a diamond-studded frog figure.

Drake had returned to England just six months earlier. On this morning, he reminisced about all of the events that had transpired.

In particular, he thought of the journals, maps and drawings that he had created during the almost-three-year voyage. Upon his return they had all been taken by the Queen's officials, on her orders. Everyone was afraid that any public disclosure of the actual events that had taken place would further infuriate the Spanish and lead to war. Everyone on the voyage was sworn to secrecy, with the threat of having all of their earned wealth seized and of being jailed if they disobeyed.

This did not particularly surprise or bother him. He assumed that when things settled down he would be given the documents back and then he would publish his story. He could be patient.

In a way, the whole restraint of most of the information was meaningless. His exploits against the Spanish had been amply chronicled in the many messages that had been sent back from the Spanish authorities throughout America to King Philip's court and to the Spanish authorities and merchants who had invested in those regions. His adventures and his bold acts of siege and piracy were well known and the information had spread throughout Europe.

Drake was the most famous man alive: a hero at home and a scoundrel, or worse, in Spain, Portugal and the Vatican.

11

The fateful voyage had not started well. After departing on November 17, 1577 they encountered heavy seas and winds such that they were driven back to Plymouth. Then followed a month of keeping the men and crews together, reprovisioning the ships, and avoiding direct contact with London in fear that the Queen would waver in her support or that Lord Burghley would cause something to happen to abort the venture. Finally, they sailed again on December 15.

For the first month they headed south, sailing around the Spanish waters to the coast of Africa where they topped up their provisions with fish, fruit and water. Also along the way they seized a couple of small Spanish ships. At Cape Verde, the group of islands off the west coast of Africa that served as a way station and marshalling point for Spanish and Portuguese ships, they seized a larger ship and, more importantly, captured a Portuguese pilot, Nunho da Silva, who had sailed between Europe and America, along with his sea charts. These were invaluable.

Over the next five months they sailed across the Atlantic and down the Brazilian and Argentinean coasts to Port San Julian, a former stopping port for Magellan, not far north of the Strait of Magellan. The trip had been difficult, beset by both heavy storms and dead-calm doldrums, both of which impeded progress. Disease and scurvy had plagued the crew. There also had been difficult encounters with Thomas Doughty, a gentleman of the Queen's court, who had been continuously seeding discontent among the crew, challenging Drake's authority, and lobbying for the return to England.

At this stop for rest and provisioning the issue came to a dramatic conclusion. Challenging Doughty publicly, and learning that he had apprised Lord Burghley of the voyage and was claiming to act with his support, all in violation of Queen Elizabeth's instructions to Drake, Drake charged him with mutiny. After a trial before a jury of officers and gentlemen, he was convicted and, following an amazingly cordial dinner with Drake, was beheaded.

This was a dramatic juncture for the voyage. Drake had quelled the dissent, ordered the gentlemen to start working with the sailors in labor and, as a result, solidified his authority and the loyalty of his crew.

Perhaps anticipating that he might face criticism or charges over the execution of Doughty, he renamed the *Pelican* as the *Golden Hind*. A hind, or small deer, was emblazoned in the crest of Sir Christopher Hatton, a sponsor of Doughty; Drake hoped the gesture would show his fealty to Sir Christopher, who could be a force to reckon with upon his return to England. Thus came about the name of one of the most famous ships in history.

The next challenge was to navigate the Strait of Magellan with its narrow passages and heavy winds and currents. Abandoning two of the smaller vessels, the fleet was reduced to three ships for the passage. Only one, the *Golden Hind*, made it into the South Pacific. One ship had turned back for England and another was lost at sea.

The journey through the Strait and into the open Pacific took three months, from late July to early November, much of it consumed by storms that drove them south as they exited the Strait proper. As a result, Drake sailed further south than anyone ever had before, latitude 56°S. He also discovered that the south shore of the Strait was actually a series of islands, not a southern continent as had been believed previously.

In late November, they stopped at an island off the southern coast of Chile for repairs and provisions. On an excursion to the mainland they encountered an Indian tribe that traded with them for some sheep, chickens and corn. However, the Indians later trapped the landing party in an ambush, apparently mistaking them for Spaniards, who had been capturing and killing natives along the coasts for years. Two members of the crew were killed and everyone else in the group was wounded in the escape. Drake was hit twice, one of the arrows piercing his face just below his right eye. Drake grimaced as he recalled that episode, also recognizing that everyone who hailed him and his crew as heroes still had no real appreciation for all of the hardships and dangers they had faced.

Early December brought their first encounter with the Spanish. They attacked the town of Valparaiso, the port that served the Chilean capital Santiago. Here they captured a ship and seized some gold, their first bounty in the Pacific. The actual siege was quite easy. The port was not defended and the inhabitants had no anticipation of danger as Drake's ship sailed into the harbor; there had never been a ship in these waters before that wasn't Spanish.

Over the next two months they continued north, capturing a few small ships and looting a few more towns. In early February he attacked the southern Peruvian towns of Arica and Chule, the first ports that served as shipping points for the treasure from the inland mines to the marshalling points in Panama for trans-shipment across the narrow isthmus and on to Spain. However, they did not capture much treasure; at Arica the ships had recently left and at Chule they had received advance notice of Drake's approach by overland runners who had arrived just hours earlier. The treasure there had been unloaded from the ships and moved inland. This news forced Drake to push north towards Lima even faster, to be sure to outpace the spreading warnings, especially since he heard that large ships of treasure were at anchor there.

Arriving at Callao, the port for Lima, they were pleased to discover that news of their presence in the Pacific had not preceded them but disappointed that there were no treasure-laden ships in harbor. After seizing what little they could find of value, they set out after the *Nuestra Senora de la Conception,* the treasure ship that had departed a few days earlier.

Over the next two weeks they pursued the ship north, stopping along the way to loot a few ships and towns; they were certainly shaking up the Spanish authorities along the whole coast of South America.

On March 1st they caught sight of their target. Again, by hiding their identity, they were able to approach very close to the unsuspecting vessel before firing a volley of cannon fire and boarding her without any serious resistance. After all, it was an unarmed merchant ship.

The treasure was enormous: gold bullion, silver bars, jewels, some belonging to the Spanish crown, namely King Philip, and some the property of Spanish merchants and investors who had backed various ventures. Drake, the crew, the Queen and all of his investors would reap huge profits from this seizure; Drake was now going to be a very wealthy man. He was also destined to be hated by the Spanish for the rest of his life.

With this prize in hand, Drake then sailed onward to the north, searching for a port to repair and provision his ship. Along the way, he did capture two other ships carrying additional treasure and, more importantly, some sea charts for the trans-Pacific voyage to the Philippines. He decided to keep one of the ships, a small frigate, which could be useful with the rest of the voyage. In mid-April, at Gualtulco in southern Mexico, they were able to secure fresh water and seize foodstuff and clothing.

The next part of the journey was beyond the settlements and knowledge of the Spaniards, or anyone else for that matter. Now it was time to carry out the Queen's secret mission and to search for the passage across the top of America and back to England.

He was about to become a true explorer rather than a buccaneer and avenger against the Spanish.

12

Francis Drake recalled that he had felt a true exhilaration as the two ships set sail from the coast of Mexico. He was going where no one had ever gone before.

Although he did not have any maps or charts to guide him to the north, at least he had the knowledge from the captured Pacific sea charts about the prevailing winds. To have sailed directly north against the trade winds would have been difficult, and prohibitively time consuming. Instead, he headed west into the ocean for more than a thousand miles and then to the northwest until he passed 30°N latitude. Only then did he head back to the north and northeast, towards the unknown coast of upper America.

Six weeks later, in early June, 1579, they reached landfall on the mountainous coastline at 50°N latitude. Although the shore was treacherous, they did manage to land a party to secure fresh water and firewood before they were forced back out to sea by a heavy fog that threatened to ground or wreck their ship on unknown shoals.

Continuing north, the weather turned very cold with the brisk winds creating a freezing sea spray. Food and ropes froze and the crew had difficulty managing the ship. Despair about the voyage north was setting in. Drake called the area "Frozen Land" and the shoreline a "Coast of Objections."

Finally, at 54°N, a large passageway opened to the east leading past a high cape to a sheltered inland passageway along a coast of high snow-covered mountains. Continuing north, they found the sea full of salmon and sea lions; they became well-fed for the first time in many weeks.

They also encountered a few Indians clad in furs, who approached them cautiously in large canoes. They made a few trades for elaborately carved wooden bowls and boxes, but the actual interaction was very limited. For the first time they saw elaborately carved posts, dozens of feet tall, standing in the villages along the shore. They appeared to depict animals, fish and birds in a uniquely smooth but chunky manner, coloured in pigments of red and green.

At 57°N latitude they were finally forced to turn back as the channels became filled with icebergs and floating ice sheets that posed a great danger for their ship, especially in the face of strong winds from the north that limited their maneuverability. However, as far as Drake could see, the main channel continued northward; could this be the fabled Northwest Passage?

They had also passed a large river mouth that flowed into the inter-island channel from the mountains, a River of Straits as he called it; perhaps it could lead to the interior of the continent. Drake was determined to return later in the season when the ice should be less severe.

Then he headed back southward in the open ocean until they reached 54°N, where they again sailed eastward through the wide passage. This time, they turned south. At 51°N, after watching the tides and currents flow, he headed further east through a very narrow channel, even encountering a stretch of rapids that could only be navigated just after high tide as the waters rushed southward. He was totally depending on his seaman's experience that such a tidal effect must surely lead back to the ocean.

After progressing almost fifty miles along the narrow channels, suddenly they encountered an inland sea that stretched to the horizon. Searching along the west coast of the sea, surely the east coast of a large island, they found a sheltered bay at the mouth of a fresh water river. Having seen numerous seals, sea lions, whales and birds, and having already caught abundant and huge salmon and halibut on their lines, Drake was sure that this heavily forested haven could be an ideal base for the English to control the many inland straits and rivers and the northern passage back home. He had never seen trees as large as grew in this place; they were more than ten feet across at the base and stretched hundreds of feet in the air in an amazingly straight manner. He called the place Nova Albion; Albion being the old vernacular for England.

The local Indian tribe welcomed him openly and they readily shared meals and gifts, but he stayed only a few days in fear that they might turn on the newcomers as had natives further south. He was certainly greatly outnumbered and their large canoes could easily outflank his ships. Before he left, as he had done at numerous locations along his voyage, he nailed a metal plate to a tree to commemorate the visit and to claim the land for Queen Elizabeth and England.

Next he crossed the inland sea to its eastern shore where they found a large valley that headed into the high mountains and delta islands that defined the outlet of a very large river. There was a flow of large salmon streaming up the river from the ocean numbering in the tens of thousands, even more. He had never before seen such a sight, which reinforced the image of the bountiful offerings that were to be found in this corner of the world. What a great heritage for England to seize!

Heading southwest, they then discovered a channel that led them back to the open ocean. They had circumnavigated a large island that was at least 300 miles in length, some three degrees of latitude.

Surveying the coastline as he went, he then sailed farther south, finding another very large river at 46°N that was protected by a huge sand bar. The sediments of the river fell to the bottom as the fast flowing waters came to a halt as they entered the ocean.

Making landfall for some provisions fifty miles south of the river, he decided then to make some lunar observations and attempt to determine the longitude of their location.

Determining latitude, which is the north-south position, was relatively easy based on observations of the sun at noon and the stars at night. Their angles above the horizon could be converted into latitude readings that were accurate within ten miles or so.

Determining longitude was much more difficult due to the rotation of the earth. It was necessary to make observations and to then compare the time of their occurrence to the time the same thing was observed at some other longitude. The problem was that there was no method to keep accurate time on board ship as it sailed around the world for years. Hourglasses were impacted by the ship's motion and the attentiveness of the crew. Even a one hour error in two years would equate to a one thousand mile error in location and the accuracy was much worse than that– it was an impossible procedure.

Scientists in England had been calculating the motion of the moon and its position relative to the stars. Making such observations at another location and comparing the angular differences would give a measure of time differences and thus longitude. Noon local time could always be determined from the peak height of the sun.

Drake had his crew lay out a grid of lines and position points over an area of a few square miles. After measuring the distances between the points and the angles of the connecting lines relative to east-west, he carefully made various observations of the moon and the stars using poles and rods as tools for determining angles. Referring to the charts that he had brought with him he calculated that they were 140 degrees of longitude west of London.

This calculation was surprising to him. Even though he knew that the maps he had with him had been based more on conjecture and rumor than fact, the consensus in Europe was that the far coast of America was at least 180 degrees west of London, perhaps even 200 degrees or more. This meant that, even if he had made an error of ten or fifteen degrees, the western coast of America was much more northerly in direction than people realized and that a journey across the top of America would be closer to 3000 miles than the 5000 miles that was suspected. This greatly increased the likelihood of success in navigating a passage during the late summer season when the warmer weather would have had its maximum impact.

Farther south again, at 45°N, they found a sheltered bay where they could carefully careen and strengthen their ship for the next stage of their voyage. Although they erected some barricades and mounted some of their guns to protect their ships and treasure while the repairs were being undertaken, the natives in the area, after some cautious approaches, welcomed them warmly. The natives danced and celebrated joyfully in various ceremonies in their village and at their common evening dinners. In fact, when the Englishmen set sail, the Indians escorted them out with many canoes and lit fires on the hills in acknowledgement. Drake decided to call the local inlets the "Bay of Small Ships" and the "Bay of Fires."

On July 23, 1579, they left the sheltered bay and headed north; they were going home across the north of America.

"How optimistic I was," thought Sir Francis.

The expectation of returning to the northern channels at 57°N that they had left in early June, finding them ice-free, and then sailing the 3000 miles across the northern Arctic sea aided by westerly winds was his dream and his plan. He would be home by late October!

It was not to be.

They encountered continuing cold northerly winds as they sailed, again needing to head hundreds of miles west before they could turn back to the northeast. Then, in early September, when they reached the channel, it was even more filled with ice floes and icebergs than in June; it seemed that the summer weather had just freed up more ice from the shores and that the winter weather was approaching more quickly than expected. The hoped-for journey through the northern passage would be impossible for the *Golden Hind*.

However, an attempt to confirm the passage needed to be made. After a candid consultation with his officers, he decided that 20 men would take the small Spanish ship that they had brought with them from Central America and attempt to make the journey. If they were forced back, they would return to the safe harbor at 45°N and wait for Drake's promised return to rescue them.

For Drake and the *Golden Hind* it meant they were going to return to England by crossing the Pacific and rounding Asia and Africa. Only Magellan's ship had ever done that.

They had no alternative. Sailing back to the Strait of Magellan was impossible with the Spaniards who would be alert and waiting to attack them, the northerly winds along the South American coast, and the fact that no one had ever been able to sail west-to-east through the Strait.

Offloading somewhere in Central America to march across the land and build a ship for the trip to England was out of the question, not only because of the Spanish, but due to the 25 tons of treasure that they had accumulated.

Aided by the captured Portuguese charts, they sailed south. First they followed the American coast below 42°N where he erected another plaque, defining the southern limit of his claim for England.

They spent a few days here, making final repairs to the ship and gathering provisions. The local natives were friendly and they interacted well. They were much different in their dress and ceremonies than the natives farther north. Here, obviously influenced by the warmer climate, they wore few clothes and even paraded around naked. They decorated themselves with colorful feathers.

After provisioning was complete, they sailed southwest to the trade-wind latitude of 10°N and then proceeded straight west.

In early November they had their first contact with anyone since they had left the American coast. They landed on a small island where the natives, after first appearing to be friendly, swarmed the ship from their many canoes and started to steal everything they could grab. Drake's crew fought the first group off successfully. A second wave of canoes carrying hundreds of natives required gunfire to be repelled; a few dozen of them were killed.

Next they encountered a large Portuguese galleon and started an attack, hoping to secure some provisions and to capture a pilot for the voyage through the myriad of islands that they would face. Drake's maps were much too general to be of much use. However, the ship was much more heavily manned and armed than Drake's and it was able to resist them.

Finally they landed on the island of Ternate in the Moluccas, a very rich group of spice-producing islands that was ruled by Sultan Babu. There followed days of feasting and trading in the lavish court of the Sultan. Drake traded for six tons of cloves, worth more than their weight in gold. He also exchanged gifts in the name of the Queen and promised to return with English forces that would help the Sultan ward off the attacks and occupations by the Portuguese, who controlled most of the East Indies.

Leaving Ternate, they then sailed south across the equator and found a secluded island where they could refurbish their ship for the long journey to Africa, past the Indonesian islands and across the Indian Ocean.

In early January, 1580, now over two years since their departure from England, they set sail in what they felt was their homeward leg, albeit a nine-month one. Just days at sea, rounding a series of islands called the Celebes, they grounded on a coral reef, and, in the most perilous time of the whole voyage, barely managed to get free. With landfall miles away and no ability to transport men, provisions or armaments in the initial darkness or the next morning while the ship was floundering, they were in real danger of perishing. Finally they were able to free the ship at high tide after jettisoning some cannons and tons of cloves.

Next they stopped on a couple of Indonesian islands where they were warmly welcomed by the natives and, after repairing the damage to the ship and gathering provisions of rice, fruit and small animals, they headed across the Indian Ocean and around the African Cape. With landings impossible to find along the treacherous coasts and buffeted by heavy winds, they did not secure fresh water or food until they reached Sierra Leone, located on the Atlantic coast north of the equator, in June. Everyone was at the point of dehydration and starvation. Thankfully, this area was rich in food, including large beds of oysters that grew at the base of mangrove trees in the shoals. They even saw the legendary huge elephants in the forest, an English first.

Now they were truly on the final leg of the journey. But, as Drake knew vividly, he was not sure what kind of welcome he would receive. Would he be a returning hero or a murderous pirate?

13

He knew that his reception would be totally dependent upon the attitude and diplomatic necessities of Queen Elizabeth. In fact, was she even alive after almost three years?

Sailing north in the Atlantic that July, passing well west of Spain and with a constant vigilance to avoid any ships, Drake developed his plan for returning home.

It would be folly to simply sail into Plymouth laden with the enormous treasure before he knew the state of affairs. If the Queen had died, or England had fallen to the Catholic sympathizers for Spain or the supporters of Mary Queen of Scots, that could be sure suicide. Better to hide the treasure somewhere and to reconnoiter the situation first; then at least he would have the means to barter and ransom his fate.

At 47°N he sailed into the familiar waters of northwest France; he had traded along these shores for years in his early apprenticeship. He anchored the *Golden Hind* in a protected bay on one of the offshore islands. Here he was just 200 miles south of Plymouth; close enough to send a small ship of reconnaissance to England but far enough away to be hidden from detection.

The crew set about offloading the treasure and hiding it on the island and along the nearby secluded coast of France. They fully understood that their wellbeing and personal wealth from the long voyage was intimately linked to Drake's fate and his generosity.

Then they beached the ship, totally scraped its hull of all the accumulated debris that had accumulated since west Africa, sealed the joints, and repaired all of the sails and lines. The canons were all cleaned, polished and remounted. Ample provisions were boarded. It was obvious to the crew that these preparations were not being undertaken just to sail home to Plymouth, just a couple of days away. The ship was being prepared for fast maneuvering and for fighting; the implications were clear.

Only then, in early September, did he approach the coast of England. Fortunately, on a hazy afternoon they encountered a small fishing ship off the south coast and Drake dispatched a crewman in a small boat to talk with them. After learning that the Queen was alive and well and that she still ruled England with her Anglican court and Parliament, he was able to sail back to France in relative secrecy. Although the story of that encounter had entered the public folklore by the time of his knighting ceremony, the timing was confused enough in the telling that it was linked to his return three weeks later.

His next decision was what to do with the treasure. He certainly anticipated that there would be many claims and disputes about its dispersal between the Queen, the investors, and even the Spanish authorities who would be expected to demand its return as the spoils of piracy. He knew that he and his crew could expect to be granted a fair share, but what was a fair share of such a large amount? He also knew that it was anticipated by everyone involved that he would siphon off some of the treasure ahead of time; that always happened with the privateer ventures. Again, what was an appropriate amount?

He estimated that the total value of the treasure was over £500,000, perhaps even fifty or one hundred percent larger than that, consisting of gold, silver, jewels and spices. That was at least twice the total annual amount the Queen was granted by Parliament to run the country. For example, he knew that the annual budget for the British navy was £10,000. The value was almost unfathomable.

He decided that he would hold back a full ten percent, leaving some of it in its hiding place in France and unloading some on a secluded shore of southwest England before sailing into Plymouth. This would assure him wealth and negotiating power whatever happened in the future.

The *Golden Hind* entered the port of Plymouth on September 26, 1580, 33 months after it had departed on the historic voyage.

He was greeted with a hero's welcome by the local population and, after the word spread to London, he was summoned to visit the Queen. Having stowed the treasure away safely in a local stronghold and leaving it well guarded by his crew, who were all sworn to secrecy about the voyage until his return, he headed to London with samples of the treasure.

He met with the Queen just over a week after his return to England.

14

"Captain Drake, welcome home to England. You must have so many tales to tell us."

"Thank you, Your Majesty. I am pleased to be here."

Over the following five hours, he related the highlights of the long voyage, answering the many questions posed by Queen Elizabeth.

"Well, Captain, there is so much more I want to hear about but we need to attend to some serious business now.

"Spain is incensed about your exploits and is demanding that all of your piracy-captured treasure must be returned. I must be very careful in dealing with those demands; Spain is much stronger than when you departed. King Philip now also rules Portugal and so controls an amazing share of the world and the riches of America, Africa and the East Indies. They have generally subdued the uprisings in the Netherlands and have a land force based there. The French are being very restrained in their relations with them. England is vulnerable to invasion.

"I will manage to avoid and deny the Spanish ambassador's demands but I must not overtly antagonize him. Therefore I will need to continue denying that you had any sanction from me or my authorities.

"There is dissension in my court about how to deal with you. Lord Burghley and others continue to greatly fear the Spanish and they would accede to many of their demands. They also are upset about the treatment you meted out to Thomas Doughty. To appease them, I will need to convene a private council to review your voyage. I will appoint Lord Walsingham to conduct the affair and I am sure it will all be resolved satisfactorily.

"There can be no public acknowledgment of your attacks on the Spanish, even though many of your exploits are already well known from Spanish sources. And, more importantly, there must be absolutely no disclosure of your travels to the northern latitudes of the Pacific. That is a secret and can only be discussed with me and the few court officials that I will confide in. Be sure that your crew and officers all know these conditions; I will treat any breach of them as reason to confiscate their possessions and to convict them of treason.

"All of the journals, maps, charts and drawings that you and any others created must be surrendered to me. They will be protected as state secrets.

"Finally, we must sequester a goodly portion of your treasure in the

Tower of London until the situation is resolved, or at least improved. If that does not happen, it may need to be returned to the Spanish.

"You should withhold £25,000 for yourself and your crew," she said with a straight face, knowing very well that Drake would have well protected his own interests.

"£100,000 can be diverted to reward the investors who backed the trip, but it must be distributed without any public ceremony. That will provide them with a very attractive return and I know they will be discreet.

"A further £100,000 should be secretly sent to my castle at Windsor.

"From what you have told me, that should leave £250,000 or so of treasure to be sequestered in the Tower. I will send my officials to Plymouth in two weeks to register that treasure and to transport it back to London."

"All of that will be done," replied Drake.

"We will talk many more times, Captain Drake. I do want to hear more about the other side of the world."

Over the following months everything evolved as the Queen had decreed. Drake visited with her dozens of times, revealing more and more of the details of his adventures aided by the many maps, drawings and paintings that had been created and were now in her possession.

The Queen was enthralled. In particular, she wanted to hear about the details of the people and their societies, which were so different from her world. She was also intrigued with the descriptions of the warm, sunny climates of the central latitudes in America and the Pacific islands, being a stark contrast to the generally dreary climate in England.

However, he lobbied in vain for permission to organize other voyages and to follow up on his discoveries; times were too dangerous for Elizabeth to permit them.

In spite of all of the subterfuges and official denials, due to the many stories that did emerge and his newfound wealth Francis Drake quickly became a national hero and an influence at court and in business.

Now he was *Sir Francis Drake*

BOOK FOUR

SEATTLE, LATE-NOVEMBER

The Set-Up

15

Herb Trawets was in his shop very early on a late-November morning. He liked to make his business connections from there, with all of his books and references handy. The time zone difference meant that he had to start calling by 6:00 am if he was going to catch the London booksellers before they closed for the day.

He had four names on his list for today. He would start with Colin Mackenzie, a longtime contact with a big antiquarian book and map shop near Piccadilly Circus in the heart of the city. He smiled as he recalled his confusion on his first visit to London when he discovered that Circus was just an old Roman word for Circle. He had envisioned a carnival setting somehow, but at least he had kept that embarrassing mistake to himself.

Colin greeted him as a good colleague, "Good morning, Yrrab," he said "it is very good to hear from you." Colin was always somewhat formal and careful to be correct in things like the time of day in Seattle and the correct pronunciation of Herb's given name.

After a few pleasantries, Herb explained that he wouldn't be in London until the New Year but he was always curious about what was new in the London book market and, in particular, if there was anything newly available in his area of specialty, the American Northwest.

Colin described a few new additions to his inventory and then said in a somewhat hesitating manner, "Actually, Yrrab, there is something that you might be interested in and that could be of help to me, although it is not strictly in your focus area. I have an absolutely stunning set of the original 1589 Hakluyt publication of *The Principall Navigations, Voiages, Traffiques and Discoveries of the English Nation made by Sea or over Land*."

He went on to summarize how this was a benchmark publication in the history of worldwide exploration up to that time and that it included some of the very first accounts of voyages by leading English captains in Elizabethan times. A description of the around-the-world voyage by Sir Francis Drake had been inserted in the text a few years later, a rarity. It also included the large folded world map from Ortelius that was seldom found in the surviving editions. The set had the original cover boards and the pages were untrimmed. The coup de grace was that it was signed on the front piece by Richard Hakluyt, a true rarity.

"There is one caveat, Yrrab. The set can only be sold to a private collector who will not divulge its source. The reason that the books are in such immaculate condition is that they were acquired by an English Lord at the time of their publication and they have been almost untouched and unread for well over four hundred years. In fact, their existence is not very well known in the book world. Now, the current generation of descendants is in need of funds and they want to sell the set. However, for obvious reasons, they want their situation to be kept confidential. Therefore we can not sell them at auction or to a public collection held by a museum or university. A discrete private sale is wanted and an American collector might offer an additional degree of confidentiality. I can not even divulge the seller's identity to you at this point but I can assure you that we can guarantee the authenticity of the set to the eventual purchaser."

Herb could hardly believe what he had just heard. He immediately recognized that this was something that he had been seeking for quite a while. He had been counseling Ray Cartwright about books for years and had sold him many excellent editions related to local history. However, there were few opportunities left to sell him any truly valuable books on that topic; the reality was that Ray already owned copies of everything that was important. That was reinforced by the experience at the fair a few weeks ago when Ray only purchased a couple of minor, relatively cheap books. Herb had been hoping to find some way to expand the scope of Ray's collection, but his attempts to date had been unsuccessful, partly because he hadn't found a topic that excited him. Maybe this was it.

"I could be very interested in the set," he replied. "How should we proceed?"

"I can not sell it directly to you, even if you wanted that. We must know the book's ultimate destination."

"If I am going to develop an appropriate customer I need something."

"You can certainly describe the set; after all there are other ones in existence that have been well documented. Then you need to test the customer's receptivity based on the assurance of the extremely high quality and attributes. Once we know that we have a serious candidate we can arrange for the necessary reviews and inspection. Remember, discretion is our priority."

"Tell me then, Colin, what level of pricing are we talking about?"

"The seller wants to realize three hundred and fifty thousand pounds, which would be five hundred thousand American dollars. I believe that for something so rare and valuable, and with the need to find a very special buyer, we should be able to realize a thirty percent selling commission, for a total of six hundred fifty thousand dollars. One third of that commission, or fifty thousand dollars, would be paid to anyone who identified the ultimate buyer."

"That is a big price. It certainly puts a big premium on the special nature of the set. However, I want to make an attempt. Can you fax me the general description of the set and a listing of its attributes? I will be careful with the information, I assure you."

"Yes, I will do that. I trust you implicitly, Yrrab. Otherwise you never would have heard about this. Keep me informed about your progress; after all, we do have other leads that we are exploring."

"Thanks, Colin. I will be in touch."

After a few more closing comments, Herb hung up the phone and let out a big breath; he wasn't sure he had actually been breathing in and out for the past few minutes. "Unbelievable," he sighed.

He immediately started to plan his approach to the Vice President. In his concentration, he totally forgot that he had intended to make other calls to London that morning. Anything else could wait.

Without even waiting to receive more information from Colin Mackenzie, he pulled down some of his reference books and opened his computer to a comprehensive antiquarian book listing service. The key phrases that described the subject publication and interested him jumped out, "extraordinary collection…comprehensive…accurate…three volumes: Middle East and Asia; Northern Europe and Russia; America…Virginia, Florida, Brasil, Peru, California…"

He knew the key to getting Ray Cartwright's attention would lie in linking it to his current interests. Therefore the comments on California were of particular importance, "…first exposure to the Pacific Ocean and circumnavigation of the world by an Englishman, Francis Drake… discovery of the northwest coast…first publication about that voyage…only revelation of that journey that has been attributed to Drake for decades afterward…details held in secrecy by Queen Elizabeth's orders…"

"That has to be the link to the Vice President," Herb mused. "The discovery of the Pacific Ocean and the ventures to the coast of North America precede but can be linked to the later explorers. "There would be so much more to collect, and to sell," he smiled. "It could cover all of the early Spanish, Portuguese and English adventures. The valuable publications of the 1500s and 1600s would make the VP's current collection of the explorers and settlers of the 1700s and 1800s seem modern by comparison."

He then created a careful outline of the presentation he would make, knowing he needed to fill in many details before he actually proceeded. He hadn't been this pumped up for many years.

A couple of weeks later, having conversed with Colin Mackenzie in London a number of times and having organized all of the relevant information into a simple folder, he knew he was ready to act.

Drake's Dilemma

One real advantage of having dealt with Ray Cartwright about books for so long, and for having developed the strong relationship as his mentor on the subject, was that Herb could actually call the Vice President.

In fact, the number he had was for Elsie Browning, but anytime he left a message or request with her he knew it would be passed on to the Vice President and that he would get a timely response. This time he simply said that he had a special book offer to describe and that he would like to arrange a meeting when the VP was in Seattle for his usual Christmas break, less than two weeks away.

Two days later a meeting was confirmed.

16

Ray Cartwright, back in Seattle for Christmas and looking forward to the visit home by all the family, was in his home. He checked his schedule and saw that Herb Trawets was due in a few minutes. He liked Herb, and had always enjoyed their discussions about books, although he was a little puzzled by the upcoming visit. Never before had Herb asked for a meeting having provided so little advance information. In the past, he would send book descriptions and prices, and then the books themselves if Ray agreed on the spot or after a few telephone questions. He only came by personally if Ray wanted to inspect and discuss a book before deciding, and that had almost never occurred since he became Vice President. Herb had just said that he had something special and that was good enough for Ray to agree to the meeting; Herb wasn't one to waste time or act frivolously.

After Herb arrived and they exchanged greetings, Herb came right to the point. "Mr. Vice President," he said, "There is an extraordinary opportunity to secure a treasure in the book world."

He then proceeded to describe the Hakluyt books and the specific situation regarding their availability. Only at the end did he mention the price.

Ray had listened to Herb's presentation without interruption. When he was finished, there was a long pause.

"Herb, that is intriguing but it would be a big change. I do recognize that I haven't been finding many exciting books lately, and I have thought about expanding my scope, but worldwide exploration seems to be too much of a reach."

"I know that, and I guess my suggestion is to think about the Pacific as a natural extension."

"OK; at least the American side of it. What if we just try to locate a copy of the Hakluyt volume related to the Americas? That's my real interest."

"We can do that. I am sure I can find an isolated volume in good shape with a little time. The cost of such a volume would only be a fraction of what we have been talking about, but, of course, it is unlikely to have the unique quality and provenance."

Herb had come to know Ray quite well over the years. He knew that the enthusiasm the Vice President had developed for antique books and his quiet pride in his collection were very real. He was sure that the uniqueness of the offer, even with the somewhat tenuous link to his previous interests, would likely prevail once he had time to think about it. So, he just continued, "Why don't I see what I can find?"

Ray smiled. "Herb, you sly rascal, you know you have piqued my interest. Already I am visualizing the books, even though I am trying to be rational about it. We know this whole subject is not really rational in the first place."

Herb said nothing. After another pause, Ray said, "OK, can you have the books sent over on approval? I need to see them before I can decide."

"Certainly; I will arrange for them to be couriered from London. I'll let you know when they arrive."

They ended their meeting then, cordially chatting about their imminent Christmas plans and exchanging good wishes. Without another word on the subject, they both knew privately that the deal was going to happen.

And that was exactly what happened.

Herb made all of the arrangements with Colin Mackenzie, who was very pleased with the identity of the customer and the discretion that could be assured.

The Hakluyt set sold itself once Ray saw it and touched it.

As requested by Herb, on instructions from Colin, Ray arranged for Maria to send the payment to Herb, Colin and the seller's bank account in three separate bank transfers.

It was a Merry Christmas all the way around.

17

February in San Francisco; the California International Antiquarian Book Fair was in its final stages of preparation. Unlike the smaller fairs in locations such as Seattle, this event was limited to members of the Antiquarian Booksellers' Associations and it attracted sellers from around the world. There were over two hundred booths set out in rows throughout the building.

Everyone liked visiting San Francisco with its laid-back ambience in a spectacular setting. The hotels and shops in the Union Square section were always a major draw, if it's OK to refer to Neiman-Marcus, Saks Fifth Avenue, Tiffany's, and the like as shops. People never seemed to tire of taking a cable car ride over the hills and down to Fisherman's Wharf to have a fabulous seafood dinner in a restaurant looking over the Bay, across Alcatraz Island to the Golden Gate Bridge.

This Book Fair alternated between San Francisco and Los Angeles each year.

In Los Angeles it was held in a very upscale hotel and convention facility on Santa Monica Boulevard in Hollywood, the site of a former movie sound stage complex.

In San Francisco, the setting was very different. It was in an old warehouse located a couple miles south of the city center, almost underneath the freeway that headed across the Bay to Oakland. The building was a full block long but very narrow; it had been a railway loading shed. Four aisles of bookseller booths were laid out for almost 1000 feet in length, although taking less than 100 feet in total width.

The ceiling was relatively high, having a hip-shaped rise in the middle that accommodated long rows of skylights. Its main feature was that it leaked when it rained, as almost always happened at this time of the year in San Francisco. This led to the ridiculous, certainly frustrating, need for dealers in the center aisle to spread large plastic sheets over the tops of their booths to protect their books, some of which were worth many hundreds of thousands of dollars. Nothing is more devastating for a book than water.

The entrance to the booksellers' layout was decorated with a large wooden arch that looked like an open book. The logos of the International and the American antiquarian booksellers associations were displayed as was the phrase "Amor Librorum Nos Unit" in large block letters. "The Love of Books Unites Us."

As always, the dealers were sizing up each other's offerings and making pre-fair deals. There was a steady hum of activity and noise, but nothing compared to the near-chaos that would occur when the doors were opened to the public buyers at 2:00 pm and hundreds of them would appear.

Again, the Vice President had arranged for early access. When he arrived, he attempted to casually wander through the displays but, of course, that was impossible. The word of his presence immediately spread through the whole place.

The booksellers at this level were used to celebrities, especially in California where people associated with the entertainment industry often showed up. In fact, most of them were simply treated as another group of well-to-do potential customers. They tended to keep their real admiration for celebrities in the book world, people such as John Dunning, an established Denver book dealer who wrote a number of best-selling mystery novels with a bookselling theme, or Nicholas Basbanes, who wrote a series of books that chronicle the history and idiosyncrasies of book collectors.

The Vice President was in a category of his own - famous, rich, public figure and book collector to be sure – but also a bit removed from the others because of his position. Certainly, almost everyone waited for him to make the first contact during his visits.

Ray had a program with the floor plan and list of dealers. He initially sought out the dealers he knew best. Due to his location near the entrance, the first one he encountered was Jeremy Boucher.

After the normal greetings Ray started to browse through Jeremy's display of journals and books about the early Spanish explorers who came to the Mexico and California coasts. This caught Jeremy by surprise as the Vice President had never shown much of an interest in that area before.

"Tell me about this one by Ulloa," asked Ray.

"He was one of the very first Spanish explorers to survey the California coast in the 1500s and therefore his journals are of great historical interest. "The fact is that even though the Spaniards controlled most of Central and South America from the time of Columbus until the 1800s, they did not explore north of Mexico very much for almost three hundred years. That seems amazing to us now, but the riches of gold, silver, emeralds and other precious things to be found in the south deterred everyone who had crossed the Atlantic and the jungles of Panama from heading north to lands of deserts and no discernible riches.

"In fact, the western coast of North America wasn't accurately defined by western Europeans until the voyage of James Cook in 1779. Descriptions of the area from the 1500s are rare. The Spaniards tended to keep any knowledge that they obtained very quiet; they considered such information to be a state secret. This volume you are looking at is in very good condition and is complete with all the original maps and illustrations. You know I am meticulous about that."

"I see on your tag that the price is $25,000?"

"Yes. However, for a serious collector and good customer like you, I can adjust that by fifteen percent."

"I'll take it," Ray said, suppressing a smile as he saw the momentary look of surprise on Jeremy's face. Of course, Jeremy was not aware of his purchase of the Hakluyt volumes and of his newfound broader interest in the Pacific. Ray had also secured some reference books from Herb Trawets last month and was already aware of books such as the Ulloa and their value.

His next stop along the aisles of display booths was at Alan Page's.

"Hi, Alan."

"Hello, Mr. Vice President, it's great to see you again."

"What's new?"

"Well not much in your area I am sorry to say."

"Oh. How about early Pacific Ocean voyages, say in the 1500s and 1600s? I have some new interests."

"Well, for sure. I have some Spanish volumes linked to Central America and Mexico."

"I was thinking a little further north, at least southern California."

"I have a few minor items. Let me show you."

As he found the books and passed them over to the Vice-President for inspection, Alan's mind was working as hard as it could to think of some way to capitalize on this new information. After all, Alan didn't call himself the Eagle Scout without reason.

"Thanks, Alan. I think I'll pass on these for now," said Ray as he passed back the three small volumes.

"You know, Mr. Vice President, if you are collecting the explorers of the Pacific Ocean you should have a copy of the journals of Magellan. He was the first European to see the Pacific from the east when he rounded the southern tip of South America in 1519. His ship *Victoria* was the first to actually sail around the world. I don't have my copy here at the fair but I can certainly arrange for you to see it very soon if you are interested."

"I would love to see it. Please call Elsie Browning at my office to arrange it."

"I'll do that. I'll be in touch soon."

The Vice President moved on and, as he did so, Alan started working his laptop computer to search his records and the various internet sites. All he had to do now was find a copy of Magellan's journal before anyone else sold one to the VP. "Ah, yes. Book scouting at the highest level possible," he thought to himself, smiling at his ingenuity in positioning the sale of an expensive book even before he had found it, let alone obtained it.

Ray Cartwright next stopped at Herb Trawets' booth. They greeted each other warmly but the Vice President did not take time to look at the books on display. He had already reviewed Herb's collection back in Seattle and had purchased a few books that Herb had obtained on his January trip to London.

Herb did say, "If you have a few minutes now, there is someone I would like to introduce to you."

"Certainly."

They headed down the next aisle to a booth with a stylized Union Jack symbol displayed. Herb caught the eye of the book dealer in the booth, who had seen the mini-procession approach, and said, "Colin, I would like to introduce you to Vice President Cartwright."

"Mr. Vice President, I am pleased to introduce Mr. Colin Mackenzie from London, one of the leading book experts in the world and a good friend who received me well on my recent trip over there."

"It's my pleasure, Mr. Mackenzie."

"I am honored, Mr. Vice President."

They conversed for a few minutes longer and the Vice President took a copy of the extensive catalogue of books that Colin offered. Although they both knew the reason for Herb's introduction, there was not even the slightest reference to the Hakluyt collection and the earlier dealings.

Then the Vice President slowly made his way out of the book fair, stopping here and there to acknowledge some past contacts and to say hello to a few dealers who displayed early exploration materials, where he collected a number of additional catalogues. Most dealers dealt in other subjects, such as famous authors, poetry, science or modern novels. He generally passed those booths with a polite wave, much to their disappointment.

18

He was at his desk taking stock of the situation.

He felt that everything had progressed as hoped for so far, but that didn't mean much, as everything so far had been generally under his control and hadn't involved any direct contact with others. The Vice President's new interest in the Pacific Ocean was a good development; that would make the introduction of the subject more natural.

The New York fair was coming up relatively soon, mid-April. It was time to start things rolling in anticipation of that.

He knew that the key to success was going to be the human factor —convincing a buyer that they could have something that no one else could have. That was the epitome for a serious collector of anything, whether it is books, paintings or baseball cards. The buyer just had to believe in the authenticity and the uniqueness of the item.

"Time to get started," he sighed, with a mixture of quiet excitement and a sense of vulnerability. It was a huge risk that he was about to undertake.

Then, looking down at the document in front of him, he broke into a sly smile.

He reached for the telephone.

19

Ray Cartwright was in his Washington, D.C. office, again in a meeting of his key advisors as they planned out his upcoming schedule. After all, the first presidential primaries were now less than a year away.

"OK," said Ray. "Where are we?"

"Everything is lining up as we would hope," replied Ralph King, his chief political advisor. "Sure, as always, there will be some other candidates for the party nomination, but they are going to be limited to those marginal ones who have a cause to promote or a constituency to serve. They won't drum up any serious support. The more mainline contenders, especially the Senate Majority Leader and the Speaker of the House, are not going to challenge you. They don't see how they can beat you and they certainly don't want to lose their current positions of influence and power."

"That is probably true," added Calvin Begg, the Chief of Staff, "but we don't want to get too comfortable. The party members, and especially those candidates for the Senate, the House of Representatives and the state governments, want to see an active primary campaign. That is how they can get some additional profile and press coverage at our expense, when they appear at the rallies and provide introductions and endorsements."

"Besides," interjected Ralph, "we can't let the other party gather all of the attention and publicity while they determine their candidate, although, again, I don't think any of the big guns are going to want to take you on this time and lose their chance for running in the future."

"That may be," said Ray, "but I don't want anyone to get complacent. Remember, in similar situations, that the same sort of advice was given to President Ford in 1976 and to the first President Bush in 1992. Then the relatively unknown southern governors, first Jimmy Carter and then Bill Clinton, ended up in the White House. And, in 2008, who would have believed ahead of time that Barack Obama was going to emerge out of the blue and defeat Hillary Clinton for the Democratic nomination and then go on to win the presidency quite handily?"

"Well, Mr. Vice President, we do have a plan and a schedule mocked up for your review. It starts right away and involves appearances at the requisite dinners, special-interest conventions and political conferences in many key states," continued Ralph.

"We have even developed a new theme for the campaign," he continued. "I believe it is a real winner, and yet it now seems so obvious to me; I don't know why we didn't come up with it earlier. The message is that, with your leadership, the future of America is rock solid. The images will be of decisiveness and steadfastness in the face of all the issues before the voters. That's been your legacy, that's what *The Vote* was all about. The key element to bring it all together, of course, is your name, Raymond Oliver Cartwright, ROC. Our tag line will be "America, ROC Solid." That logo will be used in all of the material, whether it is print, radio or television, and it will be used to punctuate your speeches."

After a pause, Ray said, "OK, I like it. Let's do it. When do we get started?"

"Well,' said Calvin with a bit of a twinkle in his eye, "there is the Ecumenical Conference in New York next month. I think I can clear your calendar if you are interested."

Ray smiled as he knew exactly what Calvin was referring to; they all knew his passion for attending the big book fairs on the side.

"Fine," said Vince Larch, the general counsel who had been keeping silent until then. "Just be sure to keep careful track of the various activities and their costs and payments – whether it is official, political or personal. We all know how much scrutiny is given to those things these days by the interest groups and the press."

With that, the meeting broke up.

20

Jeremy Boucher was back in his bookshop in Ohio after the trip to the San Francisco Book Fair, contemplating how to proceed.

He had been pleasantly surprised when Vice President Cartwright showed his new-found interest in the exploration of the Pacific coast of North America in a much broader context than previously. He had been very fortunate to have that volume of the Spaniard Ulloa's early expedition to California, since he did not actually focus very much on that area of collecting, with his main area of expertise being the eastern U.S. and the Revolutionary and Civil wars.

Now, he needed to plan how to best capitalize on this new information. The New York Book Fair was coming up in April, just six weeks away, and he knew there was a good chance that the Vice President would be there; he seldom missed that big event.

The trouble was that there were not that many available, valuable books on the subject that met Jeremy's high standards. Publications before the late 1700s were scarce, and there was limited focus on the Pacific. As he had told the Vice President, the Spaniards had controlled the area for a long time and they did not publish much, preferring to keep their knowledge secret and to focus on their exploitation of Central and South America with the vast riches of gold, silver and jewels.

He decided that his planned trip to London and continental Europe next month would provide the best opportunity. He didn't think he could locate what he wanted just by perusing the internet and making a few phone calls. He needed to ferret out books from the voluminous inventories of the many antiquarian dealers over there.

"Yes," he thought, "I need something special to catch his attention and to further stimulate his interest."

Alan Page was both pleased with himself and nervous.

He was pleased about how his spontaneous initiative with Vice President Cartwright to sell him a first edition of the Magellan document had paid off so well. Right after the San Francisco Fair he was able to locate a copy with an antiquarian bookseller in Madrid. After the normal posturing and negotiating, he was able to purchase it for a twenty percent dealer's discount, all subject to his inspection of the journal.

Then, there was a whirlwind of activity and logistics. He had it shipped to Phoenix and, after a couple of phone calls to the Vice President's office, he sent it on to Washington, accompanied with a very complete note that described the book and its importance. In a similar manner to what he had done with the La Perouse journals years before, he also included a copy of a modern reprint which had been published by the Yale Press and that was a nice piece of art in itself. It contained an English translation to enhance the Vice President's enjoyment of the historic document.

He received a short phone call from Ray Cartwright soon afterwards and, after a short discussion about some of the historical specifics, they made a deal. When it was all said and done, Alan had made a profit of $20,000 without any risk or exposure of his own money. It was one of his finest moments as a scout.

He was nervous because he was also contemplating his next encounter with the Vice President, hopefully at the New York Antiquarian Book Fair. He had been rehearsing his initial approach for some time, but he knew it would all depend on the reaction he received when he was able to explain himself in more detail in a follow-up, if that happened. Nervous, to be sure; he didn't want to spend the next few years in jail!

Herb Trawets was also thinking about the New York Fair. His year was off to a good start and he surely wanted that to continue.

His trip to London in January had been productive and he had followed that up with some good sales at the February fair in San Francisco, all on top of his ongoing dealings with his major customers.

He also recalled his exciting dealings with Colin Mackenzie in London the previous December that led to the private sale of the Hakluyt volumes to Ray Cartwright. As a result he had also sold the Vice President a few other related volumes and reference books, but nothing very significant.

Herb had to admit to himself that he had not been as quick to capitalize on the Vice President's new interest as he should have been. Jeremy Boucher had jumped on the opportunity with his Spanish publication at the San Francisco Book Fair and Alan Page had created a sale out of thin air.

He knew about the Alan Page sale of the Magellan journal from the Vice President himself. When Ray was considering the purchase, he had called Herb for advice. This was not at all unusual. When a book dealer and a customer develop a close and ongoing relationship, the book dealer is quite prepared to offer good and candid advice about a book that the customer is considering from another dealer. His professionalism ensures that he gives good advice and, as a result, the relationship becomes even stronger. This means that, in the longer term, that dealer maintains a privileged position which leads to more sales.

Herb decided that he had better call Colin Mackenzie again, as well as some of his other contacts in London, to see what he could dig up. Of course, they also were now aware of the Vice President's expanded horizons and some of them would be in New York, but they didn't have any special inside connections that often made the difference when dealing with someone so busy and protected.

BOOK FIVE

LONDON, 1588

The Tarnished Hero

21

"Sir Francis, the Spanish flotilla has been sighted approaching the English Channel. It is surely their invasion armada; there are more than 100 ships. The Queen has ordered the navy to mobilize."

"Fine," he said, as he rolled his last ball across the lawn bowling surface at his Plymouth club and gathered himself for the challenge ahead.

As he headed for the harbor in Plymouth and the waiting English fleet, he was very focused and determined. He was looking forward to confronting the Spanish navy, unlike many fellow Englishmen, and even the Queen, who had been dreading this day for over twenty-five years. For Sir Francis this was the culmination of his vendetta against Spain that had started twenty years earlier when he was betrayed in the Caribbean.

He was also confident that the new ships of the English fleet, which were smaller, longer, lower, nimbler, more stable and armed with many broadside guns, would be able to outmaneuver the larger, slower Spanish ships whose tactics were to close on enemy ships, grapple them with hooks and ropes, and then board them with a swarm of marines.

He also had time to reminisce about the seven years that had passed since his around-the-world voyage and his knighthood. So many things had happened, with many ups and downs.

He had purchased a large manor home near Plymouth, Buckland Abbey, and had created a lavish lifestyle with his wife Mary. He had also invested in many other buildings, lands and businesses. He served one year as Mayor of Plymouth, a somewhat ceremonial position, but one that reflected his new-found place in the upper business and social circles. He was also elected as the Plymouth Member of Parliament for a term that allowed him to interact with the leading politicians and policy makers.

A sad period occurred when Mary died unexpectedly in 1583; she had seen so much positive and exciting change in her life after Francis returned in 1580. He remarried in 1585, this time to Elizabeth Sydenham, the young daughter of a rich aristocratic family, which also served to increase his social standing. She was 20 years old; he was in his early 40s.

For years after his return he had lobbied the Queen and her key advisors for a return voyage to the Pacific which would follow up on his discoveries and claims. He visualized colonies on the west coast of America and new alliances with the American natives and in the Spice Islands of the western Pacific, where he believed the Portuguese were vulnerable.

Although he knew that the Spanish had somewhat reinforced their American territories from Panama down the Atlantic to the Strait of Magellan, and up the Pacific to Chile and Peru, Drake believed that they could not stop a concerted English effort.

However, the Queen would not let him leave England; she wanted him to be close in case war broke out with Spain.

In 1581, he had helped plan an attack on the Azores in support of the exiled pretender-king of Portugal, which would give England control of the critical Atlantic way station. They had amassed ships, arms, provisions and investors who foresaw profit in assailing the Spanish shipping. The Queen ordered its cancellation in fear of stimulating an all-out war.

In 1582, he was instrumental in organizing an East Indies voyage that was designed to go through the Magellan Strait and to the Spice Islands, but also to again secretly sail to northern latitudes and to further the knowledge of those Pacific shores and inlets. Led by Edward Fenton, who had sailed with Frobisher to Greenland and the shores of northeast America, the four-ship foray was a disaster. With dissension in the officer ranks, disease rampant, and a disastrous encounter with a Spanish galleon off the eastern shores of South America, they turned back to England without even reaching the Strait of Magellan. Drake was disgusted.

Over the following couple of years the Spanish had strengthened their European position: ports were blockaded against the English trading ships and some were seized; the Netherlands was being brought under control; France was in disarray. England was becoming isolated and vulnerable.

Finally, in 1585, the Queen gave Sir Francis a commission to attack the Spanish interests in the Caribbean, as much in the hope of gaining badly needed treasure as for harassing the Spanish.

It was a very large undertaking with 25 ships and 2000 men, at a cost of £60,000. The adventure had lasted ten months.

They had missed the Spanish treasure-laden flotilla at sea and had been repelled at the Canaries and Cape Verde. They did capture Santo Domingo and Cartagena, but after long negotiations they realized very little value in ransom. The Spaniards had been forewarned and most of the valuables had been removed from the cities.

On the return voyage to England, they attacked and destroyed the Spanish town of St. Augustine in Florida and they rescued the struggling and starving English settlers at Roanoke in the Virginias. Overall the adventure was a huge financial failure.

It had generated some national pride in England over the capture of Santo Domingo, but it also created chaos and anger in Spain, which led to an increased determination to invade England. Spain began planning a foray that would see their navy control the English Channel and their army invading from bases in the Netherlands.

Fearful of England being undefended, Queen Elizabeth denied permission for any other Caribbean ventures.

In late 1586 Lord Walsingham, utilizing a network of spies and informants, uncovered a Catholic plot, supported by Spain, to kill Queen Elizabeth and install the Scottish Catholic Mary Queen of Scots as Queen of England. In early 1587 Mary was beheaded in the Tower of London on the orders of Queen Elizabeth. Relations between England and Spain were at the boiling point.

After extensive lobbying, in the spring of 1587, the Queen approved a plan for Drake to attack Spain itself, hoping to disrupt their preparations of an invasion force and to seize valuables. It again was to be a privateer operation, financed by wealthy investors and merchants.

A fleet of 24 ships and 3000 men sailed on April 1, 1587.

Three weeks later they entered the southern Spanish port of Cadiz and, after scattering the defenders and destroying more than 30 ships, seized valuables and supplies. They had truly "singed the beard of King Philip."

Next, further northwest along the coast at Cape St. Vincent, they again captured the port, this time sinking almost 50 ships and as many fishing boats. They also destroyed a large quantity of supplies such as planks and barrel staves that would hinder the Spanish navy's logistics and provisioning for years.

Then, further north again, they blockaded the port serving the Portuguese capital of Lisbon, capturing a large naval ship and driving the defending forces inland.

The final coup was at the Azores Islands, where they captured the large caravel *Sao Felipe* laden with gold, silver, jewels and spices returning from the East Indies.

The English venture was totally successful, both in achieving a huge return for its investors and in delaying the Spanish attack on England for a year. The Spanish military was in disarray after the attacks and the priority for Spain was then diverted to enhance its fortifications and defense preparations in case the English returned.

Nevertheless, the Spanish were determined to achieve revenge against the English; it was just being delayed.

Francis Drake knew all of this as he reached his flagship in the Plymouth harbor and prepared to sail out against the Spanish fleet. He only hoped that their emotional determination had caused them to be less prepared and less formidable than they might have been; England's freedom was at stake.

22

On July 20, 1588 the Spanish Armada entered the English Channel, sailing steadily east in an impressive formation that could easily be observed from the English shore. Seventy-five naval ships stretched in a wedge formation over a length of more than two miles, with another 50 supply and support vessels in the protected interior positions. The ships carried 30,000 men and over 2,000 cannons and mortars.

The Spanish intent was to sail the length of the English Channel to the Dutch coast where they would escort the waiting Spanish army in an assault on England.

Over the next week there were a number of intense, multi-hour naval battles, but no decisive results. The English were able to attack the Spanish from a distance with their faster ships and much more agile cannon mountings but they inflicted little serious damage. The Spanish were unable to cause much damage to the elusive English ships and could not manage to grapple and board any of them. Nevertheless, the Armada continued its relentless eastward passage along the Channel.

Drake did manage to capture a large supply ship that carried most of the Spanish fleet's money that was destined to pay the armed forces in the Netherlands. One other Spanish ship was destroyed in a fire that broke out onboard.

On July 27th the Spanish fleet reached the French coast at Calais, where they could anchor in a bay with some protection for the first time. They were just a few miles from the English coast at Dover and a few miles from the Dutch coast where the Spanish army was to be collected.

However, to the surprise and frustration of the Spanish naval admiral, the Spanish army was not ready for deployment. In fact, it had no means to rendezvous with the Armada. The flat bottom boats that they would need to depart the shallow Dutch shores were not seaworthy in the stormy English Channel.

Sir Francis Drake knew that the time had come to make a decisive move. They could not wait for the Spanish ships to reorganize and arrange some logistical solution to the army's problem.

The English floated dozens of small ships that had been set on fire into the Bay of Calais. Fearing that their ships would be burned and destroyed, the Spanish fleet indeed sailed out into the Channel, where they faced the English navy in an intense naval battle that lasted most of a day.

This time, Drake urged his ships to engage the Spanish more aggressively, close enough that their cannons were much more effective, but still out of the reaches of the Spanish boarding tactics. Four Spanish ships were sunk, others were disabled and captured, and over 2000 Spaniards were killed, wounded or captured.

The Spanish fleet was driven into the North Sea where the winds and currents carried it away from the English shores in disarray. The English had successfully prevented the Spanish invasion.

Over the next few months, the remnants of the Spanish Armada sailed north of Scotland and then south down the Atlantic, west of Ireland, to return home to Spain. By the time they did get home they had lost 60 ships and 15,000 men, many of them in ship wrecks on the rugged Irish coast as well as due to rampant disease.

In England, Francis Drake and the naval leaders were treated as heroes, but with some reservation. Yes, they had driven off the Spanish Armada, at least for now, but, in reality, the English navy had had limited success in actually attacking and destroying the Spanish ships. The Spanish had been defeated as much by the weather and their own poor planning and logistics as anything else. They might come back again better prepared and more effective.

Francis Drake was incensed by the criticism and second-guessing that arose within the Queen's court. To him, the naval actions had been truly heroic; England had driven off the most powerful nation in the history of the world, both in terms of its control of countries and continents and by the scale of its enormous wealth.

Over the next six months, Drake rallied support and lobbied the Queen and her key advisors to organize a follow-up attack on Spain in order to eliminate the threat of another invasion attempt.

There was a great deal of support for the undertaking but based on many different reasons.

The Queen and her council, including Lord Burghley now, wanted to pursue the remnants of the Spanish Armada and destroy as much of it as possible. It was believed that the ships, many of them damaged, were at anchor in northern Spanish ports such as Corunna and Santander.

The Portuguese Pretender, Dom Antonio, and his supporters wanted the English to attack Lisbon. They believed that the Portuguese would rise up to welcome them and support them in the ousting of the foreign Spanish army and authorities. This would give the English a critical ally and base of operations against the Spanish in the future.

The English investors and merchants wanted the pursuit of the Spanish to lead to the plundering of Spanish cities and the capture of the Azores, so that England could control the seaways and attack treasure flotillas returning from America and the East Indies.

Finally, in February, 1589, Queen Elizabeth gave her permission for the force to sail against Spain. Preparations consumed the following two months, with a great deal of confusion and contradictory decisions by the Queen and her authorities.

In mid-April they set sail, again somewhat prematurely for fear the Queen would cancel her permission. It was the largest English naval force ever amassed: 180 ships, 13,000 sailors and 4,000 marines. They had many ship board cannons and plenty of arms for the soldiers, but they sailed without taking any heavy siege guns, which would be required if they were going to attack land-based fortresses. They dared not wait.

The ships were also much under-provisioned for such a large force and an expected long campaign. They were going to need to secure water and food along the coasts of Portugal and Spain.

The voyage started poorly. Bad weather and stormy seas delayed and dispersed their fleet; some ships even defected and turned back. Provisions were consumed and new supplies were not obtained.

Having been driven farther south than planned, they did manage to reach Corunna in northwest Spain and attacked. The Spanish had been forewarned and there were few Armada ships still in port to be destroyed. The army did defeat a small relief force that the Spanish had sent to the city but it failed to siege the main inland upper town; they did not have enough firepower. They razed the lower port city and confiscated some provisions, but these did little good to alleviate their problem since the bad weather forced them to stay in the port for more than two weeks.

Then they sailed south to Portugal, intent on attacking Lisbon and all but ignoring Queen Elizabeth's ordered priority to pursue and destroy the Spanish navy.

The English marines were landed in order to attack the city overland while Drake led the ships into the open bay and towards the port. Both forces captured small towns on the way but they were stymied at Lisbon itself. The expected uprising of the Portuguese to support them with men, arms and provisions did not occur. They refused to commit themselves against the ruling Spanish forces until they could see that the English were successful in their invasion. It was an impossible condition since, without their help, the English were ineffective.

After three weeks of attacks and counter-attacks, the English retreated, having lost many men in battle. The lack of siege guns had cost them dearly; the Spaniards could not be dislodged from their positions.

Most of their remaining force was in poor condition due to disease, an all too common result of large groups being confined together in small spaces with inadequate provisions.

Their next target was the Azores but heavy winds, sick crews and more defecting ships prevented that.

The fleet disbursed and returned to England in failure. The Spanish had not been damaged and England had lost 10,000 men. Huge financial losses resulted and there were many confrontations over the sharing of the limited spoils that had been captured.

England's national pride and international presence had been diminished. Sir Francis Drake's personal reputation and heroism was tarnished.

After months of naval inquiries and legal disputes with the investors in London, Drake returned to the quieter life of his home in Plymouth in late 1589.

BOOK SIX

NEW YORK, APRIL

The Approach

23

New York weather in April is always a bit of a crap shoot. In many years it would be great, as spring would bring sunny skies and the emergence of fresh green grass and flowers in the parks. This was not one of those years. The skies were dark with heavy clouds, the wind was blowing steadily and the rain only varied from showers to thunderstorms.

The book dealers arriving for the New York Antiquarian Book Fair were feeling a little depressed as they organized their materials. It was always a bit of a hassle, even in a spacious place like the Park Avenue Armory. There were a couple of hundred dealers all trying to maneuver the entrances and aisles at the same time, hindered by the multitude of boxes they all transported from place to place. Books all have one thing in common – they are heavy.

The weather affected the mood in a practical way as well. They knew that it could reduce the attendance of potential customers at the fair. The decision to come was always a discretionary one for customers and the logistics of Manhattan, even in good weather, were challenging. Those people from the city knew taxis came at a premium in the rainy weather and those from out of town knew that traffic just became more impossible than usual.

Even though New York is an amazing city to visit, most of the dealers had been here many times before and the novelty had worn off. This was reinforced by the fact that the fair stayed open well into the evening on the Friday and Saturday of the three day event. Having been on their feet for long hours, few dealers hit the Great White Way.

Jeremy Boucher was quite relaxed, in spite of the weather. This fair was always good for him, as the demand for Revolutionary and Civil War material never seemed to wane. He often joked that he wished that Presidents Washington and Lincoln had done their own shopping – even a hand-written grocery list would sell for a good price.

Herb Trawets was also feeling fine. Although demand for his Pacific Northwest specialty wasn't quite as high here as in California, he certainly had a broad enough general selection to entice many buyers.

Alan Page was neither relaxed nor calm. He had carefully set up his booth, as always, but, unlike essentially every other book fair that he had ever attended, he was not cruising the aisles to search out hidden gems in the collections of the other dealers. He stayed put, mentally visualizing his hoped-for encounter with the Vice President.

Ray Cartwright arrived on the scene, as was usual now, about 10:00, two hours before the noon opening to the public. He was upbeat as his political speech the previous evening had gone very well and the "ROC" campaign tag was catching on with the public according to early polls

As the vagaries of chance would have it, the lottery for dealer booth locations at the fair this year had resulted in Jeremy, Herb and Alan all being well back from the main entrance and so he did not see them for a while.

As Ray worked his way through the aisles, he was easily and often distracted by various book sellers with items of interest. From Simon Katz, an upscale dealer who was actually based in New York City, he purchased a fine book related to the early settlements in the Oregon Territory. From Graham Maltsby, an Australian dealer who specialized in Pacific explorers, he obtained a first edition of William Coxe's *Account of the Russian Discoveries between Asia and America* that was published in 1780. This was one of the first relatively accurate descriptions of the Alaskan coast ever published in English based on the journeys of the Russian explorers such as Bering. The final stages of the voyage of James Cook that approached the same coasts from the south was still in progress at the time that Coxe was published, although Cook himself had been killed in Hawaii in 1779. Ray's Pacific Ocean collecting horizons were continuing to expand.

Ray was also attracted to a display of very colorful maps that were displayed in the same booth. They were generally from the period 1550 to 1800 and showed the different stages of knowledge about the American west coast over time. Although many antique book collectors also become quite involved with antiquarian maps, and vice versa, Ray had never paid much attention to them as discrete objects which had been published separately, as compared to those maps that were often included with the books and journals of explorers. He left the booth thinking to himself that he should learn more about that aspect of collecting history.

Arriving first at Jeremy's display, and then Herb's, Ray was running short on time and so he just exchanged general pleasantries. In spite of their searches over the previous month, neither of them had uncovered any books of high interest to him. They both gave him their printed lists of books that were with them at the fair and he agreed that he would study them when he had some time. Naturally, they were both somewhat disappointed that they had not at least had a chance for a longer conversation; after all he was their most famous customer and they knew that they gained some respect and guarded jealousy from their fellow dealers because of that.

When he reached Alan's booth, after the opening greetings he started to give the same explanation about running out of time and that he hoped to see Alan again soon in the future. Somewhat out of character, Alan essentially cut off the Vice President in mid-sentence, "Oh, Mr. Vice President, I was so looking forward to seeing you. I have located an extremely special publication that I know will be of interest to you and I was hoping to get the chance to tell you about it."

"What is it?" Ray asked

"I'm sorry; I can't tell you all about it here. It involves a very sensitive and discrete situation, which I know you can appreciate from other dealings you've had in the past. Is there any way that I can get a few minutes with you to discuss it?"

This took Ray aback a bit. Although he'd known and dealt with Alan a number of times in the past, he had never been approached in this direct but ambiguous manner before. However, his curiosity was aroused and he knew that Alan had been the source of some of his favorite books, such as the journals of the La Perouse and Magellan voyages.

"Well, I must rush away now. I will be in Arizona in a couple of weeks to address a party convention as part of my national travels. Will you be back home then? I'm sure that I could find a few minutes to talk."

"That would be great."

"OK, call my office, as you did with that book last time, and they can set up a time."

"Thank you. I will do that."

Ray turned and left for the exit with his security entourage in his wake. They looked around somewhat nervously as the main doors were opened and the crowd of keen book buyers surged down the aisles.

Meanwhile, Alan simply sat down in the chair at the back of his booth and stared into space. He didn't even notice that his shirt was soaking with sweat and that his breath was coming in short, fast gasps. However, he quickly came out of it when the customers started to gather around his display and he had something to distract him.

Later, when things slowed down a bit, all he could think of was the ancient phrase used by Julius Caesar when he crossed the Rubicon River on his way back from Gaul to take over the Roman Empire, *Iacta alea est*, "The die is cast." He realized that he hadn't totally lost his sense of humor, perhaps gallows humor he thought, as he also recalled the gladiators' salute, *Morituri te salutant*, "We who are about to die salute you."

Then he looked up a phone number in his daily journal.

24

Two weeks later, the Vice President had just returned to his hotel suite in Phoenix, fresh from a series of meetings with local party leaders and a de-briefing session with Ralph King, his political advisor, who had accompanied him on the trip. They were pleased at how everything was progressing and knew that the speech at the state convention that evening would be a successful event. Arizona was an area of solid support for Ray.

He noted on his daily itinerary that Alan Page was scheduled to meet with him this afternoon. Ray recalled the somewhat strange comments that Alan had made at the New York Fair and briefly wondered what that was about, but he knew that he was always interested in good books. "I guess that I'll just have to wait and see," he thought to himself.

An hour or so later there was a knock at the door and the on-duty secret service agent announced that Alan Page was there for his appointment.

"Hello, Mr. Vice President."

"Hello, Alan, come on in and take a seat. It's good to see you, and I am a little curious to know what this mysterious book thing is all about."

"Well, Mr. Vice President, it is a very complicated and certainly unusual situation, but I think you'll also find it intriguing."

"OK, let's get right to it. Already you have my attention."

Taking a bit of a sigh, Alan started the story. "First of all, I must repeat what I told you in New York. This is a very sensitive and discreet situation; in fact, even if we do not proceed with an arrangement, I must ask you to keep our whole discussion secret from absolutely everyone. It is our faith in your discretion that has led me to be here today."

Ray looked Alan straight in the eye, and with a hint of suspicion on his face and in his voice simply said, "I will certainly be discreet but I guess I must also be cautious. If the situation seems uncomfortable, I'll simply terminate our conversation."

"Fair enough."

"It all starts with Sir Francis Drake in the late sixteenth century," continued Alan. "I am sure you know the story of his epic journey around the world that involved both pillaging Spanish ships and towns and undertaking new explorations in the Pacific.

"He's credited with sailing up the west coast of North America as far as Northern California and Oregon – the first Englishman to do so.

"You also know, I'm sure, that when Francis Drake returned to England all of his journals and maps were confiscated by Queen Elizabeth since she was concerned that the public dissemination of Drake's descriptions of looting the Spanish would enrage the Spanish and could lead to war. The situation between England and Spain was very tense in those days, fueled by the Spanish King's ambition to conquer large parts of the world and the religious zeal of the Catholics to obliterate the separate Anglican Protestant leaders of England, which had started with the English King Henry VIII, Elizabeth's father.

"In fact, over his whole lifetime, which lasted for sixteen years after that epic voyage and which included his later heroic leadership against the Spanish Armada, he never published anything. The only sources of information about the journey were small leaks to friends and a few discreet conversations he had with the leading mapmakers of the day.

"The first publication of the journey was titled *The World Encompassed* by Sir Francis Drake in 1628. That was more than twenty years after Drake's death and the Sir Francis Drake referred to there is his nephew, who had inherited the Knighthood. That 1628 document was based on the writings of the ship's preacher and other members of the crew, not Sir Francis Drake's own journals, although it was widely known that he did review and edit them before he died.

"All of Drake's journals and documents that had been confiscated by the Queen were destroyed in a fire in 1698. There have been no surviving Sir Francis Drake original documents relating to the voyage ever found."

After that, Alan paused. There was complete silence for a moment as the unspoken implication of what he had just said sunk in.

"Are you suggesting that such a document does exist?" asked the Vice President, as if on cue.

"Yes."

Again…a long pause.

Ray simply raised an eyebrow as a query.

"This is where it gets very complicated and sensitive," continued Alan. "We are now talking about a document that has no historical reference. It's being offered by someone who will not disclose his identity and who insists that the purchaser absolutely promises to never divulge that he has it or even that the document exists."

"We are talking about an original Sir Francis Drake document?" Ray asked directly.

"Yes."

"And what price level are you suggesting?"

"Two point five million dollars," replied Alan with a hint of breathlessness.

The Vice President leaned back in his chair and stared at Alan. "You are saying that you have something for sale for 2.5 million dollars, an item that has no established authenticity, from someone who will not identify himself, and that I would need to keep secret forever?" he said in a low voice filled with skepticism.

"That's right."

At that moment there was a quiet knock on the door to the room and the stationed secret service agent poked his face in and said, "Mr. Vice President, your next appointment is here."

"Thank you," Ray replied, looking up at the agent. After the briefest of pauses, he continued, "Please tell them that I apologize but that I will be a few minutes longer."

"Fine, Sir," said the agent as he withdrew and closed the door.

Alan wasn't aware of it, but that interruption by the agent was just a pre-arranged process that the Vice President had established which allowed him to end meetings that had gone on long enough or that he wanted to escape gracefully. Ray realized that his answer meant that he was actually interested in what Alan Page was saying, no matter how improbable it seemed.

Turning back to Alan, he asked, "What does the document look like?"

"Well, I haven't actually seen it, but ..."

"What! You haven't seen it! How do you know it exists? How do you know it's real? How do you know this isn't a hoax?"

"I guess I don't, really, but then the worst case is that I make a fool of myself with you and probably lose the chance to deal with you again. It seems worth the risk."

"Who are you representing, then?"

"That's the whole point of my involvement. I can't tell you who it is; that keeps their identity protected. I was contacted to make this approach because people know that I could get access to you, but on the condition that I do not reveal who is offering the document. The seller sees you as someone who would have an interest in the document, has the necessary money and can be trusted to keep it all confidential. The seller needs money but that can't be disclosed publicly; I think you know how that can occur from other dealings in the past."

Alan continued, "I can tell you that the document is described as an eight page, quarto sized document, printed on plain heavy duty paper and bound between simple boards that were typical of the time. In other words, it was printed on a single piece of printer's stock and folded in four which creates eight sides or pages of text. Each page would be a bit larger than today's standard 8 ½ by 11 page.

"The text is described as a summary of Drake's around-the-world voyage of 1577 to 1580 which he wrote shortly before his final voyage in 1595. He died on that voyage in early 1596. It's claimed that there are some startling revelations in the document; I was not given any details."

Everything in Ray Cartwright's persona and history as a scientist, a businessman and a lawyer cried out to his internal consciousness to simply say "No" to Alan and to avoid this offer as being too bizarre to be worth considering. However, at a deeper level he was struck with the all-consuming "collector's disease," which simply means the overwhelming desire that serious collectors of anything, whether it be books, art, stamps or baseball cards, develop about obtaining something special – my God, this was truly an opportunity of a lifetime, if it was true. And, surely, he would be able to do some research and checking before he actually paid any money.

"If I am interested, how do we proceed? How do I get to see the document?"

"If you agree with the conditions of secrecy, it will be delivered to your hotel in Vancouver, Canada when you visit there in a couple of weeks. You can bring it home with you to study. Then, if you don't want to proceed further, you can simply return it – instructions would be provided at that time."

This information surprised Ray even more, as if everything up to this point hadn't been enough. He was going to Vancouver to represent the United States at a ceremonial presentation by the Queen of England.

25

For the next ten days, it seemed to Ray Cartwright that, although his time had been busy with various political appearances across the western United States, whenever he had a spare moment he could think of nothing else but the conversation with Alan Page and the upcoming trip to Vancouver.

Sitting in his home library in Seattle, surrounded by the familiar and comforting bookshelves that held his collection, he again glanced through the handful of books he had obtained recently about Sir Francis Drake. They included a couple of biographies, some history books about the Elizabethan period, and a modern publication of reproduced maps from the sixteenth and seventeenth centuries that showed the evolution of knowledge about the world in general and the Americas in particular. Some of them showed a trace of Drake's supposed route around the world, usually depicting his northern point along the west coast of America at the latitude of northern California. He also noted that many maps, starting in the mid-1600s, depicted California as a large island which historians had trouble explaining. That anomaly persisted in maps for more than one hundred years.

As he tried to visualize, for the umpteenth time, what the document would really look like and what insights it might contain, his mind drifted to the upcoming trip to Vancouver.

The Queen of England was on an official visit to Canada and was scheduled to cut the ribbon at the official opening ceremony for a new learning facility at the mouth of the Fraser River in Vancouver. It would depict the early explorations of western Canada, both overland and via the Pacific Ocean. It was to be named *The David Thompson Historical Interpretive Centre*. Yes, Ray recalled, the Canadians spelled words like *center* in the English fashion of *centre*. It was named after the famous explorer who first determined the geography of much of western Canada and the far northwest of the United States between 1792 and 1812, more than two hundred years ago. He has been called "The greatest land surveyor who ever lived."

Since the historical displays included a fair amount of material about the U.S. Pacific Northwest, the U.S. was invited to send an official representative to the ceremony. Ray was the overwhelmingly obvious choice, of course – Vice President, resident of the area, collector of historical books about the same subject, and a politician in the beginnings of a campaign where any publicity and photo opportunities linked to foreign affairs would be beneficial.

The agenda showed that, after a brief courtesy visit with the Canadian Prime Minister, he would attend a state dinner where the Queen would be present. He would stay in Vancouver overnight and then attend the official opening ceremony before returning to Seattle.

He was keenly looking forward to the brief trip, probably as much for the delivery of the promised document as for the official events.

The trip to Vancouver proceeded as planned. Flying out of Seattle on Air Force Two, the modified Boeing 757 that was usually used for Vice Presidential trips, it was only a half-hour flight to Vancouver.

He and Anne were greeted at the airport by the Canadian Deputy Prime Minister, a politician from Alberta, the western prairie province that probably has the most in common with the United States, politically and culturally. After a few cordial exchanges of pleasantries, they were taken by limousine to their hotel, the Pan Pacific in the heart of Vancouver, on the large inner harbor called the Burrard Inlet. Their suite had a great view of the busy waterway with the comings and goings of large cargo ships, local ferries, seaplanes that serviced travel to other communities along the coast, and various pleasure boats. They could also see the Lion's Gate Bridge, the large suspension bridge that spanned the entrance to the inlet, as does the Golden Gate Bridge in San Francisco.

Ray liked Vancouver. It was like Seattle in many ways. Both cities were located on the inland waterways of the Pacific Coast, but Vancouver seemed more open, since the Strait of Georgia that lay between its mainland location and the large offshore Vancouver Island was much wider than the narrow channels and close-in islands of Seattle's Puget Sound. They were of a similar size, Vancouver's metropolitan area with two-and-a-half million people versus three-and-a-half in Seattle, and they both had an active arts and cultural community, often dedicated to works of the Pacific Northwest.

Both cities offered a great lifestyle. Over the years, Vancouver has been rated as the best city in the world to live in by *The Economist* magazine, certainly always in the top few with cities like Zurich and Vienna.

The most noticeable difference was a function of Canada's stronger history with Britain. This showed in cultural, language and political things.

As opposed to the American republic, with its two separate legislative bodies, the House of Representatives and the Senate, and its independent President, Canada had a parliamentary form of government where the

Prime Minister ran the legislative House of Commons and also ran the administration with a Cabinet drawn from the elected House.

The Queen was still the legal Head of State, a ceremonial function with no political power. She only visited Canada every ten years or so, usually to conduct some ceremony to mark a historical occasion. The Queen's continuing involvement with Canada confused, and amused, Americans in general.

In the late afternoon he had a one-hour meeting with the Canadian Prime Minister, Robert Durocher, a fluently bilingual French Canadian from the eastern province of New Brunswick. It was cordial as the Prime Minister was committed to working cooperatively with the United States on trade and security issues and Ray was relatively knowledgeable about Canadian affairs and political sensitivities. The unspoken context of the meeting was that both of them were expecting to be in power in their respective countries for a number of years after the next U.S. election.

That evening Ray and Anne attended the gala event in the hotel's Grand Ballroom, where over two thousand people gathered to see the Queen and other key dignitaries, first in a formal receiving line, and then over dinner. Everyone was dressed in their finest.

The Vice President was seated on the left side of the Queen, with the Canadian Prime Minister on her right. Anne was seated beside the Prince. Dinner-time conversation was expectedly polite and reserved, focusing mostly on comments about the new interpretive center and various historical events. The Vice President felt very comfortable with those subjects and was pleasantly surprised with the Queen's knowledge. He did flinch slightly when the Queen said, "We in Britain have been interested and involved in the Pacific coast of North America ever since Sir Francis Drake's voyage in the late 1500s," but there were no follow-up comments as the conversation moved on to the exploits of James Cook and George Vancouver.

On returning to their suite after the dinner, Ray was disappointed that there was no sign of a package having been delivered in their absence.

The next day they all reconvened at the new interpretive center for the official opening.

Prime Minister Durocher initiated the formal ceremony with a general welcome to everyone and with a brief history of the exploration and settlement of the west coast as a key element in the creation of Canada in the 1800s.

Then Ray Cartwright was invited to say a few words. He simply summarized the common experiences of explorers from both the American and British sides in the early 1800s that eventually led to the peaceful negotiation of their current common border along the 49th parallel, often cited as "the longest undefended border in the world," which was still true in spite of the increased world tensions that had built up over the previous decades.

Finally the Queen, after some preliminary comments, quietly and directly said, "In the name and spirit of all the brave explores and adventurers who came to these shores and lands more than two centuries ago , I declare *The David Thompson Historical Interpretive Centre* officially open."

This was followed by a tour of the facility for the dignitaries and attending guests in small groups.

Shortly after the tour started, Ray was standing in front of a large wall map that depicted the routes of the various explorers. It spanned the Pacific coast from the mouth of the Columbia River, today's border between Oregon and Washington State up to the northern reaches of the Alaskan coast. The map showed the overland routes of David Thompson, Simon Fraser, Lewis and Clark, and a handful of others. It also showed the sea routes of Cook, Vancouver, La Perouse and other European explorers. In the northern waters it showed the routes traveled by the Russian explorers such as Bering and Kotzebue in the 1700s.

One of the members of Ray's group introduced himself as the High Commissioner from Britain to Canada, Lord Southley. Ray recalled that the diplomats exchanged between former British colonies were called High Commissioners, not ambassadors.

In conversation, Ray learned that the fellow was actually a member of the Royal Family, somewhat removed from the Queen's direct lineage. He was an avid historian of British history related to North America. He described how he would spend hours in the Royal Archives reading the ancient reports and documents from the times of the early explorers. It was this avid interest that had led to his appointment as High Commissioner to Canada.

While they were chatting, Ray heard the man next to him quietly, but determinedly, say, "They still don't believe."

Ray turned to him and with a questioning look on his face said, "Hello, is something wrong with the map?"

The man introduced himself as Jonathan Robinson, a geography and history professor at the University of British Columbia who had extensively studied the exploration of the Pacific coast. He went on to say, "I fervently believe that Francis Drake sailed up the Pacific coast beyond the Queen Charlotte Islands, about 750 miles north of here, in 1579. His journey should be shown on that map, but all of the traditionalist historians still refuse to accept the accumulated evidence."

Ray asked, somewhat skeptically, "Surely the historians delve into those ideas thoroughly; why don't they agree?"

"Ah, historians, and I am one! Too many of them just want to be the biggest expert in some small segment of history. It's Read, Study, Know, and Teach. Once they have established a story as fact, they never change their minds; it would deny all of their expertise and self worth. It's not like in science where new discoveries are welcomed and celebrated. The fact that new scientists make advancements on Einstein, who advanced Newton, who advanced Galileo, and so on, does not take away from the achievements of the earlier ones. For historians, if your expertise is challenged, your whole worth is jeopardized.

"For example, my work was stimulated by a book, *The Secret Voyage of Sir Francis Drake*, written by Samuel Bawlf early in this century. Just based on newspaper articles about his book, some traditionalists immediately called Bawlf irresponsible, sloppy and confused; he was described as pedestrian or as an amateur. For them, his years of research didn't matter, without even taking the time to read it. Reactions can be amazingly vicious."

Ray responded, "Well, there have been many stories about historical events that have been proven false, especially ones about military and political events. Recall the old saying that "only the winners get to write history.

"Also, I wouldn't be so generous to the scientists. For example, Darwin was attacked and censored for decades, even longer. The second and subsequent editions of his work were seriously amended due to the academic and social pressures he faced.

"And, to be fair, there are frauds and incompetencies – remember the excitement about cold fusion a few years ago? I think it was the famous physicist Max Planck that said, "A new scientific truth does not triumph by convincing its opponents and making them see the light, but rather its opponents eventually die, and a new generation grows up that is familiar with it."

Lord Southley, who had been listening to this, spoke up, "I am aware of Bawlf's work and it fascinates me as well. It is too bad that all of the original Drake material was lost in the Whitehall Palace fire. If only his records had survived; we would know so much more. I have personally delved into many of the historical documents from Elizabethan times. Everyone keeps hoping that some long-lost documents from the era will be found, filling gaps in our knowledge about those times; the fire was devastating."

Ray wanted to ask Robinson to elaborate on Bawlf's findings, there seemed to be so much to learn. However, at that moment, his security detail flagged to him that it was time to leave. Ray immediately decided that he would get a copy of that book as soon as possible.

Ray and Anne returned to the hotel to get ready to head to the airport and back to Seattle.

This time, there was a package waiting for Ray, a very thin wooden box, somewhat larger than letter sized paper in area. The security agents had scanned it and, deeming it safe, placed it in his room, since he had told them that he was expecting a package.

He immediately opened it and stared down at the thinnest book he had ever seen – four sheets of paper between two relatively heavy pressed board covers, bound with a leather ribbon. Opening the cover, he actually shivered with anticipation as he read, in elaborate early-English script:

A Brief Discourse On A Voyage Around The World

1577 – 1580

Sir Francis Drake

London, 1595

BOOK SEVEN

LONDON, 1594

The Frustrated Explorer

26

Sir Francis Drake was frustrated. He was in his London house, contemplating his future plans.

It was late 1594 and he was no further ahead in getting the Queen's commission to undertake another adventure against the Spanish in America, or of being allowed to publish the stories of his earlier expeditions.

In 1592 he had returned to the Queen's court and the close interaction with the rich aristocrats and merchants in London, after spending more than three years on personal and public projects based in Plymouth.

Those three years after the ill-fated post-Armada attack against Spain had been productive. He had significantly increased his personal land holdings and had gained control of many businesses, such as corn grist mills in western England

He had also assumed many public positions, from Deputy Lord Lieutenant in the local political administration, to the leader of military defense and public works projects in Plymouth, and as a magistrate who oversaw and judged many criminal and business legal actions.

His local reputation and status was never higher and he was always treated as a national hero, but he knew that the memories of his exploits were fading over time as new events occurred.

The conflicts with Spain had persisted, although not on a grand scale. The Spanish continued to disrupt English trading and to seize ships from time-to-time. Scores of privateers from England continued to harass the Spanish ships in the Caribbean and the Atlantic, but there were no concentrated attacks on their cities or large flotillas.

The Spanish had continued to improve their defenses in America, although Drake believed that they were still vulnerable. He was actively promoting another large scale attack but support was difficult to obtain. The Queen continued her cautious ways and his main benefactor in her court, Lord Walsingham, had died in 1590. Lord Burghley continued to wield great influence.

There had been no sustained or successful follow-up on his discoveries in the American Pacific Northwest or in the East Indies. There had only been two English expeditions to the Pacific since then.

The most significant activity had taken place without his involvement or even knowledge, which irritated him even to this day.

In July, 1586, just days before Drake returned from his large, relatively unsuccessful ten-month attack on the Spanish Caribbean, Captain Thomas Cavendish had departed on a voyage to the Pacific that closely mirrored Drake's earlier one. The voyage had been organized in his absence, obviously with the permission of the Queen.

Cavendish sailed south in the Atlantic, through the Strait of Magellan and up the western coast of South and Central America. In the passing he had sunk 19 Spanish ships, burned the city of Acapulco and had captured a treasure-laden Spanish galleon. He then crossed the Pacific and returned to England, via the East Indies and around the Cape of Africa in September, 1588, shortly after the Spanish Armada had been defeated. Cavendish had received a public hero's welcome as had Drake before him.

Drake had learned from private briefings that Cavendish had also sent his second ship north along the American coast to learn more about Drake's discoveries and the hoped-for western entrance to the Northwest Passage. Nothing had been heard back from that crew in the ensuing six years. They had obviously perished, as had been the fate of the crew that Drake had left in the north Pacific in 1579.

Aside from the personal angst that Drake felt about Cavendish's voyage, he was also angry that Cavendish had not learned anything new about the Pacific or the East Indies. To him, that voyage had been a waste of time and resources.

The second voyage, led by young Richard Hawkins, son of his early mentor John Hawkins, had departed over a year ago in the summer of 1593. The Queen would not allow Drake to leave England with the Spanish threat always being present, but he had been involved in advising in the preparations of that small two-ship expedition, which was planning to gain additional knowledge about the north Pacific shores. However, word had just reached London, via Spain, that Hawkins had only made it through the Strait of Magellan and to the Spanish coast of Peru where he was attacked by a Spanish naval group. His ship was captured and destroyed and Hawkins himself was being held prisoner. The venture had achieved nothing.

In addition to his frustration at the Queen's lack of support for another expedition under his leadership, Drake was also upset that many of the details and accomplishments of his voyages were still kept secret, even though it had been 22 years since his first major success against the Spanish in the Caribbean and over 13 years since he had returned from his trip around the world. The amount of information that had surfaced about that epic voyage was remarkably sparse; Drake and his crew had obeyed the Queen's edict very carefully.

Over the first couple of years after he returned he privately advised some of the English mapmakers, but the changes to their maps were very general. He coached them in placing islands south of the Strait of Magellan, making the western shores of South and North America trend more northerly, showing the upper coast of North America about 140° west of England and widening the expanse of the Pacific.

The major map makers of the time, Hondius, Ortelius and Mercator, complained to Drake and various English officials about the lack of information. They discussed among themselves that there must be some very good reasons for the secrecy, including speculation that Drake had actually returned from the Pacific across the north of America via the fabled Northwest Passage.

He had created some relatively simple hand-drawn maps for friends for their private use but that was quite unsatisfactory. Then, in 1583, a Dutch map by Van Sype surfaced showing Drake's around-the-world path, including a terminus of his northern travels along the Pacific coast of North America at 57°. This violated everything that the Queen had decreed.

The Queen met with Drake and Lord Walsingham that year and established firm rules for Drake to follow in the future. He was still forbidden to publish any accounts of his voyage or to issue any maps of his own. He could give some guidance to other mapmakers but in no case could he disclose that he had sailed any farther north than 50° and he could not give out any information about the possibility of entrances to a Northwest Passage. Allowing the name Nova Albion to appear north of the Spanish territories was permitted, and even encouraged, as it would establish future rights for England.

The various commemorative items that were offered to the public over the next few years, maps, medals, plates, etc., adhered to those rules; the trace of his voyage always stopped short of 50°N.

The major map makers such as Ortelius steadily added more details to their maps of the Pacific coast, including offshore islands, deepwater bays and large inland rivers. True to Drake's undertaking, these features were located well south of their actual position. In fact, many of them were shown near 40°N, not far north of the Spanish territories and in a region that Drake had never visited at all, since he had sailed far out to the west in the Pacific in order to catch the westerly winds that could carry him to the more northerly latitudes.

The Van Sype images disappeared from use due to a lack of support from Drake; no other mapmaker repeated the northern terminus.

In 1587, Ortelius and historian Richard Hakluyt issued maps that showed the coast continuing north of 50°N with many inlets, islands and rivers. It also showed the coast starting to trend westward above 60°N. These details were not attributed to Drake; in fact, everything was labeled in Spanish, giving the impression that Spain was the source of the information. A track of Drake's voyage was not shown. Therefore, without attribution, the maps were assumed to be illustrative or hypothetical at best. Of course, Drake knew better.

Sir Francis had initiated some action in an attempt to get Queen Elizabeth's permission to publish the details of his voyages. Working with his former chaplain, Philip Nichols, as an editor, in the late 1580s he had undertaken to write the stories of his two major successes in the western hemisphere, the 1572-1573 raids in the Caribbean and the 1577-1580 voyage around the world. However they had languished in his possession for years as he could not get any support from Walsingham.

The document that Drake had created was based on the journal kept by Francis Fletcher, the chaplain on the voyage. Drake and Fletcher had maintained a strained, but functional, relationship during much of the voyage. As a devoted Puritan, Drake took his religion very seriously and ensured that church services, prayers, bible readings and hymns were an integral part of life on his ships. When the *Golden Hind* floundered on the reef in the Indonesian Spice Islands, Fletcher had announced that this was God's retribution for all the wrongs that Drake had committed, including the execution of Thomas Doughty. This infuriated Drake, who then had Fletcher chained and imprisoned on the ship. He also confiscated Fletcher's journals, concerned about what they said about him. When he returned to England and was ordered to surrender all of his journals and charts to the Queen's officials, he conveniently forgot to include the Fletcher material. Fletcher himself had no way to know the fate of his works.

Now, years later, that journal had provided Drake with many useful details to supplement his own memories about the voyage. Even so, his new document, which he titled *The World Encompassed*, still adhered to the Queen's rules on disclosure; it was simply silent about the journey to the far north. He covered up the gap by saying that he careened and provisioned his ship near 38°N and exaggerating the time it took to do that and to sail across the Pacific. Similarly, to conceal the time he spent on the coast of France before landing in England he stretched out the time spent sailing across the Indian Ocean and up the western shores of Africa.

By 1588, Drake had renewed hope that his voyages could be published. After all, he had just led the English successfully against the Spanish Armada. Richard Hakluyt, with the endorsement and encouragement of Lord Walsingham, was creating a major publication called *The Principal Navigations, Voyages and Discoveries of the English Nations*. Drake allowed

Hakluyt to review some of his own writings about the voyage, which led Hakluyt to announce in early 1589 that his upcoming publication would include the first descriptions of Drake's historic voyage.

However, in the fall of 1589, just prior to the publication of Hakluyt's volumes, the Drake material was removed. The order had been issued by the Queen and delivered by Walsingham. Hakluyt had to announce that the promised material would not be forthcoming, implying that it was due to Drake's refusal to release the material since he was planning his own publication.

Drake had been mortified. He had actually hoped that Hakluyt's edition would pave the way for his more elaborate journal.

In a lengthy follow-up with Walsingham he could get no better satisfaction. Walsingham simply said that the Queen was again concerned about the Spanish, since they were rebuilding their navy. Drake suspected that it was also due to the Queen's displeasure about the failure of his post-Armada raids. She could be fickle and punitive in her feelings and decisions.

At that point Drake retired to Plymouth. Over the next few years little new had been published in the way of stories or maps.

Upon returning to the Queen's court in 1592, Drake had picked up his lobbying for action. By then, he reasoned, surely the Queen would no longer object to the publication of the Caribbean venture; after all that was two decades in the past and it was hardly going to infuriate the Spanish any more than they already were. Therefore, he printed the story of that venture, titled *Sir Francis Drake Revived*, and presented it as a gilded bound gift to the Queen for New Years 1593, a year ago. He had even noted that it was a special year for both of them, he was turning 50, his golden year, and the Queen was going to be 60, her diamond year. He also gave her a diamond studded gold bracelet.

However, she had still not given him permission to publicly publish it and he feared that she never would. This told him that she would certainly not allow him to publish his account of the around-the-world journey, even in a heavily abridged and edited form.

Finally, in 1593, the Queen had agreed to the publication of the abridged version of Drake's voyage which had been created by Hakluyt five years earlier, although the accompanying map was a reversion to older images of the Pacific coast. The tract of his voyage on the map was terminated at 42°N, his supposed landing point. This publication was intended to satisfy Drake, but, in fact, it further irritated him.

27

Now, late in 1594, after two frustrating years in London, Sir Francis was determined to make something happen.

Over the next six months he intensified his recruitment of support from the investors and merchants in London to mount another attack on the Spanish in the Caribbean. He certainly hoped that such an additional venture, with naval success and plundering of riches, would convince the Queen to allow him to undertake another voyage to the Pacific.

The Queen's support for the Caribbean enterprise wavered on and off over that period, since she was always concerned about further Spanish attacks on England. With her approval in one of her positive periods, Drake had assembled a large fleet by May, 1595, but he could not get permission to sail. The continuing delays depleted the provisions and disheartened the assembled seamen, but Drake held them at the ready, to ensure that he could depart as soon as the Queen allowed it. He didn't want her to have time to change her mind again.

During that period Sir Francis decided that he should put his affairs into better order, since there was always a risk that he would not return. His estate was quite large and he had entered into an elaborate marriage contract with his wife and her family that stated that his estates would pass on to her. Nevertheless, he wanted to ensure that his brother John and his close nephew Francis also received significant value and so he created a new will.

As he was pondering his financial legacy, he also considered his personal legacy as an adventurer and explorer. The Queen's continuing insistence that he could not publish his memoirs bothered him. Even if his heavily edited version of the voyage around the world, *The World Encompassed*, was issued someday, the true nature of his accomplishments in the Pacific would never become public. His place in history would be incomplete.

He knew that his escapades against the Spanish were very well known, even if not from his perspective, due to the many reports and stories that had emanated from Spain and its colonies in America. It was the time he spent in the northern waters that would never be revealed. As well, his reputation as a sailor and navigator would be tarnished by the erroneous information about islands south of 50°N, his being forced back by ice at 50°in June, and taking more than two months to cross the Pacific. There was also the fact that he had exaggerated the time required to sail from

Indonesia to England by two months in order to cover up his landing in France.

Perhaps he should create a supplement to his *World Encompassed* document that would correct the record. Of course, this would absolutely violate his agreement with the Queen to never reveal those facts; she would be furious and very vindictive if she were to find out that he had written such a document. In the past, she had banished noblemen from her court for deemed disobedience and sometimes had their assets seized. She had even executed Mary Queen of Scots, her royal relative, when she decided that Mary was plotting against her. If he was going to do it, he would need to do it secretly and secure it well.

He reached for his quill and paper and started to write.

Three months later, when word reached London that a Spanish treasure galleon laden with treasure was damaged and stranded in Puerto Rico, the Queen finally gave her permission for the sailing venture to go forward. In August 1595, the English fleet, under the joint command of Drake and John Hawkins, set sail from Plymouth. It consisted of 2,500 men on 27 ships.

The voyage did not start well, which was becoming the normal situation. Underprovisioned, due to the haste of their departure in fear that the Queen would change her mind again, Drake diverted to the Canary Islands to secure food and water. When he landed his force to take possession of the city of Las Palmas, he was beaten back by the local forces. Having lost men and time, he was forced to gather water and food from a remote part of the island.

Crossing the Atlantic, the fleet reached the island of Guadeloupe at the end of October. Unfortunately two of the smaller ships became separated from the main fleet and were attacked by a Spanish fleet that had been sent from Spain to repel the English attackers; the long preparations and delays in sailing from England had allowed spies to report back to Spain about the planned English venture. One of the English ships was captured. Now, the Spanish were aware of their actual presence and, undoubtedly from the interrogation of the captured crew, alerted to their plan to attack the treasure ship in Puerto Rico.

When they reached their target in mid-November, they found that San Juan's fortifications had been significantly strengthened, the passages into the port were well blockaded and the Spanish naval fleet was waiting for them. The treasure had been safely stowed onshore. In spite of that, Drake attempted an attack. Although they had some success and even sunk the largest Spanish ship, they were no match for the total firepower that the Spanish had amassed. They sailed away in defeat.

More critically, they had lost their most important weapon, the element of surprise. Word of their presence quickly spread to all of the Spanish settlements in the region.

Also, ominously, Sir John Hawkins, the scion of English adventurers, succumbed to a lingering sickness and died at Puerto Rico. Although this allowed Drake to assume total command of the fleet and thus bring some decisiveness to their plans, it also seemed to reduce the fervor of the crews and to dissipate their enthusiasm for the venture. Nothing had gone right so far. The hoped-for financial rewards from success were evading them.

The next six weeks brought more failure and frustration. Continuing along the Spanish Main, they attacked and severely damaged the city and port facilities at Rio de la Hacha, Santa Marta and other smaller towns, but in every case the populace had fled into the interior lands and almost everything of value had been removed.

After those delays, he arrived at Nombre de Dios, the city on the Panama isthmus that was the gateway to the overland route to the Pacific, and the location of his greatest Caribbean success two decades earlier. Again, he found the city essentially deserted. However, the larger disaster was his attempt to send a force of almost 1000 men overland to the port of Panama. Halfway across the isthmus, hampered by the jungle overgrowth and bogged down in the muddy terrain, a Spanish force ambushed them, driving them back and inflicting many losses.

The English forces sailed from Nombre de Dios on January 4, 1596, heading to the island of Escudo to regroup and plan their next attacks on the Spanish centers in Nicaragua. The troops were disheartened and pessimistic. Their ranks were filled with seriously sick people, having been confined in close quarters with poor provisions for most of the previous five months. Every day several sailors died.

Over the next three weeks the crews worked at refurbishing and reprovisioning the ships, but progress was slow and ineffective. On June 23, the fleet set sail towards Panama again, where Drake hoped the Spaniards had let down their defenses after routing them earlier.

Drake himself had fallen ill in mid-January and was becoming weaker with each passing day. As the fleet gathered near the offshore island of Buena Ventura to organize their planned attack, he became very depressed and then too weak to leave his cabin.

Early in the morning of January 28, 1596, Sir Francis Drake died and was buried at sea.

The fleet returned to England, defeated and without any treasure.

BOOK EIGHT

SEATTLE, MAY

The Temptation

28

Ray Cartwright was still staring at the title page of the document when Anne said, "It's time to get going to the airport. What have you got there? It's certainly caught your attention."

"Nothing really," replied Ray. "It's a small document that a book dealer sent over. It will be a nice addition to my collection. OK, let's go," he said as he stuck the document in his small briefcase. He would have to inspect it later, when he got home.

The trip to the airport and the flight back to Seattle were quick and uneventful. On arrival in Seattle there was the usual routine of clearing U.S. customs. The Vice President and his staff carried diplomatic passports and were exempt from the process other than being recorded as arriving.

The news media members who accompanied the Vice President filled out the necessary forms and turned their passports over to the plane's steward, who greeted the immigration and customs agents as they came to the plane for a cursory process. The customs agent conducted a brief walk through the rear compartment of the plane, greeting everyone from the list he had been handed. Then he left, picking up a small brown paper bag from the shelf near the exit. He always appreciated their thoughtfulness in leaving him a small box of Cuban cigars when they returned from these trips.

As Ray prepared to leave the plane, he knew that he was a little tense and probably fidgeting a bit; he just hoped no one noticed. He easily rationalized that he was not doing anything illegal since he had not actually bought anything and, in any case, it was just an old used book. He knew he was ignoring any thought that it was possibly a British national treasure, it might be stolen, and that it was worth millions.

After arriving home, Ray and Anne settled in and had dinner together, talking a little about the past two days as they recalled the pomp and protocols around the Queen, but also noting how she handled the constant activity and interaction with strangers with ease and grace. "Even if she didn't have a hereditary position, she would have made a good leader anyway," mused Anne.

This turned the conversation to their own upcoming political activities, and the acknowledgement that, with the election year approaching, they would soon be entering an even more frenetic schedule of travel and public events.

Drake's Dilemma

After dinner, Ray retreated to his library, which was quite usual; he often had government or political documents to review, or he just wanted to enjoy a few minutes of peace with his books.

Tonight it was different. He immediately went to his desk and extracted the small box containing the document from his briefcase.

For a moment, he thought that he should call Anne in and explain what was going on and solicit her advice; he had always shared major decisions with her. Although he tried to rationalize that it was not a big deal and that she didn't really want to get involved with his book-collecting hobby, he knew that, in reality, that wasn't the reason. She would undoubtedly advise him to back away from the book offer as it presented a political risk. He didn't want to do that.

Opening the box, this time he noticed a small note. It simply said "Please be advised and reminded that you are not to show this document to anyone, including Alan Page."

Then, after staring at the covering page one more time, he started to read with a sense of excitement and anticipation.

A Brief Discourse On A Voyage Around The World

1577 – 1580

Sir Francis Drake

London, 1595

By the grace of our Ever-loving and Generous Anglican God and her most Excellency, Queen Elizabeth of England and all of her domains, I, Francis Drake, humble lord of the Realm, with certain great trepidation and plea for understanding, do hereby record certain aspects of the great expedition around the world that I and my brave officers and crew undertook in the years of our Lord 1577 until 1580.

I have strictly and constantly adhered to the express wishes and direction of Her Majesty related to disclosing details about that magnificent venture so as to preserve the secrets of the nation and to mitigate the wrath of its mortal enemy, the evil and treacherous papist-state of Spain and its vindictive King Philip.

Thus and therefore, I have obeyed the Royal Directives and have severely limited the information of geography and navigation that has been shared with close friends of the Court and the Nation.

I have caused to be written an elaborate account of the said voyage, again in strict adherence to the Royal Directive, and do trust and pray that the day will arrive in the reasonable future when it will be aligned with the Queen's wishes to have it disclosed to the public. Such an event, I am certain, will give rise to great joy and pride for the people of England.

That account of the voyage I have titled *The World Encompassed* and have dedicated it wholly and unreservedly to Her Royal Majesty, who has encouraged and supported my many ventures, albeit often in diplomatic secrecy. That treatise has been secreted away, pending my return from the forthcoming new adventure to the Spanish Main and the Caribbean, so as to ensure that it does not inadvertently come in to the hands of the enemies of Her Majesty or those who would give comfort and support to Spain.

Nevertheless and notwithstanding the Royal Directive, I am here undertaking to describe certain aspects of the voyage and to document certain discoveries that were made, so that if something were to befall myself, or the enemies of the Queen were to be successful, there shall be a record of them. I do fervently hope that the day will arrive when the Journals of the voyage will be released and returned by Her Majesty, such that many more details of the travels can be disclosed.

These revelations must be read and understood in the context of the descriptions contained in *The World Encompassed* which I will not attempt to repeat herein.

The description in that treatise regarding the early stages of the voyage across the Atlantic and the dealing with the mutinous behaviour of Sir Thomas Doughty is adequate, as is the description of the brave deeds by the officers and sailors to effect passage through the treacherous Strait of Magellan.

The violent storms that greeted our passage into the Pacific Ocean did truly buffet our passage and thrust us south as to reach fifty-seven degrees of southern latitude. Most assuredly, this also did allow us to observe that the lands to the south of the Strait were truly islands, and were not adjoined to some massive southern continent. I do not know or understand why Captain Thomas Cavendish has been so ready to cast doubt and aspersions of those observations; surely the lack of such sightings by him during his subsequent, but ineffective, voyage through the passage and around the world can not be taken as testimony to the facts.

The voyage along the Spanish coasts of America from Chile to Peru to New Spain and to Mexico is also well described otherwise. It is well justified to repeat the admiration for the skills and fortitude of the brave English sailors.

It is also worthy of the repetition that the damage to the Spanish was immense, from the raiding of their cities and ports, to the capture and destruction of many ships, to the seizure of Spanish treasure which has been faithfully conveyed to Her Majesty and the loyal supporters of the venture.

The navigation along the Pacific shores of Southern America showed that the coasts proceeded in a near northerly direction, contrary to the maps of Master Abraham Ortelius prior to this time. This has been corrected in subsequent charts as encouraged by my words. It is an obvious fact that this knowledge was well known to the Spanish and therefore its disclosure had neither impact nor importance to the security of England.

Following upon the seizure of the vast treasure from the *Nuestra Senora de la Conception*, it was imprudent and dangerous for the successful completion of our journey and mission to continue into the Spanish territories of Panama and New Spain, and thus we continued northward to the coasts near Gualtulco in Spanish Mexico to careen and provision our two ships, the *Golden Hind* and the Spanish bark that had been seized off the coast of Guatemala.

Leaving Gualtulco, we thereupon advantaged the winds and the current and sailed far to the west and then back to the northeast for a distance approaching two thousand miles, again encountering landfall at latitude near fifty degrees.

As will be shown in detail when the Journals of the voyage are examined, we then proceeded northward, encountering rugged shores, deep channels, inland water courses behind large islands, and the inflow of large rivers from the mountainous eastward interior. One particularly large river I named The River of the Straits.

Upon reaching the latitude of fifty-seven degrees in early June, 1579, we were forced to turn back south by the presence of huge ice flows and terrible headward freezing winds and rains. However we could see deep, wide channels trending north and east into the snow-capped mountains and we were determined to return and to continue the search for the Northwest Passage across the northern reaches of America when the conditions improved at the end of summer. This was our sacred mission as secretly decreed by Her Majesty prior to our departure from Plymouth some one and a half years earlier.

I must note for history that on this journey we had reached the fifty-seventh degree of latitude both in the south and the north, a feat never before accomplished in either direction by any mariner.

Returning south along the outer Pacific shores, we entered a deep passage eastward at fifty-one degrees and followed a narrow channel, encouraged by the ebb and flow of the tides. At one point, we were required to wait for the highest tide to carry us over shallow rapids, certainly a momentous decision that could have stranded us on the other side of the world.

Once free of the narrows, we discovered a very large inland passageway, flanked by high mountains on both the eastward mainland and the westward island. As we were to discover later in our journey, this island extended in a north-south direction for three degrees latitude, from fifty-one degrees to forty-eight degrees.

The waters were filled with large fish such as salmon and halibut and teeming with fur-bearing seals, sea lions and otters. Large groups of whales and porpoises would follow our ship. The skies were filled with white-plumed eagles.

The waters were surrounded by forests on all sides that displayed trees of a size never before seen — they stretched hundreds of feet into the air in a straight line and had a girth at the base that could not be closed by the outstretched arms of six men. It would take but a few of these trees to build a whole ship and to fashion its masts.

In the midst of this passage, along its western shores, we encountered a large well protected bay, fed with abundant fresh water from a large inflowing river. Here we encountered a large tribe of natives who were very friendly and welcoming. Trading goods and tools that we had carried along, we received valuable furs and precious stones as well as good hospitality and provisions. Surely this place would be the ideal location of a Pacific base for the English utilization and control of the Northwest Passage. I named this territory Nova Albion and claimed the territory in the name of Her Majesty, leaving a plaque of iron and copper to note the event.

Our presence had attracted many hundreds of natives who arrived in increasing numbers daily and so we sailed away south, somewhat in anxiety since we were becoming so outnumbered and were surely isolated half a world away from England.

Sailing south, we noted a very large River of the West flowing into the passage from the mainland to the east at forty-nine degrees. We then reentered the Pacific through a narrow passage at forty-eight degrees, with mountain-filled islands on both flanks. There was an exceedingly high mountain to our rear, on the mainland, which had a brilliant white snow-covered peak even at this midsummer time.

In all, with our departure, we had identified at least four large islands along the Pacific coast from forty-eight degrees to fifty-four degrees, of which the largest was the one we had just departed.

Needing to repair our ships and provision them for the return north, we sailed south, encountering another very large river inlet at 46 degrees although entry in to its waters was blocked by churning waters over underwater sandbar accumulations. We dared not risk our ship.

However, we did make landfall south of that point and there did undertake to determine our longitude by means of geometric lunar observations such as practiced by the astronomer William Bourne. After careful measurements and surveys, I determined that we were some 140 degrees of longitude west of London. Even if the observations contained some measure of error, this established that the western coast of America had trended much more northerly than had been depicted on maps such as those of Master Abraham Ortelius. This also leads one to conclude that the passage across the northern parts of America will be much shorter than feared heretofore.

We then continued south to forty-five degrees where we careened our ship and gathered provisions as described in detail in *The World Encompassed*, but as noted, well north of the location stated therein. The natives here were friendly and helpful, but they were not the same ones described in *The World Encompassed*. Those scantily clad natives were actually encountered farther south as I will relate below.

The reality of our voyage and its disclosure to this time is that, in the cause of secrecy, the latitudes of the northern Pacific events have been placed ten degrees south of their actual location. We never encountered the shores of America between the northern reaches of Mexico and forty-two degrees north latitude. I explicitly state this here such that when future explorers and adventurers come to these waters they do not presume that I was lost or incapable of determining my latitude.

We departed on the 25th of July, but our journey then was back to the north, not yet across the Pacific

We had hoped and envisioned that the summer heat would have freed the northern passages from ice, but, upon our return to the inland channels at fifty-seven degrees, we found them even more ice infested. The summer sun had simply dislodged more ice from the frozen shores. The *Golden Hind* could not proceed.

Here, a crew of twenty brave and noble sailors agreed to continue north in the smaller Spanish bark that we had trailed along since Peru, hoping to breach the northern passage and to return thereby to England that fall. Sadly, they have never been heard of since.

Returning south, driven by favorable winds, we made a final landing on the shores of America near 42° N, where we gathered final provisions for our journey across the Pacific Ocean. It was here that we encountered and socialized with the natives who deported themselves nearly naked and who adorned themselves with colourful feathers. The description of these natives being at the site of our earlier stop for repairs and provisions has been a necessary part of the deception about the latitudes that we actually visited.

I placed a final metal plaque there, claiming all the territory north of that point in the name of the Queen for England.

Then we headed south and west, crossing the Pacific in forty days, not sixty-eight, reaching the first islands of Indonesia in desperate need of water and food. The travels through the archipelagos of the south Pacific, Indonesia and the Spice Islands were as described elsewhere, including the elaborate encounter with Babu, the Sultan of Ternate, and the near-disaster of running aground on the reef near Celebes.

It was there that the true nature of Francis Fletcher came to light. He had been the Parson of the voyage, although his leadership of prayer, sermon and hymnals had always required strong guidance. At the time of the mutiny of Thomas Doughty he had been an apologist for him and now, with the ship in desperate peril, he had the audacity to suggest it was God's retribution for that court martial and many other acts of commission over the previous two years. Such insolence and subordination could not be tolerated and he was removed from his duties and chained in his quarters as a traitor to the mission. His journals, filled with fabrications and distortions, were seized and secreted away.

The continuing trip across the Indian Ocean and around the Cape of Africa was as uneventful as described, although the total journey from the southern islands of Indonesia back to England was almost two months shorter than stated.

As a prudent precaution, in the occasion that the Queen had died or that the Spanish-loving Catholic forces had deposed her, we made landfall along the northern coast of France to totally repair and provision the *Golden Hind*, in preparation for the possibility of the need to flee enemy occupants of England or to battle our way to the sanctity of Queen Elizabeth.

Only when we were thus prepared, and after discerning that the Queen was truly alive and in control of England, did we sail into Plymouth port on September 26, 1580, after a journey of almost three years.

July, 1595

Francis Drake

$$\Omega$$

Ray Cartwright sat staring at the document he had just read, almost numb, as he realized the historical significance of what it said in terms of Francis Drake. He had really sailed up the Pacific coast as far as the southern reaches of Alaska!

Ray immediately admired the way that Sir Francis Drake had written the document. "Jeez," he said to himself. "This guy wrapped himself in God and country; he violated the Queen's directive in the name of history; he made sure that his reputation as a sailor and navigator was preserved; he politely skewered competitors such as Cavendish; and he did it all for the glory of England. He should have been a politician."

Then his brain kicked in, and he was flooded with questions and doubts:

"If this was true, why hadn't it been revealed a long time ago?"

"Who would own such a document and keep it secret?"

"Why would it surface now, in this strange manner?"

"Was it even real? Maybe it was a fake and this was all a con job on him?"

"Is it real, but stolen property? By who? From where?"

"Shouldn't he just run away from the whole situation as fast as possible? Could it cause a scandal for him and compromise his ambition to become President?"

"Maybe it was even a political set-up, designed to trap him."

He had trouble breathing for a minute; he realized that he had been hyperventilating.

Then, staring at the thin, almost fragile document again, he thought, "What if it is real and I can have it, even if I must keep it secret?"

The collector's disease was just as real for Ray as anyone.

"Did this really present the opportunity to have an important, one-of-a-kind item?" he wondered.

Then the guilt seeped in to his consciousness. "How can I play any part in suppressing such an important historical document? Doesn't this violate everything I believe and stand for?"

"But… that was not really up to him. If he declined the opportunity, it would simply disappear into some other collection." He had given his word.

"Besides, what harm was there in at least pursuing this whole thing a little further?" he concluded.

29

The next morning at breakfast, his mind was still churning with all of the issues.

"You seem distracted this morning," said Anne. "And you were tossing and turning all night. Is something bothering you?"

"No, not really," he replied. "I guess I'm just starting to get hyped about the election. I am wondering if we are overdoing the ROC thing. I think I'll give Ralph King a call later and talk it all through again."

"Anyway," he continued, "I'll take a little break from it all this morning and spend some time with my books. In fact, one of the book sellers that I deal with, Alan Page, is coming by later this morning to show me something."

"That seems like a good idea. It'll give you a break"

A few hours later, the phone in Ray's library rang and the security agent announced that Alan had arrived.

"Hello, Mr. Vice President," he said.

"Hello, Alan" replied Ray. "Come on in and have a seat."

As Alan entered and seated himself, there was an expectant silence in the room. Ray noticed that Alan was quickly scanning his desk and the tables by the chairs, obviously hoping to get a glance at the document itself; Ray remembered that Alan had said that he had never seen it.

Then Alan looked up at the Vice President expectantly, not knowing quite what to say.

Ray started, "Well Alan, the document arrived as promised in Vancouver and I have looked at it. It's fascinating but I have a lot of questions." He didn't offer to show it to Alan; remembering the note that warned him about doing so.

"OK," said Alan. "What can I add to what we already discussed?"

Ray's engineer / lawyer background kicked in at that point as he formulated his questions for Alan. He remembered the axiom that you need to be careful what you ask, in case you don't really want to know the answer.

"Well, the very first issue is that given all of the need for secrecy that you have demanded how can I be sure that the document is authentic? It could be a fake, a counterfeit."

"To be sure. That is what my contact expected you to be concerned about. He also gave me some instructions on how you could partially verify its age and source. Apparently the very last page simply shows an elaborate scroll design, typical of the era. He suggested that it would be acceptable to take the tiniest sliver of paper from the last page and to scrape a small amount of ink from the scroll itself which you could have dated by some respectable scientific institution without needing to show them the actual document.

"In fact, he did that himself and I have an envelope here with laboratory tests that state that the document dates from the late sixteenth or early seventeenth centuries. Of course, you would be expected to have your own tests conducted."

After a pause, Ray said, "That would be a start, but it certainly wouldn't be definitive."

At that point he went to his desk and extracted a small box from a drawer and brought it to the sitting area. He could sense Alan holding his breath as he opened the box and extracted the document. Without showing him the front page or any of the content pages, he turned to the back of the last page and looked at the scroll design that was printed there again. It included the letter Omega, Ω, the Greek symbol for *The End*.

"OK, what else can I do?"

"Again, my instructions were to repeat that you can not show the actual document to anyone. However, he suggested that you might test the general concept of the contents with experts about Sir Francis Drake, just to confirm the possibility that it is authentic."

"Possibility…possibility; that's hardly going to prove anything. What about it's provenance; where did it come from? Does the seller really own it?"

"That is the crux of it all, I guess. I can not tell you anything about its source. As I said earlier, the secrecy of the source is the only reason that I became involved. In fact, and I didn't tell you this explicitly last time we talked, I have not met the supplier myself; all the contact with me has been by telephone."

"What?" exclaimed Ray, looking at Alan as if he had just said he was a visitor from Mars. "That is even more incredible. How can you believe it's authentic?"

"I can't, as I told you before. I'm just a messenger in this. He said it would be up to you to decide if you were interested."

"Well, surely the seller told you how he came to have the document… its source? What did he say about that?"

"He said that the document had been uncovered in an old family home that was being renovated. Once the seller realized what he had, he knew that, if he divulged it, he would be pressured to donate it to the British national archives. He would not be able to realize any monetary value, and he apparently needs money."

"That's a convenient story. You don't know anything about the source at all, do you?"

"No, just that the person seemed very knowledgeable about antiquarian books, me and you, and your interest in the subject. He spoke with an English-like accent."

That last statement hung in the air as Ray thought back to the delivery of the book in Vancouver at the time of the British royal visit. The subtle implication that the source was linked to the Queen or at least to the Queen's court was too much to say out loud.

"So they entrusted all of this to you, just on faith?"

"Well, in fact, they haven't entrusted much to me at all. I have the general story, all from an anonymous source, and I have made contact with you, which, as I said, just puts my reputation with you at risk. They didn't trust me with the document itself; that went directly to you. This is my first glimpse of it."

"And, what kind of receipt would I receive to show that I had bought it?"

"I will give you a simple receipt that states that I verify that you received and paid for the document. I would be able to do that since you obviously have it in your possession and I would be given confirmation from the seller that he had received payment."

Ray sat back and said nothing for a couple of minutes. He silently reviewed all of the questions and concerns that he had before. Very little had been resolved in this meeting. Again his conscious being was calling out, "No, No...Bail-out! Bail-out!" And again he couldn't say that out loud; he was too mesmerized by the possibility, no matter how irrational that was.

"I need some more time to think about this. Can I keep the document and call you in two days?"

"Certainly. That was a hoped-for request."

At that point, Alan departed and Ray was left to his thoughts, all the time looking at the document.

30

Most of the next two days were consumed with political activities, both in person and on many phone calls. His schedule for the coming months was filling in quite solidly.

Nevertheless, he was able to locate a specialty research laboratory in Los Angeles that could provide carbon dating and chemical analyses which could be used to verify the age of the document, all for a significant fee of course. They even agreed to send an expert to his place to collect the samples when Ray explained that he could not send the actual document in question to them. Being the Vice President did attract some perks.

The next step was a little trickier to pull off. He decided to consult with his mentoring bookseller Herb Trawets, knowing that it was going to difficult to explain the situation with the promise of secrecy to the sellers. He decided that the easiest way was to call ahead and tell Herb that he was going to drop by his shop, which Ray had done many times over the years.

When he arrived at the shop, just after nine o'clock the next morning, Herb greeted him warmly and they retreated to the small sitting area in the rear. Being so early, actually an hour before the shop's normal opening time, there were no other customers around, as Ray had planned.

Once the usual pleasantries were taken care of, Ray started to lay out the situation for Herb in a careful and abridged way.

"Herb, if you had the chance to buy an antiquarian book that has no historical reference and no verifiable ownership provenance, what would you do?"

After a pause, Herb replied. "I guess I don't understand. Often a book's provenance is difficult to determine - books don't come with serial numbers; but I don't know what you mean by it having no history? Every book has some history."

"What if there was just one copy of a book printed and it was stored away for a very long time?"

"Just one copy? How long ago are we talking?"

"The 1500s. England."

Herb's face displayed a puzzled look. "A single copy? The 1500s? No record of it? How can that be? For one thing, printing a book in those times was quite an elaborate process; why would there only be one copy? There would be no profit in that."

"It would have been a private document."

"Well then, I guess I would be very skeptical. I certainly would have it inspected by many experts, both in terms of the physical characteristics of the book and definitely in terms of the content. What kind of book is it that interests you so much?"

Ray started to squirm in his chair. This conversation was getting away from him. "I can't show the book to you; the seller is demanding strict secrecy as he doesn't want what he is doing to be known. It's a bit like the situation we had with the Hakluyt set last year."

"And what is the book about?" Herb repeated.

"Sir Francis Drake."

"Wow. How could such a document both exist in the first place and survive without being known?"

"I guess that's the question I am facing."

"I am getting out of my depth here, but, again, I would be very skeptical."

"Is there someone else we could talk to?"

"We could call Colin Mackenzie in London, I guess. He knows a lot about the era. I could try now if you want. There is an eight hour time zone difference and so it is late afternoon over there; he might still be in his book shop."

"OK, let's do it. But, Herb, you must recognize by now that I am being very careful with what I say; the seller needs to maintain privacy at all costs."

"I understand, but you can't proceed without some verification, surely? It must be expensive."

When Ray didn't respond any more, Herb turned to his phone index and dialed the number for Colin Mackenzie.

Colin was in. Herb covered off the front-end niceties and then said, "Colin, I have Vice President Cartwright here with me and we have been discussing books on exploration from the Elizabethan era and wanted to get your input on books relative to Sir Francis Drake. Of course, you recall that the Vice President purchased the Hakluyt volumes and he is asking whether there are any additional documents from Drake's time that describe his voyage around the world. I gave him a general summary of what happened in those days, but I think you could add a lot. Do you mind speaking with him?"

Of course, Colin Mackenzie was very pleased to have been contacted in this way. Over a period of about fifteen minutes he described the Elizabethan situation and how Drake's documents had been confiscated. He also repeated the story that none of them had survived due to a fire at

Whitehall Palace in 1698, such that any published documents were based on the stories of others, with the most complete being the one published by his nephew in 1628.

Then Ray started to ask a few questions. "Is there any way at all that some of Drake's own works could have survived?'

"I certainly wish that was possible," said Colin. "They would be invaluable, but I don't see how it could have happened. Surely over four hundred years they would have been found, and, if so, they would have been received with great fanfare and historical interest. They would likely have ended up in the British Museum and been carefully preserved."

"Things can get lost in old buildings and libraries. Couldn't that have happened with Drake?"

"As far as we know everything that Drake created was confiscated by the Queen's court. I would think that they kept things well organized. Then the fire happened over 100 years later. Of course, when we are talking about events so long ago, anything is possible; people do find forgotten Rembrandts and Van Goghs in attics."

"There seems to some debate about how far north Drake actually went up the coast of North America," said Ray, changing the course of the conversation.

"The consensus by historians is that he traversed as far north as present-day Oregon. There are some scholars who claim he went much farther north in an attempt to discover a passage across the top of North America, but that has never been established. There is a Canadian author, Bawlf by name I recall, who published an extensive study that claimed just that. It is still a controversial subject."

That reminded Ray Cartwright about his encounter with the historian in Vancouver at the opening of the *David Thompson Centre*. In the rush of the past few days he had forgotten about it. He must get a copy of that book about Drake's secret voyage.

"Doesn't the appearance of California as an island on many maps in the 1600s and 1700s give some support to the Drake northern voyage theory?" Ray then asked.

"Bawlf and others certainly try to make that case," replied Colin. "However, you need to remember that exploration of the region and mapmaking was quite limited in those times. The misinterpretation of the California Baja peninsula as an island is a little hard to understand but the Spaniards controlled the area and didn't explore that area much. Also, mapmakers in Europe would often rely on fanciful stories and rumors in creating their maps of far-away places. Right up until the late 1700s, two hundred years after Drake and just before the voyage of James Cook, the whole west coast of North America was often shown as having great prominences, bays and rivers that do not actually exist. The California Island was just a variation on those things."

After a few more general questions and comments Ray thanked Colin for his time and advice and they hung up the phone.

"Thank you for positioning the conversation the way you did, Herb. It avoided most of the awkwardness."

"You are welcome," said Herb, "but I can tell that you are not fully satisfied."

"You are right. Colin seems like a fine fellow but he does seem committed to the traditional thinking about Drake."

"He is British," Herb replied, trying to keep a straight face.

Ray smiled. "Thanks again, Herb. I'll go back home and think about all of this some more. I'll be in touch."

31

Back in his library, Ray Cartwright wasn't sure what to do next. Certainly Herb and Colin had increased his caution. Alan Page wasn't going to be any more help. He was also sure that the laboratory tests would not prove anything; after all, the seller had suggested that he do that.

He recognized that he had reached the point where he really wanted the document to be real; he coveted having such an item. He knew this could affect his judgment.

He found himself getting into a form of double-think. The seller would know that he would consult people like Herb and Colin and could easily guess what their advice and cautions would be. Nevertheless, the seller was confident enough to propose the whole deal to him, which meant that it was real. Didn't it?

He had asked his local assistant to locate a copy of Bawlf"s book, *The Secret Voyage of Sir Francis Drake,* which he would read as soon as possible. He considered who else he could consult. There was Jeremy Boucher in Ohio, who was a real perfectionist and could perhaps give him some other ideas on certifying the book. There was also Simon Katz in New York, who had a breadth of world-wide experience, but he wondered what he could contribute beyond what he already knew from Herb and Colin.

He decided to call Jeremy.

It was now late afternoon in Ohio and Ray caught Jeremy Boucher at his office in Columbus. He was surprised, and certainly pleased, when he realized that the Vice President had called him directly.

"Jeremy, I am sorry to bother you but I could use your advice on a situation that I have come across. I have been offered a book from the sixteenth century and I wonder how I can determine if it is authentic or not."

"Mr. Vice President, I would be pleased to look at it and to give you my opinion. I have quite a bit of experience in examining that kind of publication as you know."

"Yes I do, Jeremy, but that is not possible in this case. The seller is being quite secretive; you know this can happen when people do not want their financial situation to become known to others," said Ray, slightly misrepresenting the facts but hoping it would be sufficient for Jeremy.

Jeremy, being reticent to challenge the Vice President by saying that he could be counted on to keep things confidential and that he would not need to know the identity of the seller, moved on to more general advice. "You certainly want to carefully inspect the book and to collate it against recorded descriptions in the many available reference publications," he said. "You must ensure that it is complete."

Ray mused that this specific advice was of no value; there was no reference or record of the document.

Jeremy continued, "If you are concerned that the book is a forgery, which can happen but is unusual in this business, you can have scientific tests done. The paper and ink can be tested. Dating techniques help for the paper. Since a forger would need to obtain very old pages for the book, likely from more than one source, you would want to compare the analyses from a number of pages. A legitimate book would have only one type of paper.

"Chemical analysis is required for the ink. Those materials were made very differently four hundred years ago. What you need to do is to have the experts look very carefully for contaminants. In the fifteenth and sixteenth centuries new inks were developed for use with the newly-invented printing presses by Gutenberg and others that followed him. They were based on things like soot, turpentine and walnut oil. Of course, a clever forger would try to reproduce those old formulae, but modern walnut oil would be likely to contain traces of modern fertilizers or pesticides; that's what you would look for."

"That's very useful, Jeremy," replied Ray. "I had planned to have analyses done but I didn't appreciate some of the subtleties. Is there anything else?"

"The other thing I can think of is the type face of the printing. The styles are always changing, and, again, that was very true in the sixteenth century. There are good reference books available about that also; the set of Dolphin compilations about *The History of the Printed Book* are particularly informative. What you also look for is some sign of wear on the type. After all, these were expensive and special items for a book printer. Unless a specific book was one of the first to be printed with a new set of type, statistically unlikely since type lasted a relatively long time, you would expect to see some small flaws. If a forger created some new type to look like an old style it might look too neat."

"Great; thanks for that. I appreciate your help. I am sure I will see you at a book fair soon. All the best in the meantime."

"Anytime, Mr. Vice President. Good luck with your campaign."

With that, they hung up.

32

For the next two weeks Ray was back in Washington, D.C. for various meetings and government activities, filling in the open spots on his calendar with political side trips to the Northeast and Midwest.

He had called Alan Page after his meeting with Herb Trawets and his phone call to Jeremy Boucher to explain that he was proceeding with the scientific tests and that he would get back to him in a couple of weeks. Somewhat to his surprise, Alan was not concerned about the timeline and told him that he could have all the time that he needed.

In that time he had located the Bawlf book and had read it through. It was a revelation in the sense that Bawlf's detailed analysis of the historical record and of the political dynamics of the Elizabethan era, plus his persuasive conclusion that Francis Drake had traveled far north up the Pacific coast of North America, were totally consistent with the secret document that he was being offered. To Ray, this either added credibility to the document or just indicated that someone had read Bawlf's work. It certainly reinforced the tremendous historical significance of the document, if it was real.

Ray was now reading the technical report that he had just received from the laboratory in California. Full of tables and charts, it concluded that everything that it had analyzed was consistent with a sixteenth century document. This included the search for the telltale traces and inconsistencies which Jeremy Boucher had mentioned to Ray.

"So there it is," Ray said to himself. "Nothing disproves the validity of the book, but nothing proves it either."

Taking a piece of blank paper, he started to scratch down all of the elements of the book offer. It looked like a combination of an elaborate line doodle and a jigsaw puzzle. However, staring at it did crystallize some of his thinking.

He started by noting that the first real issue, perhaps the only issue for him, was whether or not the document itself was legitimate. He didn't know what else to do to test that question. Obviously, if it was a fake he was being set up as the victim of a huge confidence game.

If it was a con, there were two possibilities. Either Alan Page's story was true and he was simply being used as a pawn by some other person or Alan himself was the perpetrator. After thinking that through, Ray decided that it was likely the first situation but that he really didn't know Alan well enough to decide if he could pull off the preparation and the acting that was required to present the deal to him. It didn't really matter though; if he was conned and he really kept the whole transaction secret, neither he nor anyone else would ever know the truth, at least not until his estate was being probated and the document surfaced!

Then he studied the possibilities of the document being legitimate, seeing if that presented any inherent clues or contradictions.

He had to be skeptical about Alan's "found-in-the-attic" explanation. If the document had been found in some old lord's manor house or ancient building, it would have been made public by the finder. No matter how high a profile or title that such a person had, and no matter what their true financial status was, they would gain the most by disclosing it publicly and putting it up for auction, fully expecting it would be purchased by the British Museum or the British government archives and be kept in the public domain. They would benefit from the publicity without any real adverse consequences. They would not need to undertake this secret process that was being proposed to Ray. Besides, they would make a lot more money in that way; the two million dollars from Ray seemed like a lot of money on the surface but a public auction would certainly generate a larger sum.

So that meant there would need to be some other reason for the process to be kept secret. Who could own such a document, have kept its existence secret, and then be willing to dispose of it secretly for two million dollars? The allusions to the Royal Family that came from the events in Vancouver certainly came to his thoughts.

How could it have been kept a secret for four hundred years? Deliberately kept secret for political or diplomatic reason, as had all of Drake's original documents? Then, somehow, not being destroyed later along with the rest of them but misplaced in the archives of some royal Castle or the Tower of London? Discovered only recently by someone in charge who needed money? All of that was possible, of course, but was it likely?

The next possibility was that those events of history, the original secrecy and the lost document for centuries, were true and that it had been found by someone who stole it for their own gain. It caused Ray to flinch when he realized that this scenario was as likely as any. Was he being set up as the receiver of stolen goods?

That raised the possibility that it was all a political set-up, a trap for him. He didn't think that that was likely; even with all the dirty tricks in politics, this didn't feel political.

Ray couldn't identify any possibilities other than those five or six, depending on which ones you discarded completely.

He also pondered the fact that the seller had approached him. Sure, he was rich and a known collector of antiquarian books, but others fit into that category. If the document was fake or stolen, surely there would be safer targets than the Vice President of the United States, who could easily alert legal authorities if he decided that course of action was appropriate.

At that moment, Vincent Larch was shown into his office, arriving for a scheduled review of some legal issues related to upcoming legislation in the Senate.

After they had completed the business items, Ray said to Vince, "I have a hypothetical situation that a friend has posed which I would like to get your opinion on."

Looking a little suspicious, Vince said, "What is it, Mr. Vice President?"

"Suppose that someone was considering buying something and, in spite of conducting a lot of checking and asking questions, he wasn't sure that the seller had a legitimate ownership in the item, would…"

"Oh boy, Mr. Vice President, please stop there," interjected Vince.

"Sir," he continued. "You know that I am your legal counsel for government activities; I can't advise you in confidence on personal matters. Besides, you are a good lawyer; I can't imagine that you aren't quite capable of giving your friend good advice.

"As an aside, I wouldn't get Calvin or Ralph involved either. You know they would just tell you to avoid any connection with well-meaning friends who may have a lapse in judgment. We have seen the political complications that such things can create before.

"I'll go now, sir." Then he added quite softly, "I know this was just a hypothetical situation and we didn't really get into it, and so I will not have any reason to record it in my daily log."

After Vince left Ray stared out the window of his office and shook his head. "What am I doing? What was I thinking? How can I jeopardize everything?" he mumbled to himself, although, even in doing so, he knew his decision was not going to be that easy. He wanted the book to be real, and he wanted to own it.

33

It was June 1st. Ray was in Denver for a political dinner and some fund raising meetings. As well, he was going to make a convocation speech to the graduating engineering class at the Colorado School of Mines, his original alma mater. In doing so, he would receive the honorary degree of Doctor of Engineering and a Distinguished Service Medal in recognition of his outstanding career achievements. Those type of ceremonies were good for the recipient and good for the university; positive publicity always helped

It also gave Anne and him a chance to visit their son and his family, a less frequent occurrence now that he was so engaged in political campaigning.

In his speech to the new graduates, after the normal thanks for the invitation and the honor, and after the routine words of congratulations to the graduates, he moved on to his main message for the graduates and, not too surprisingly, to the media that were covering the event.

"You have worked hard and succeeded in your studies over the past four years. Congratulations again. You have had a great deal of fun, I am sure – university days do not change that much from generation to generation.

"I know that you have developed a sense of rivalry with your fellow engineering groups: Chemical Engineering, Civil Engineering, Mechanical Engineering, and so on. I also know that you have had a sense of competition and maybe even a sense of one-upmanship on other faculties and other schools. You know…the business guys, the lawyers, the arts types in history or literature, the social sciences…

"Let me tell you now, and encourage you to embrace it fully: those other disciplines will be more important to you in the future than any of the other engineering disciplines. The environmental concerns, the community impacts, the legal structure, the need to finance projects will all impact your work in the future; and so they should.

"You must embrace these other inputs as real and necessary, because they are. They are not impediments or restrictions on your projects or your businesses; they are legitimate dimensions for your work. Generations past, mine included, have often fought against those concepts. Don't do that; move forward.

"Early in your careers you will be busy and focused on establishing your professional credentials, on making some money and finally getting some material things of your own, and on settling down and raising a family. Everyone does.

"There is more to it than that though. Look out to your communities and your fellow citizens. Maybe in the beginning it is coaching a community kid's team or helping in the hospitals and schools. Later, maybe it's getting involved with community associations or school boards. Who knows, maybe you want to be President."

That brought a loud wave of laughter and cheers from the assembled crowd.

"You can make this country and the world a better place. You have the talent and the skills. Have the determination and the courage to apply them."

There was thunderous applause as he stepped back from the podium.

He had called Alan Page a few days before the trip to Denver. Alan had agreed, quite easily of course, to fly up from Phoenix in order to meet with the Vice President directly. Neither of them broached the subject of paramount interest on the phone.

The morning after the speech and the related dinner of honor, Alan arrived at the Vice President's suite in a downtown hotel. He entered the room with a look that seemed to be a mixture of suppressed excitement, caution, and some trepidation, quite a combination to convey.

"Hello again, Alan. Come on in."

"Hello, Mr. Vice President. It is good to see you and congratulations on your honorary degree. I understand from the morning paper that your speech was very well received by the graduates."

"Thank you."

This was followed by a long pause. Alan Page did not know what to say next.

Finally, Ray Cartwright resumed talking. "Alan, is there anything more you can tell me about the document and the offer?"

"Not really, sir. I have heard from my contact a few times over the past weeks, but that was only to check in and to get an update on the conversations I have had with you. There is nothing I can add about the document."

After another pause, Ray said, "I certainly wish there was more to be had about the history and the provenance of it."

Then he continued, almost in a whisper, "What do we do next if I decide to buy it?"

The ensuing silence was so pronounced that Alan thought that he had stopped breathing and that his hearing had failed.

Then he said, "The next step would simply be for you to transfer the funds, less my commission, to a bank account in the Bahamas, which I can provide to you. Then it would be all done. You already have the document and we won't need any other paperwork."

"Ohmygod," said Ray suddenly. "I forgot. I don't have any money!"

At times, in novels, you will read a passage saying that a character's jaw dropped to the floor in surprise. Alan Page's jaw came as close to that image as is physically possible for a human being.

34

Ray Cartwright and Alan Page stared directly at each other, still in total silence.

"What did you say?" Alan finally said, forgetting any form of protocol.

"It's the trust arrangements," started Ray. "All of my money is tied up in a blind trust due to my political position. I can access the money for personal purchases such as books but it would involve my personal administrator, Maria Rodriguez. The situation would even require the insurance underwriters to inspect the material. That all hardly lends itself to secrecy.

"As well, they would need a bill of sale, proof of ownership, and a third-party certificate of authenticity and value. That means that the whole process can't happen."

All of the color had drained from Alan's face.

"Surely there is something you can do," he pleaded. "You have a fortune."

"I do, but I don't."

Then Ray added with a chagrined look, "I don't suppose the sellers would wait for nine years?"

That spooked Alan even more.

Ray finally said, "Give me a little more time. I will try to figure something out."

Alan left, saying that he would need to talk to his source again and to find out what they had to say. Ray sat in his chair, lost in thought. In spite of the predicament, he smiled when he realized that he had pursued the deal with Alan without consciously saying, either to himself or out loud, "I want to buy it."

It had just happened.

Surely there was something he could do!

He knew that, in spite of his half-joking comment to Alan, the seller was not going to wait for many years to deal with him. There were certainly other people in the world that he could approach with the same offer. He would not have to worry about Ray interfering with or spoiling any of their other activities. After all, the only thing he knew about the seller was what Alan had told him, very little, and he had gone too far to be willing to risk his own reputation, even if he just backed away now.

He still hadn't told Anne anything about his dealings with Alan Page and, in any case, there was nothing that she could do about raising large sums that would be independent from the intense scrutiny that he always faced.

He thought of Brian Butler, his partner in *TickerTreat*, who certainly had lots of money and a good relationship and loyalty to Ray, but he could not think of any way that he could approach him about the current situation. The need for secrecy about the deal and the need to be absolutely circumspect with others regarding his political image precluded involving Brian.

"How can I secretly round up two-and-a-half million dollars?" he muttered, almost laughing out loud. "I don't even have anything that I could sell privately, certainly not for the amount involved with the Drake document."

Then, a new idea flashed into his mind. "What if I buy something that's legitimate and then quietly return it for a refund?" Then he sagged, "How could something like that happen in complete confidence?"

Nevertheless, he couldn't shake the concept out of his mind. "How? How? How?"

He started to make a list, in sort of a doodle, on his ever-present notepad: valuable…verifiable…returnable…credible…confidential…

"How would it work? Who could he possibly trust?"

A name came to him – "Herb... Herb Trawets."

"What could Herb possibly arrange? Could he get access to very valuable books? Could he arrange some form of swap transaction? Could they do some kind of bait-and-switch? How could he approach Herb and what would he say?"

There were many imponderables but Ray started to think that even a poorly thought-out plan, with many pitfalls, was better than no plan at all. The overwhelming need would be to protect himself from some form of leak or backlash from the people they would need to deal with; that would be politically fatal.

Although he wasn't sure exactly how he would proceed, or even if he actually would try it, he called Elsie Browning, his executive assistant, and informed her that he needed to change his travel plans. He wanted to head back home to Seattle that afternoon for a few days before returning to Washington. That was one advantage of being Vice President, even one in the early stages of an election campaign; no one really cared about or noticed his comings and goings that closely, unlike the President. Anne was staying over in Denver anyway to have an extended visit with their grandson.

Next he called Herb Trawets at his store and told him that he would be in town tomorrow and that he wanted to drop by in the morning.

Herb was full of curiosity, of course. He naturally assumed it was a follow-up to the meeting he had with the Vice President a few weeks earlier and the phone call they had placed to London. "I wonder what he wants from me now?" he mused.

After the call to Herb, Ray called Alan Page, who had just returned to his Denver hotel room.

"Alan, I just wanted to tell you that I am working on a solution to our problem but I will need a few days more to figure it out."

"OK, Mr. Vice President. I will be in touch with my contact right away about these new developments. I'll get back to you but I am sure that a little time won't make a difference now."

After Ray hung up, he again wondered to himself, "Could this all be a hoax masterminded by Alan Page? If so, he is certainly cool and collected with it."

35

Ray spent all that afternoon, including the flight from Denver to Seattle, and that evening in his library, thinking through how to approach Herb Trawets.

He had to keep everything as simple as possible and ensure that Herb was not inadvertently drawn into doing something unethical. Ray decided to simply use an edited version of what was happening, leaving out some of the awkward circumstances of his deal and fabricating a few details. He knew that Herb would be curious and quite thoughtful about what Ray was saying and doing, especially because of the earlier meeting they had that led to the call to London. Ray decided that he had to rely on Herb's natural reticence to speak out too directly to the Vice President. It was not going to be easy.

When he arrived at Herb's bookstore the next morning their greetings were warm and cordial but very quickly a silence settled over them as Herb awaited what the Vice President had to say.

"Herb, I need your help," started Ray, looking Herb straight into his eyes.

"It is complicated and sensitive," he continued. "It does follow on from the subject that we discussed a while ago. I have done a lot of research and testing and have decided that I want to purchase the book that has been offered to me. The problem, as I told you before, is that the seller is demanding the utmost discretion and secrecy, which I must honor or else I can not purchase it.

"Normally, that would not be an issue for me, but in my current political position I do not have as much freedom to act. My funds are tied up in a trust arrangement and I need to involve a number of people to access significant amounts of money. In this case I need two-and-a-half million dollars."

As Ray paused, Herb looked at him with a look that was a combination of surprise and amusement. He couldn't help saying, "Well, Mr. Vice President, maybe I could just get it for you out of my petty cash."

Herb immediately pulled back in embarrassment at having said something so frivolous, but Ray simply smiled and said," I wish it was so, Herb, but I am hoping that you can help me anyway."

Herb stared at him.

"First, tell me, what books are there in the collecting world, in my area of general interest, that would have a price tag of millions?"

Herb paused and tried to think the question through. "Well, there aren't many. Sure, there are valuable books, but very high prices tend to be in the hundreds of thousands of dollars, not millions. For books to be so valuable they would need to be of special historical significance, be rare, and be in good shape. Such books tend to end up in major museums or national archives, funded by government grants or large endowments. Not many are in private hands and available for sale. I would need to do some research to identify anything that might be available – perhaps a very old, intact world atlas that has some historical provenance. But, if I might ask, I don't see how having another very expensive book would solve your problem of accessing funds."

"I was thinking that perhaps I could borrow such a book, and, since it would not need to be closeted in secrecy, I could use it to release funds from my trust accounts. In effect, I would buy it and then return it for a refund."

Herb looked flabbergasted. "You mean you want to take out a multi-million-dollar book as if it was in a public library, and then use it to obtain cash?"

"Sort of. But, of course I would be quite willing to pay a lending fee to the owner and also pay you a handling commission."

Again Herb was speechless for a minute, being both amazed by what he was hearing and suddenly excited about the possibility of earning a sizable fee. Then he said, "I don't know if something like that could be arranged or not. As I said, I don't even know what book or which dealer or source might be willing to do such a thing; I would need to do some research."

"Of course. To start, why don't you try to identify any available books that might fill our needs? Then, before you approach anyone specifically about the arrangement, let's talk again."

"OK. But, Mr. Vice President, are you sure you want to do this? It seems very unusual and risky to be buying the secret book in such a convoluted way."

"Herb, I appreciate your cautions and your advice, but I have just about decided to go forward. Can you check out your sources and contacts in the next day or so? Can I call you tomorrow afternoon?"

"Of course, I'll see what I can do."

36

Ray returned to his home office, planning to make a number of political phone calls and to arrange a couple of local meetings with supporters. First, he called his Washington, D.C. office to talk with Elsie Browning about various administrative matters and then to talk with Calvin Begg and Ralph King about political activities.

At the conclusion of his conversation with Elsie, she said. "There is one other thing Mr. Vice President. I had a call from the FBI Director's office and they asked if you would be available to meet with an FBI special agent in Seattle while you are there. They said it was a routine inquiry that did not involve you directly but that they thought you might be able to give them some relevant information. They didn't elaborate."

"That's unusual, but sure. If you contact them, I could make some time this afternoon, say about 3:00."

"OK, I'll call them and confirm it back with you."

As Ray then followed up with his calls to Calvin and Ralph, he found himself getting easily distracted as he pondered what the FBI visit could be about. He couldn't help but wonder if it was related to his book dealing.

The time to 3:00 went quickly as Ray continued to make his calls. Then the secret service agent on duty announced that FBI Special Agent Wilson was there to see him.

Agent Wilson entered the room saying, "Mr. Vice President, thank you so much for giving me a few minutes of your time. I know you are busy and so I will try to make it quick." As he said that, he showed Ray his badge and handed him a business card that said *Efrem Z. Wilson, Special Agent, FBI, Seattle.*

Ray couldn't help but smile slightly at the name on the card and say, "No problem, Agent Wilson, but can I ask you, does the Z stand for Zimbalist?"

With a resigned shrug Agent Wilson said, "Yes it does. You are very observant. My father was also an FBI agent. He was a big fan of the television series *The FBI* in the early 1970s and he named me after the leading actor. It has been a bit of a downer for me, especially during the FBI training days when the other recruits would rib me about it, calling me *FBI Man* in a lyrical manner."

Ray smiled at that and then asked, "What can I do for you, Agent Wilson?"

"Well sir, it relates to a book purchase."

Ray sensed that he was holding his breath as he waited for elaboration.

"I believe that you purchased a set of old books by an author named Hakluyt late last year. Is that true?"

"Yes," Ray replied with a sense of relief.

"The FBI is cooperating with Scotland Yard in England regarding a suspected money-laundering operation. We are tracing the flow of funds related to your purchase. It appears that the original seller has inflated the amount he received, presumably to camouflage the actual source of those extra funds which were likely from some illegal activity."

"I am curious about how Scotland Yard could detect such a thing."

"Apparently it was a fortuitous event. There is a young auditing clerk in the British government's tax department who has a personal interest in old books; he attends book fairs and auctions and monitors historic books as a hobby. When he happened to be reviewing the recent tax return from the seller, the large sum involved in the Hakluyt sale caught his attention. Just as a personal curiosity he started to do a little research about the books and it seemed to him that the sales price was surprisingly high and so he passed on his thoughts to his supervisors. They followed up with Scotland Yard, who it turns out were following other leads about money laundering. That all led to this tracking down what actually transpired in your deal."

"I remember the transaction clearly; it was a big step for me in the scope of my collection. I purchased the set for 650 thousand dollars. It was organized by a London book dealer named Colin Mackenzie; my contact was arranged through Herb Trawets here in Seattle, the owner of Herb's Books. Surely Herb is not involved in money laundering!"

"No, not at all. In fact the tax records of both Herb Trawets and Colin Mackenzie are quite consistent with your recollection. They are not involved. I have one last question for you, sir. It is a little sensitive, and I certainly do not want to presume anything, but I must ask it. Did you make any other payment to the seller?"

"No, why would I? I was paying full value already. In any case I didn't even know the identity of the seller; it was all represented through the book sellers... Oh, I understand your question now; presumably if I made an extra payment it would be to help the seller avoid some commission to Colin and Herb. Of course, if that had happened, it would make the seller's tax return legitimate, wouldn't it? Anyway, that didn't happen and I wouldn't do anything to tarnish my relationship with them; they are the source of many of my best collection volumes."

"Thank you, Mr. Vice President. This has been useful and it helps us close the loop on the case. We appreciate your assistance. We may need to follow up to get an affidavit signed to be used as evidence, although the documents from Colin Mackenzie will likely suffice"

"That's fine. I am always available to help law enforcement activities. I have one more question, out of curiosity. How much did the seller claim he received?"

"The return showed four hundred thousand pounds, or eight hundred thousand dollars, which is three hundred thousand more than he actually received after the book dealers' commissions."

"That is significant all right. I can see how it caught the young auditor's attention."

At that point they wrapped up their meeting and agent Wilson left.

Over the next few hours, alone in his library, Ray revisited all of the issues related to the Drake document. He realized that he had to think everything through much more carefully; his desire to get the document had clouded his thinking. There were more risks and pitfalls to his dealings. His idea of just swapping funds from a phantom purchase seemed too vulnerable now.

The different considerations were almost mind-numbing.

What if the document was a fake? Then, in the final analysis Ray would be shown to have been duped. That wasn't good, but neither was it a fatal problem. That wouldn't create any legal or political problems for him, especially since nothing should surface for a long time, even in his lifetime.

What if it was stolen? This would be a bigger problem. First of all, if that was discovered, the document would be seized and returned to its rightful owner. Then he would face a more intense scrutiny about his actions, but there was not really any significant legal problem for him that he could see, just political ones. He would just look less competent for not having checked more thoroughly. However, the phrase *interstate transportation of stolen goods* did cross his mind.

He had transported the document across the Canadian-U.S. border. That could be a problem but, again, he thought that he would be OK. He didn't own the book then and he wasn't bringing it back to sell it, but rather to possibly buy it. He realized that this train of thought could just be a rationalization.

What if it was real, but was part of another money-laundering scheme; after all, he had been implicated in the one case already. If that was the case, it could be said that he should have been more careful, but, in reality, he could never be expected to know what a seller was going to do with the money he received; that was impossible to know.

However, if that was the situation, and he were to receive another visit from the FBI as had just happened, he would have trouble showing how he had paid for it if he undertook a bait-and-switch process. His paper trail would be for the wrong book; one that he would not even have.

That also meant that when someday his collection was being reviewed again, even if it was not until his death and in an estate probate, his records would not show any history for the Drake document and the phantom book would be missing in spite of having invoices and insurance papers. That would be a problem for his legacy, which he would like to avoid. But what if it all came out sooner? How could he handle that?

Then he took the box out of his locked drawer and opened the document. Staring at the pages, he didn't read the words; he had already done that a dozen or more times. Instead, his mind visualized Sir Francis Drake, sitting in a similar situation, contemplating his own life and legacy while he created this document. Somehow, Ray felt a bond that reached back across the centuries.

Ray finally decided that he had to take a break and move on to his other activities for a while. Perhaps some new idea would surface later. Again he did note to himself that he was working very hard to find a way to buy the document; he was not going to just give up and tell Alan Page the deal was off.

37

Herb Trawets spent a busy afternoon searching for something that would meet the needs of the Vice President's situation.

He had seen some very valuable books over the years, often at the major book fairs, but he couldn't immediately think of anything in the two million dollar range that was in the Vice President's area of interest, even peripherally.

He decided that he would start by doing an electronic search of the various bookseller services on the internet. Then he would consult the various catalogues that he always picked up at the fairs and received in the mail from dealers around the world, since not everything was posted on the general sites. Finally, he would do some searching on the various booksellers' individual websites for updates. He hoped that one idea or lead might lead to others as he progressed through the materials.

He started with the specialty internet sites that listed books for sale; books of every type and description. He went to abebooks.com, bookfinder.com, addall.com and a few others. Since he didn't know what he was looking for, he simply made searches by categories, always specifying that the lists start at the highest prices. He used key words such as explorers, voyages, and atlases. He tried names such as Lewis and Clarke, Drake, Cook, and Vancouver.

Herb had a great deal of experience in the book selling business and had seen many expensive books but looking for a two million dollar item was certainly new to him. In fact, the brokering of the Hakluyt volumes between Colin Mackenzie and Vice President Cartwright was the most expensive item he had ever dealt, by quite a margin.

As he had anticipated, the searches did not uncover many items in the price range he was searching. There were a few atlases listed over a million dollars, the most relevant one being a Ptolemaic atlas issued in 1513 by Waldseemuller at a price of $1.2 million. This atlas was a landmark item, containing 48 woodcut prints, a few in color. What made it of particular attraction was that it was the first atlas to have a map devoted to America, labeled *Tabula Terre Nove or Map of New Lands,* based on the journeys of Columbus and a few others over the ensuing twenty years.

There were some non-atlas books priced over a half-million dollars but there were no books with a price over a million dollars. As he had said to the Vice President, for a book to demand such a price it would need to be of very special significance and very rare, meaning that most such items end up in museums, universities and national collections and are thus unavailable to a private collector. Any collector who had such an item was unlikely to sell it. It would be a fortuitous happenstance to find something like that at a specific time.

Herb's browsing of his bookseller catalogues did not surface any further leads. One thing he did note from his searches online and in the catalogues was that a limited number of dealers seemed to dominate the very expensive book market, a few in England, one in Australia, and a couple in New York. A name that surfaced constantly was Simon Katz in New York.

Although the Vice President had suggested that he make some direct contacts with some key people about available books, without disclosing what Ray was contemplating, Herb balked at that idea. He first wanted to talk to the Vice President again. There were a number of problems with the Vice President's plan that were beginning to bother Herb.

First, it appeared that he would need to obtain at least three books in order to achieve a value of two-and-a-half million dollars. That likely meant that a number of dealers would have to be involved, not a good formula for secrecy.

Second, he didn't know how he could arrange with a dealer, or dealers, for such expensive books to be bought and then returned for a refund. At this level of collecting, the dealers would be pleased to send books to a collector such as the Vice President on consignment for inspection. Then, after a decision was made to purchase the books, an invoice would be issued and payment sent. It would be unusual to first pay for the books and then get a refund; that would involve the needless multiple transfers of large sums of money, often complicated by currency exchange changes.

Even if such a transaction could be arranged, the accountants in most established firms would insist on sending the refund to the same source that paid the invoice in the first place, namely the Trust that managed the Vice President's affairs.

Based on those concerns, it seemed to Herb that he shouldn't call anyone yet. It was better not to prematurely complicate any messaging that might be required. He decided that he would continue to do his own research and wait for the Vice President's call that was planned for the next day.

The next afternoon the Vice President actually returned to Herb's Book Store rather than just phoning; he needed to talk things through with Herb Trawets as no new ideas had come to him overnight.

When he walked in, Herb looked up in surprise and then greeted him warmly. The only customer in the store at the time was also surprised to see the Vice President, and he nodded politely in acknowledgement. Ray nodded back and said "Hi," but didn't elaborate. The customer quickly felt awkward in the presence of the Vice President and the sight of his bodyguards and limousine out in front of the store and soon left. At that, Herb turned over the "Closed" sign in the window and turned back to Ray.

"Mr. Vice President," he said. "I have not had a great deal of success in locating an appropriate book for your planned transaction and I have developed some reservations about the doability of it." Herb went on to describe in detail the results of his searching and the concerns he had about the logistics of the bait-and-switch plan Ray had proposed.

"Herb," replied Ray after hearing Herb out, "I have similar concerns. To be frank, I don't have any other ideas how to proceed to free up the funds and keep the actual purchase secret. I guess I just need to go back to the seller and explain that I need to share the information with other people if I am going to be able to proceed; people that can keep a secret.

"If you come up with any other ideas or leads, let me know. I'll be in touch if something else develops on my part. Thank you so much, Herb, for all you have done and for your well-thought-out advice."

When Ray got back home he left a voice message on the answering machine at the number that Alan Page had provided him, asking Alan to call. "My God," thought Ray, not for the first time, "this is really consuming me."

38

Alan Page, back in Phoenix, picked up the message from the Vice President very shortly after it was left, but he paused for a few minutes before returning the call. What was the Vice President going to say and how would he handle it? He would need to contact the seller immediately after the upcoming conversation; he felt the deal and his opportunity for making a huge commission slipping away. Somehow, he had to broker an arrangement; that was what he was supposed to be good at. However, he didn't have any idea how to make the Vice President's funding problem go away.

Alan's involvement in this affair had started with a phone call last March, just three months ago, between the Los Angeles and the New York book fairs. He was in Arizona.

The voice on the phone started with, "Mr. Page, I have a proposition for you that relies on your involvement and contacts in the antiquarian book business. It could pay you very well."

Alan was a bit taken back by the immediate directness, without any introduction or preamble. He did not recognize the voice; in fact it sounded somewhat artificial. He wasn't very good at recognizing accents but it sounded to him like either an Englishman trying to sound American or the reverse. There was a hint of a British accent but the overall sense from the phrasing and pace seemed American. Maybe it was a Canadian accent?

Alan responded, "I am always interested in a business proposition. I'm sorry, but I didn't catch your name."

"That doesn't matter for now. If you want, just call me Frank. What I have is a very sensitive situation and for that reason I can not reveal who I am. I have an extremely important and valuable document that needs to be sold privately and discreetly. For personal reasons, the sale absolutely can not be known publicly."

"That's not unusual," replied Alan. "Often people want to raise funds without public awareness."

"I understand that. This situation is a bit more complicated as I will describe in a minute, But, first, I need to establish that you can get direct access to Mr. Ray Cartwright, the Vice President of the United States, who I believe would be an ideal purchaser of the document."

This question made Alan sit up straight in his chair. "I have had dealings with the Vice President," he replied cautiously, "but it would need to be something very special for me to contact him directly."

"I assure you that this is special," replied the voice. "It is a document written by Sir Francis Drake in 1595 that presents a summary of his voyage around the world fifteen years earlier. It discloses some important new facts about that voyage."

This was followed by a silence. Alan wasn't an expert in Sir Francis Drake, but he did know that there wasn't any original material attributed to him. "How can that be?" he then asked. "There is no such document as I recall."

"This document was discovered relatively recently in an obscure corner of an Elizabethan era mansion library. The owner wants to sell it privately, because, if its existence became known, he would be faced with immense political and social pressure to donate it to a museum or the National Archives. Selling it publicly is not an option for him."

"How can you know that it is legitimate?" asked Alan. "Is there any ownership provenance? Any historical reference? Any corroborating evidence at all?"

"Not directly, no. We have conducted various technical tests which all show the document to be of the proper age and style. Of course, we assume that the Vice President will want to do the same thing. That is acceptable, but, and this is critical, he can not show the document's contents to anyone. If that were to become known, even in a rumored way, then the whole arrangement could collapse."

"I guess I understand that," replied Alan. "I would be able to give him whatever advice I can, based on discreet inquiries."

"Actually, that's not true. You won't be able to see the contents of the document either."

"What!"

"That's one of our conditions."

"Do I understand you correctly? You want me to sell a document to the Vice President that I haven't seen, for which there is no verifying documentation, all based on a conversation with someone I don't know."

"Correct."

"How could I possibly do that?"

"I agree it would take quite a large amount of chutzpa; you would be putting yourself out on a limb. However, I also believe that once the Vice President sees the document he will want to acquire it. It's your access to him that led to this call, plus your reputation as a free-wheeling salesman and negotiator. We know about your recent sale of the Magellan set to him."

That caused Alan to pause again. "They have certainly done their homework," he thought to himself. Then he asked the critical question, "What is the asking price and what sort of commission would I earn?"

Alan heard a very small sigh on the phone, and he could almost see a smile on the unknown face. He was a good enough salesman himself to sense when the hook had been set with a potential customer; this time he was the fish.

"The owner wants two million dollars. We will be earning a fifteen percent commission for doing the research and arranging all of the logistics. You will be paid ten percent, that's two hundred thousand dollars, for making the contact. That makes a total selling price of two-and-a-half million dollars."

"That's a lot of money."

"To be sure, but it's actually a fraction of the document's true value if it could be sold publicly."

Again there was an extended silence as Alan mulled over everything he had heard. Then, "Can I think about this for a bit?" he asked.

"Sure. I'll call you back again at this same time tomorrow. Just be sure to keep all of this to yourself. If we pick up any sense of a leak, you will never hear from us again."

"OK, I'll talk to you tomorrow."

Alan hardly slept that night as he churned everything he had heard over and over in his mind. By noon the next day he had decided that he would pursue the deal further. He rationalized many things: the worst case was that he would make a fool of himself with the Vice President, but even then, he could protect himself by being candid – he was a messenger, not a seller or authenticator. This same rationale convinced him that he would not be doing anything illegal even if the document was stolen or a fake. "Yes, the mind can rationalize anything if enough money is involved," he mused.

When the second call came, he learned more details about the planned process – the delivery in Vancouver, the eventual transfer of funds to the Bahamas, and so on. It was stated that the payment to him, if a deal was made, would be directly from the Vice President as a deduction from the money transfer. Thus there would be no financial record between the seller and Alan.

He was also given a phone number to make future contact as things proceeded, both to report progress and to pass on any questions or issues that arose. The number had a 212 area code, New York City. It was explained to him that the phone was a pay-as-you-go cell phone that had been purchased in one of the busy electronics shops on Fifth Avenue with plenty of prepaid minutes to cover their upcoming communications. The number could not be traced, as it was simply shown as being purchased by a Frank Drake with a false New London, Connecticut address. Alan had thought that was one degree too cute, but said nothing.

Since all of that had occurred just two weeks before the New York Book Fair, Alan had decided to make the first contact there, quite confident that the Vice President would show up as he almost always did. If not, he could then start a contact through Cartwright's Washington office, which he preferred not to do. Of course, it had all worked out as planned until the Vice President shocked him with the money-sourcing problem.

The issue had surprised his contact, Frank, as well, which Alan could tell from the silence when he passed on the news. However, Frank had quickly recovered and told Alan to assure the Vice President that he could certainly have more time to work out that issue, which he had done.

Now Alan was about to phone the Vice President back and find out what had developed in the past two days.

The Washington operator connected Alan to the Vice President in Seattle quite quickly.

"Hello, Alan," Ray said when he picked up the phone. "Thank you for calling back. I am afraid that I don't have any positive news for you; I haven't sorted out how to arrange for the funding of the purchase yet. Have you or the seller come up with anything?"

"To be candid, Mr. Vice President, we haven't been working the problem directly. We've been assuming that you would be able to solve it, given a few days to address it." Alan's mind was wheeling as he tried to find a way to keep the deal alive and to buy time. "I'm sure the seller can be a bit more patient. Let me contact them and see if they have any ideas, now that we know your current status. Also, perhaps, a new concept will come to you."

"OK, Alan. Thank you. Call me back again when you have checked things out."

They both hung up the phone with glum looks on their faces.

Alan called the New York number and left a message. When Frank called back, he passed on the news.

Frank seemed calm about it all and simply said, "I can give him a little extra time because it is easier to keep this confidential if we don't need to involve someone new. However, we can't delay forever. Alan, it's time to earn your fee. Remember, it was your ability to deal directly with the V.P. that gave you this opportunity. That might not be the case with another buyer; my next candidate is not in your realm of contacts."

BOOK NINE

LONDON, 1628

The Publication

39

Sir Francis Drake was very pleased. Finally, *The World Encompassed* was *being* published.

It had been over thirty years since his uncle, the original Sir Francis Drake, had died on his ship in the Caribbean. His legend as an explorer, adventurer and naval hero against the Spanish had persisted, but the details of his voyages had never been published; there had just been the short Hakluyt version.

Until her death in 1603, Queen Elizabeth had forbidden any publications. Her successor King James, the protestant son of Mary Queen of Scots, had continued the ban, being unwilling to provoke the Spaniards needlessly. Minor military actions on the high seas and at various coastal towns had continued between the two countries although there had not been any major battles.

In 1625, just three years earlier, James had died and was succeeded by his son, Charles. King Charles was much more defiant of the Spanish and less concerned about the publication of documents such as Drake's. After all, he believed devoutly that he was anointed by God and had the divine right to rule England; he had nothing to fear from Spain.

This had been tested two years earlier, when Sir Francis received permission to publish his uncle's description of the Caribbean raids of 1573. This was the document that Drake had presented to Queen Elizabeth on New Year's, 1593, and which had remained secret ever since. The publication, which was a detailed account that ran for over 25,000 words, included the covering letter Drake had originally written to Queen Elizabeth and a new, short, covering letter that the current Sir Francis addressed to King Charles.

In that new introduction, he had been meticulous in acknowledging that the document was King Charles's by right and succession, and that its current publication would cause no present damage. He even compared it to the writings of Caesar and suggested that its release could stimulate the uncovering of more historical information. Yes, he had done everything he could to pave the way for the release of the more important story of his uncle's historic around-the-world voyage of 1577 - 1580.

The publication of *Sir Francis Drake Revived* was a huge success with the public, and they were openly asking for more. And so, now, King Charles had given his permission.

The document that he had assembled was significant; it ran for over 40,000 words. It was essentially the document that his uncle had created in the late 1580s with the help of Francis Fletcher's journal. However, he had also attempted to include additional material from whatever sources he could find.

He had the abridged publication by Hakluyt from 1593, but it contained nothing that was additive since it had obviously been based on Drake's own work. Similarly, the major publication by the De Bry family in the late 1590s of two dozen volumes covering all of the significant historic voyages of exploration just summarized the Hakluyt material. There were a few other minor stories that he picked up from various sources, but that was all.

He had searched everywhere in his manor homes, the same ones that his uncle and then his father, the first Sir Francis's brother, had occupied, but found nothing new. He recalled hearing from his father that shortly after the news of his uncle's death reached England, officials from Queen Elizabeth's court had visited and searched the premises, for what he did not know.

Also, the homes had been controlled by Sir Francis's wife Elizabeth who had vigorously contested Drake's last will that gave many of the properties to his brother. Her death in 1598 had cleared away that problem, but who knew what had been found during that intervening time? Thankfully, *The World Encompassed* document had been left with his father, who had secreted it far away from the Buckland Manor estate.

He was a little annoyed that King Charles, in spite of permitting the new publication, had not allowed him to see his uncle's original journals and charts, which were still secreted away in the royal archives. Access was denied with the simple declaration that they were still too inflammatory to the Spanish to be publicly released.

As he had read and edited the document, a couple of anomalies caught his attention, but he had been unable to find any information to resolve them.

The first thing was that there was no description of the two-month journey across the Pacific after their departure from the cold American coast on July 23, 1579. There was just the simple sentence, "And so having nothing in our view but air and sea, without the sight of any land for the space of full 68 days together, we continued our course through the main ocean till September 30th…"

This was odd because there were detailed descriptions of the whole journey over the previous year and a half, and they were sailing in waters that were new for everyone. Why hadn't Drake at least described the weather and the prevailing winds and sea states, let alone the actions and demeanor of the crew on that long voyage segment, since he later reported that they were struggling for survival when they finally reached the first western Pacific islands?

It was also hard to understand why the voyage across that section of the Pacific Ocean had taken him twice as long as Thomas Cavendish ten years later. Drake was certainly the superior sailor and navigator; what had delayed him that wasn't worth mentioning?

There was a similar dearth of description, and an unexplained long time, for the last part of the journey from Indonesia, across the Indian Ocean, up the African coast and back to England. The journey took six months and was described in five very short paragraphs. The paragraph that described their landing at Sierra Leone for water and provisions after a prolonged time at sea was just one sentence long, "The 22nd of the same month, we came to Sierra Leone, and spent two days watering in the mouth of the Tagoine, and then put to sea again; here also we had oysters and plenty of lemons, which gave us good refreshing." Forty words out of forty thousand; how did that make sense? He didn't even describe the elephants or the oyster trees that they saw there and which they often talked about later when they returned to England; there was no secret about that part of the journey.

Young Sir Francis also wrestled with the map of the world that he was including with the publication of *The World Encompassed*.

The knowledge of world geography and the shapes and relationships of the continents and oceans had developed a lot since Abraham Ortelius had published his map of the world in the first atlas, almost 60 years ago in 1570. The exception was the Pacific coast of North America; no one had been back there since his uncle's trip and the maps from various mapmakers were very inconsistent.

He had examined every map that he could find that had been published since 1580 and talked with every mapmaker that he could locate, although the legendary Flemish ones such as Abraham Ortelius, Gerardus Mercator and Jodocus Hondius, contemporaries of his uncle, had all died years earlier. He knew from word-of-mouth stories that had been passed down over the decades that his uncle had influenced them in the 1580s and 1590s.

He could see it in the evolution of the maps over that period – the disconnecting of South America from some imaginary Antarctic continent, the trending of the American Pacific shores in a northerly direction, the widening of the Pacific Ocean and the presence of some islands along the North American coast.

He found various maps that had been drawn over the years to

depict the actual path of his uncle's journey, and, again, there were many inconsistencies. A few maps showed that the ships had sailed well north of 50°N, but most stopped south of that latitude. That was consistent with his uncle's document that said they had turned back due to ice and cold winds at 48°N and had returned to about 38°N to make landfall, where they encountered friendly natives and refitted and provisioned their ships. This was the land that had been named Nova Albion and claimed for England.

However, three years ago, a new development in mapping the American coast appeared. In 1625, Henry Briggs, a London mapmaker, had issued a map of North America that showed California, on the Pacific coast of North America, as a very large island; it stretched more than 1500 miles from 24°N to 44°N. He had attributed it to a "Spanish Chart taken by the Hollanders," although he never produced such a chart. The implication was that the Dutch navy, which was starting to assert itself in the western Pacific, had taken it from a Spanish ship, although the Spanish had never published anything that identified California as an island. Lower California had always been shown as a long peninsula and no one had raised the possibility of it being an island before.

Young Sir Francis had met with Briggs a couple of times. He found him to be relatively evasive about the source of the map, claiming that he had seen it in Antwerp. Nevertheless, he found Briggs's story to be compelling. He made a good case for the map, arguing that the Spanish had always kept secret everything they could about the Americas and that their forays north of Mexico had never become public.

He also claimed that he had talked extensively to the Flemish mapmakers, including descendents of the famous ones. They passed on tales about how many of the maps in the late 16th century had been influenced by Sir Francis Drake, including the concept of their being islands and large inland rivers along the coast north of the Spanish settlements.

John Speed, one of the most respected mapmakers in England had repeated Briggs's California-as-an-island depiction in 1626.

Therefore, Sir Francis Drake showed California as an island when he published his uncle's *The World Encompassed*.

BOOK TEN

SEATTLE, JUNE

The Decision

40

That evening, after Ray Cartwright's phone call with Alan Page, there were three restless people. Ray, Alan and Herb were all consumed with trying to find a way out of Ray's financing dilemma.

The next morning, a few new developments occurred.

First, Ray received a message that Jeremy Boucher had called from Ohio.

When Ray phoned him back, Jeremy was initially polite and apologetic for bothering the Vice President. He continued, "Mr. Vice President, I know it's not really my place, but I haven't been able to get our earlier conversation out of my head. I gave you some advice about how to test a book for age and authenticity but I have thought of another point, if you are still interested and pursuing the matter."

"To tell the truth, the matter is somewhat in limbo at the moment, but I certainly would like to hear any other advice that you have to offer."

"Well, when we talked before, I mentioned testing the paper and ink and inspecting the type face. I didn't remember to mention testing the glue that holds the book to its binding. Glue can be even more difficult than ink to reconstruct without some telltale traces of modern chemicals. You know the old tales about turning an old nag of a horse into glue, but there is some truth to it. Animal bones and parts were definitely ingredients. Modern animals would almost certainly have traces of modern chemicals from their feed, even if it is just natural grass exposed to the modern atmosphere."

"Thank you for the thought, Jeremy. However, the item I am considering isn't glued together. The individual pages are held between binding boards with a leather ribbon that is threaded through a series of slots in the boards and the pages."

"That is certainly unusual. Normally the large sheets, which have a number of pages printed on them, would be folded to the page size format and then sewed together and glued between the covers. I have never seen the type of binding that you describe, but I have heard of something similar being used for very special small documents that were printed in very limited quantities. The method is just not practical or durable enough for larger volume editions. Cutting and trimming the pages was not usually done by a printer."

In an indirect way, this new information from Jeremy just reinforced for Ray that the document was likely to be authentic; after all it was one-of-a-kind. "Thanks again, Jeremy. The document is a very limited edition."

"That's fine. I thought the glue concept might be useful. Is there anything else I can help you with?"

"No, I don't think so. I appreciate your thinking about my situation and making contact."

Just before Ray hung up, on impulse, he added, "Oh, Jeremy, I was having a conversation the other day with some people about antiquarian book collecting and my interest in the early explorers. They asked me just how expensive books like that could get, and I said they could be many hundreds of thousands of dollars. They wondered if there were multi-million dollar books and I admitted that I didn't know the answer. Do you?"

"There are certainly some very valuable documents from the 1400s and 1500s. This was the era when world-wide exploration was growing and the printing methods were improving. Although many exploration documents were relatively mass produced by the later 1500s, the earlier ones were often quite limited in their creation and their survival rate was low.

"Perhaps you recall the 1507 Waldseemuller World Map that was purchased by the Library of Congress when it was offered in auction from a private German collection in 2003; it was the only surviving copy of that map. It is the very first map that used the name America. It sold for ten million dollars."

"Is there anything in the couple-of-million range that relates to the actual exploration of America?"

"There would be first editions of the earliest explorers' journals, in excellent shape, and with a provenance of having been presented to the Queen of England or the King of Spain, or some other high dignitary, but those are very rare and usually housed in institutions.

"I guess there could be sets of books which would be worth well over a million dollars, if the collection was complete and consisted of first editions in good shape. I don't know if such a set actually exists in a private collection."

"Thanks again, Jeremy. I'll tell my friends your answer. I am sure I will see you at a book fair sometime soon."

"You are welcome, sir. Good luck with your campaign."

Second, Herb Trawets decided to be more proactive in searching out possible expensive books for the Vice President's purposes. He called Colin Mackenzie in London.

"Hello, Colin," he started. "I was calling to get an update and to get your advice on something."

"Hello, Yrrab," Colin replied. "Everything is normal, I guess. I have a few new books in your general area of interest, but nothing particularly special. I can send you an e-mail description of them."

"Thank you, Colin. My specific question is whether or not you know of any very expensive books that might be available related to the exploration of western America or the Pacific coastal areas. By expensive, I mean over a million dollars, even a million euros."

"I haven't had anything even close to that level since the Hakluyt volumes last year and those were barely half-a-million dollars. It sounds like your favorite politician is on the prowl."

"Not quite, but something similar," lied Herb. "I expect such items would only surface from old, established families going through some form of financial or generational change, as happened last time."

"That is usually the case for rare books. I haven't heard anything specific recently, but there was a bit of a rumor going around some of the dealers at the New York Book Fair in April that Simon Katz was onto something big. I never heard anything after that."

"OK, thanks again. Do keep in touch."

After they hung up, Herb considered calling Simon Katz in New York, but decided that he had better talk to the Vice President first.

Third, Alan Page, who did not know anything about Ray Cartwright and Herb Trawets' idea of raising money through a buy-and-return scheme, started to formulate a concept whereby the Vice President could sell a portion of his collection, albeit likely a large portion, to some dealer who would agree to hold the books for a long period and then resell them to the Vice President later, at an appropriate increase in price. Maybe the Vice President could even keep them in his home, sort of a lease deal. He couldn't develop any details since he didn't know the real extent of the Vice President's collection nor any controls that were on it. However, at least it was an idea to share with the Vice President; it might stimulate something.

41

Ray Cartwright was sitting in his library, contemplating the things he had learned from Jeremy Boucher, but still no further ahead with a plan. "Thank God," he thought, "I can still disappear from the political process for brief periods." Less than three days had elapsed since he had returned to Seattle from Denver. He would be returning to Washington tomorrow morning.

As he was contemplating the next few days, Elsie Browning called from his Washington office and they spent almost an hour going over various meeting schedules and travel plans. He had actually talked with Calvin Begg at some length earlier, before Jeremy Boucher called. The three hour time difference between Seattle and Washington, D.C. was a benefit sometimes, just not when some eager staffer decided to call early in the morning Eastern Time.

In closing, Elsie said, "The switchboard just informed me that Alan Page and Herb Trawets have called and asked you to call them. I guess you are busy book hunting again; it's better than animal hunting these days, at least politically."

"I'll call them. Thanks. See you tomorrow afternoon."

He decided to call Alan Page first, thinking he should know the status of things before proceeding with Herb. Alan answered on the first ring.

"Mr. Vice President, thank you for calling back so quickly," he said after Ray's greeting. "I have been thinking about the situation and have an idea that might lead to a solution." He shared the ideas that he had developed that morning about leasing out his books for near-term fund raising.

"Thank you, Alan. I will think about those ideas. There may be something there that I can work with. I'll be back in touch soon, within a day or so."

"Fine, Mr. Vice President. I'll wait for your call."

After hanging up, Ray thought about what Alan had said. It was a similar idea to the one that he and Herb had talked about, but it involved using his existing collection rather than some new entity as the leverage. One problem was that, although he had a very impressive collection, including many famous explorers and the Hakluyt set, his total value in the books was well short of two-and-a-half million dollars. And, how could he pull such a transaction off in private?

Next he called Herb, who immediately described his conversation with

Colin Mackenzie. "So, Mr. Vice President, I could call Simon Katz and try to find out what he might have of high value, but I still don't know what to say to him about your situation and any proposal you might put to him."

"I don't either anymore, Herb," replied Ray. "But at this stage we have nothing to lose, as long as you just make your inquiry a general one. Perhaps Simon will say something that will help us."

Herb smiled to himself a little at the Vice President's use of the words *we* and *us*, as if Herb were now part of some secret conspiracy. "OK," he said. "I'll call him right away and then call you back."

"Fine," Ray replied. "Just call the receptionist number that monitors my local calls; you don't need to keep going through Washington when I am in town."

After they hung up, Herb searched out Simon Katz's number in New York and dialed. It would be afternoon there. After first talking to a general clerk – Simon Katz's store employed a staff of about ten – he was connected.

"Hello, Simon. This is Herb Trawets in Seattle. How are you?" he began.

"Just fine, Herb. It's a beautiful sunny day here, much better than the weather we had for the book fair in April. How can I help you?"

"Well Simon, I am on a bit of a fishing expedition actually. I have a client who is planning to celebrate a big occasion and he is looking for something special related to the early exploration of America, and in particular, the west coast. "

"I always have a good selection of great books; you know that Herb," replied Simon with a bit of a lilt in his voice. "I wonder what big event could be coming up?" he continued, knowing full well that Herb Trawets was a prime supplier and a mentor to the Vice President.

Ignoring that comment, Herb went on, "I am looking for something truly special; say a million dollar item, or even two million or more."

"Wow," said Simon. "That's impressive. I could gather a selection of books of relevant interest, say eight to ten, which would add up to that kind of money."

"I was hoping for just a book or two, or at least a companion set of some kind."

"You know, I almost had my hands on something that would have been perfect a couple of months ago but it all fell through. The sellers couldn't agree on taking action."

"Tell me about it."

"I guess I can. There are a few sensitivities with the people involved, but I can share the gist of it. I assume you know about the De Bry collection of voyages that was published over a few decades in the late 1500s and early 1600s?"

"A little."

"There was a set of books issued by Theodor De Bry and his sons in the period 1590 to 1634. They actually published two sets of books, one called *Great Voyages about the Americas*, in fourteen volumes, and one called *Small Voyages about the East Indies*, in twelve volumes. De Bry was determined to stimulate Queen Elizabeth and the leaders in her court to become more active in the exploration and colonization of the world. He had a similar attitude as Hakluyt. It was an amazing compilation."

"That sounds like the perfect thing that I have been seeking," interjected Herb. "Do you actually have access to such a set?"

"Not really. There is a set around, but the family that owns it can not agree on selling it. It is one of those inter-generational things. The patriarch of the family, who is in his 70s and controls most of the family assets such as the set of books, is contemplating donating the set to the university library at Harvard, his alma mater.

"His two sons, in their early 40s, prefer to sell the books and to generate some additional money. That is why they contacted me in the first place; they wanted to get a sense of the set's value. They tried to convince their father that, if they sold the books by auction, they would raise a good sum of money and that, inevitably, the books would end up in an appropriate location since a foundation or a large public collection would likely be the successful purchaser.

"The father didn't agree. He felt that selling the books would look too crass and he was hung up on the books going to Harvard specifically, not somewhere else. As far as I know, that's where it now stands; I don't think they have actually done anything one way or the other."

"That's fascinating," said Herb. He couldn't think of anything specific to do or say as a follow-up right then, but it intuitively seemed to him that there might be something in this for the Vice President to pursue. "What was the appraisal value that you gave them?" he added.

"Herb, as you know, I had to be very careful about that. I told them that I would be interested in purchasing the set and thus it was inappropriate for me to give them a definitive appraisal as that would create an ethical conflict of interest.

"What I did was lead them through some of the bookseller websites and past public auction records. That showed that there had been a few sets sold over the past four years between a half-million and eight hundred thousand dollars, but in every case the sets were missing a couple of volumes and some of the books were second editions. Their set is complete and is all first editions. Some of the illustrations were even hand colored at the time of publication, meticulously done in the pastel shades of the time with gold and silver enhancements. As well, the books had an established provenance of having been presented to a member of Queen Elizabeth's court.

"The general impression I left with them, without being specific, was that their books could be worth one-and-a-half million dollars, perhaps a little more."

"Simon, that is exactly the kind of thing I have been looking for. If you get any further indication that they are going to sell it, please contact me. Also, if you can locate anything else that meets my criteria, please call."

"I'll do that, Herb. It's always great to talk with you. I'll be in touch if anything surfaces."

Herb decided that this information was worth sharing with the Vice President, even though he didn't have a plan forward after that. When he called, Ray Cartwright said he would come by Herb's shop about mid-afternoon.

42

When they were seated in Herb's store, just after 4:00 pm, Herb repeated what Simon had told him about the De Bry set in New York.

Ray stared off into space for a while, as he digested what he had heard. Something about this situation and the concepts that Alan Page had put forward to him that morning started to gel into an idea.

"What if I could buy the books on some kind of deferred basis but use them as a distraction for securing funds?" he mused to himself. "How could that work?"

Then, out loud he said, "Herb, it seems to me that this lead is worth pursuing. We need to develop some kind of plan and storyline that would appeal to these potential sellers; it has to be one that would allow us to establish the value and free up the funds but delay the payment."

"That seems like a lot to ask."

"I know, but let's talk it out.

"The younger generation of the family wants money and they are concerned that they will get nothing out of the books if their father simply donates them to Harvard. Therefore, they might be receptive to getting money for the books on a deferred basis.

"The patriarch of the family wants to look magnanimous and to give something significant to his alma mater. If we could accommodate a temporary assignment of the books to Harvard, say ten years, that might satisfy him. Remember, I am also a Harvard graduate, and so we can work in that angle. Ten years from now, he will be in his eighties and I will be retired from public life, even if I become President for two terms."

Herb could hardly breathe. If he thought that he was getting close to the Vice President this morning, this conversation was beyond belief. The Vice President was actually sharing personal thoughts about becoming a two-term President and how he would contrive to move money around for over a decade. "He certainly wants that book," he thought.

"Mr. Vice President, if I can ask. Even if this idea can work, the value of the books is still barely half the amount of money that you said you needed. And how do you get money released from your trust without actually having a set of books to show and an invoice from the seller?"

"I don't know exactly, but we know that the value of very expensive collectible things is always subject to a lot of variation and surprises. We would need to show that the books are something special and thus worth a significant premium over other sets that have been sold. As far as releasing funds from the trust, we will need an actual invoice; I guess that is where you will come into play."

Herb gulped. "I guess so, Mr. Vice President," he said with a tone of hesitation and doubt in his voice.

"Don't worry, Herb. If we get that far I will ensure that you are not at risk. Now, what do we do next?"

"Well, I guess we need to make contact somehow. I can call Simon Katz back and arrange for some kind of approach to the owners, but what should I tell him?"

"He certainly knows, or will quickly figure out, that I am the customer that you are representing. Therefore, I think you should tell him that up front.

"Then, you emphasize that I am a serious collector of books such as the De Bry set, which he already knows to a degree, and that I am very, very interested in the set. The next point to be made, which I hope will get his attention and will motivate him to contact the owners, is that I can be very flexible regarding the timing of the actual purchase and that I am supportive of giving Harvard some access to the books. This has to be the hook to get Simon convinced that he can approach the family again. As you well know, he would love to score a large commission for brokering a deal such as this and to get a closer connection with me."

Herb listened to this and, as a momentary distraction, felt a sense of pride and excitement that this engineer-lawyer-businessman-politician was capable of thinking through such complicated issues on-the-fly so quickly. "He'll make a great President," he thought.

"Alright, I will call Simon in the morning. It is now 5:00 pm here and thus 8:00 pm there. Shall I call you locally again when I have talked to him?"

"No, I will be leaving for Washington, D.C. early in the morning. I will call you when I get there. Thank you for getting involved like this, Herb. I really appreciate it."

As Ray was leaving the shop, he noticed a large coffee-table-sized book titled *Historical Maps of the Americas*. Picking it up and browsing through it, he realized that the maps of the sixteenth and seventeenth century totally aligned with the revised story of Drake's travels and discoveries, if you studied them with that premise in mind.

The details that emerged over the decades from the time just before Drake's around-the-world voyage until his death had to reflect Drake's input. No one else had sailed there.

He noted the Ortelius map of 1570, published before Drake's historic voyage, which showed South American separated from Antarctica only by the Straight of Magellan, the distorted coast of South America, the bulging prominence of North America in the northern latitudes, and the narrow Pacific Ocean.

The Ortelius map of 1587, after Drake's voyage, corrected many of those errors, and showed many large coastal rivers in the north. The 1589 version also showed a chain of islands off the Pacific coast, north of 50°N latitude

An earlier Dutch map by Van Sype in 1583, although of poor quality, showed the track of Drake's voyage around the world; its northern terminus ended with a drawing of a ship in the north Pacific spanning latitudes well north of 50°.

Briggs map of 1625 was unmistakable as it prominently showed California as an island for the first time. This concept was repeated by Jonathan Speed in 1627, who also showed an indefinite coast of north America well east of the earlier versions of Ortelius and others.

Sir Francis Drake's nephew's 1628 *The World Encompassed* continued the Californian island image, essentially repeating the Speed version..

Many maps through the rest of the 1600s, and even some English maps as late as the 1740s, continued to show California as an island, even though the Spanish had definitively shown it was a peninsula in the very early 1700s.

To Ray, that just confirmed that Drake's influence was profound and long-lasting - he wanted the document even more.

Ortelius - 1570

Ortelius – 1589

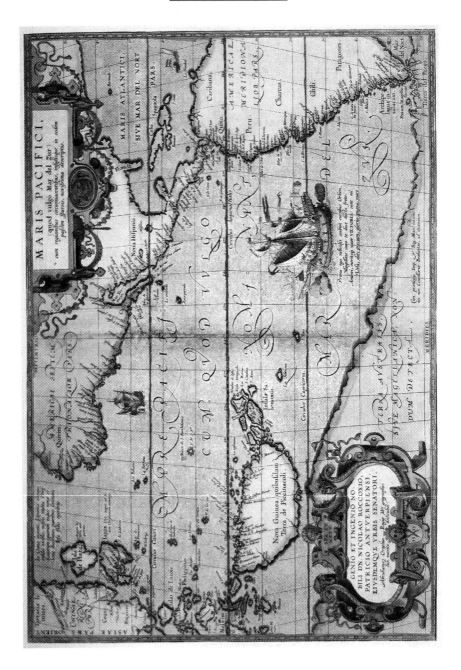

<u>Van Sype (The Dutch Map) – 1583</u>

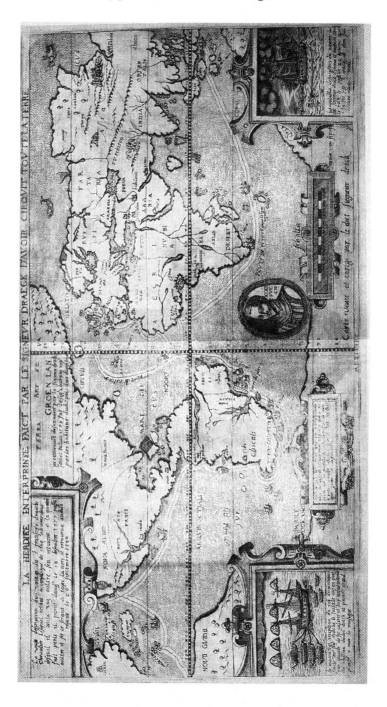

Briggs – 1625

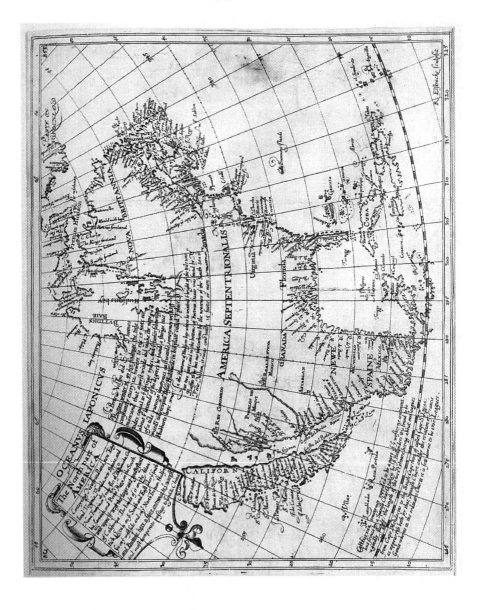

Speed – 1627

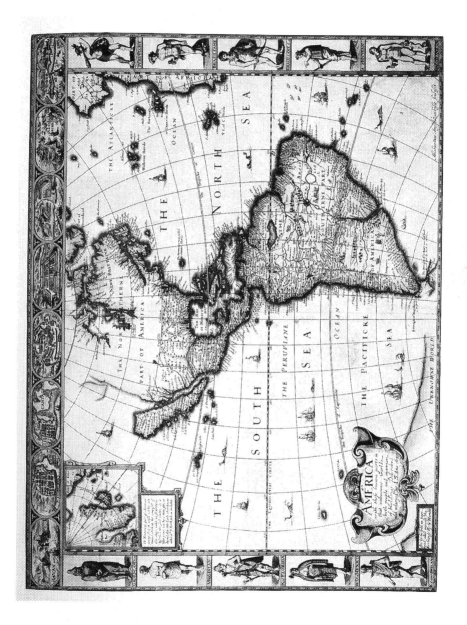

Drake's "The World Encompassed" – 1628

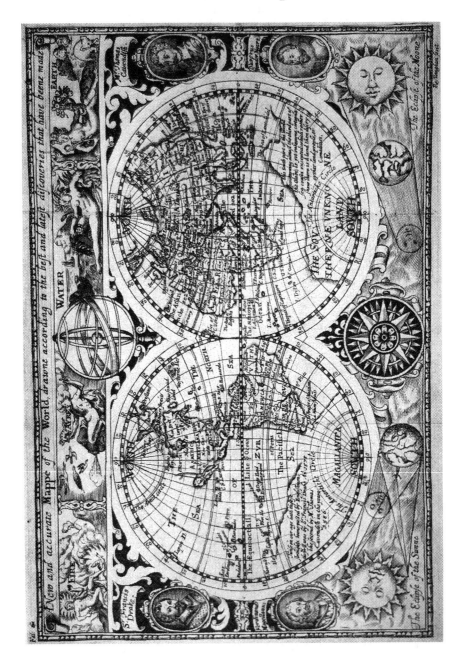

43

The next morning Herb was in his shop early, ready to call by 10:00a.m. Eastern Time, the opening hour for Simon Katz's bookstore.

"Hello again, Simon," he started. "I want to follow-up on our conversation yesterday. I have been talking to Vice President Cartwright, as I think you guessed. He asked me to call you to investigate whether he might be able to work with the family that owns the De Bry set to find a common agreement."

He then went on to explain the concept of the Vice President purchasing the books on a deferred basis and thus accommodating them being lent to Harvard for ten years.

Simon Katz had listened to Herb's presentation without interruption. As Ray had predicted, he immediately thought of the large commission that he could earn if a deal could be brokered and the benefit of getting closer to the Vice President.

"Herb, that is a fascinating idea. I don't know if it will be acceptable to the family or not, but I am certainly willing to contact them. I would guess that there will be a lot of details to be worked out if they want to go forward, but let's find out if they are interested at all. I will get back to you when I have an answer."

Simon sat by himself for a few minutes after he had disconnected the call from Herb. The approach to the owners would need to be carefully managed. He hadn't told Herb the whole story; in fact, the dispute over the books had created a lot of tension and anger within the family. To reopen the issue required tact. Also, it was the sons who had contacted him initially, without their father's knowledge; they should be the ones he contacted first. That was probably the best anyway; they might be willing to seize on any plan that would generate money, even if it was delayed.

He placed a call to John Armstrong, the younger brother, in Boston. John had been the more temperate of the two brothers; Robert Jr., called Bob, was the one who had become fully engaged in the intense discussions with their father, Robert Armstrong Sr.

"Mr. Armstrong," he began. "I am calling you to follow up on the discussions that we had a couple of months ago about the set of De Bry books. Something has come up that I think will be of interest to you."

"Simon," John Armstrong replied, "I am not sure that I want to reopen that issue within the family right now. Things have sort of settled down between my brother and my father."

"I know it was a difficult time for all of you," Simon continued. "However, I do believe that this new development might be of interest to all of you. Anyway, if you can spare me a few minutes, I can lay out the situation for you."

"Sure, why not? I have some free time right now."

Over the next few minutes Simon described the approach he had received from Herb Trawets, playing up the fact that the Vice President was involved and, as a Harvard alumnus, was supportive of giving it access to the books.

"That is certainly an innovative approach," said John. "I am quite impressed with the various solutions it presents for our differing preferences within the family. Let me think on it a bit and then test it with my brother and father. That may take a few days, at least, as I will want to raise the issue in an appropriate time and manner. We do have a family dinner this coming weekend; that may present the opportunity. I will call you back early next week, if that's OK with you."

"That would be great, Mr. Armstrong. I'll wait to hear from you. Do call sooner if you need any other information."

After that, Simon called Herb in Seattle and conveyed the information. Later that afternoon, Ray Cartwright phoned Herb from Washington and learned of the developments. Ray then called Alan Page and explained that something was developing and that he would be back to him early in the week. Alan, of course, then left a message for Frank.

Then they all waited for the results of a family dinner in Boston. It was a long few days for everyone.

44

John Armstrong called Simon Katz on Monday morning.

"Simon, we had a long and very calm discussion about the De Bry books last night after dinner. Father has decided that he would be willing to hear more about the proposal, but that he wants to hear it directly from the Vice President so that there are no misunderstandings. Be assured, if we make a deal, you will be paid a generous fee."

"It is unusual for the seller and the buyer to interact directly in these situations but this is an unusual situation to be sure. I will pass your request back to Herb Trawets and see what they say in response."

Again the chain of phone calls occurred. After a brief conversation, Ray Cartwright told Herb to say that he would be pleased to meet with the sellers but that he would want to know who he was dealing with beforehand; to this point Simon Katz had not disclosed their identity. The Vice President didn't say it directly, but it was obviously important to him that the sellers could be counted on to be very discreet about the eventual deal that he would be proposing.

After another series of calls between Ray, Herb, Simon and John Armstrong, it was agreed that their identity could be disclosed and that the Vice President was willing to meet with them in Boston in one week's time. Ray had the flexibility to schedule a political fund-raising trip to New England at the same time, which would avoid any questions about why he was going to Boston.

It was also agreed that Simon Katz and Herb Trawets would join them for at least the first part of the meeting. Ray needed some experts present to be sure he understood what he was dealing with exactly.

The next Monday morning at 10:00 am the Vice President entered a downtown Boston office tower and headed to the reception area of Armstrong, Armstrong & Armstrong, Attorneys-at-Law.

Ray had done some research on the Armstrongs over the previous week. Robert Sr., the current patriarch of the family, had been born in the early days of the Second World War, making him a little older than the baby-boomer generation. His father was a lawyer and he followed in those footsteps by attending Harvard Law School after earning a general business degree at Boston College. He joined his father's relatively modest practice in the 1960s and became the driving force to expand the firm's reach into the higher echelon of commercial law, particularly during the heyday decades of mergers and acquisitions that generated large fees. His sons, born in the 1970s, followed an almost identical path. Thus the current name of Armstrong, Armstrong & Armstrong was established.

Herb Trawets and Simon Katz were already waiting in the reception area. They had actually met for breakfast earlier to coordinate the activities and to be sure they had the same understanding about how things would proceed. They had arrived at the Armstrong offices more than fifteen minutes early; they certainly weren't going to keep the Vice President waiting.

They were all shown into an ornate board room where introductions were made all around.

"Mr. Vice President," started Robert Armstrong, "welcome to Boston and to our offices. We are quite honored to have you visit. We certainly wish you every success in your upcoming political activities."

"Thank you, Mr. Armstrong, the pleasure is mine. After all, we are here to discuss a passion of mine, antique books related to the exploration and discovery of America."

"Quite right. Perhaps we should start by having you look at the books. They are laid out on the credenza at the end of the room."

With that, everyone stood up and walked towards the display. There were twenty-four books. They were about the size of today's legal paper and varied in thickness from about half-an-inch to a little over an inch. The covers were leather, obviously old, with a remarkably small amount of wear showing. The edges of the pages were rough, almost tattered; this was referred to as *uncut*. In fact, those edges were special to a collector. Old books were originally printed in that form and, usually, trimmed smooth when they were bound for the original customer. Sometimes it happened centuries later when they were rebound due to wear.

With a nod from Robert Armstrong, Ray picked up one of the books. He had done some research on the De Bry books, and so it was no coincidence that he chose the eighth volume of the Americas set, the one that described the voyages of Drake, Hawkins, Cavendish and Raleigh, published in 1599.

Staring at him from the title page was a drawing of a world map that showed Drake's route around the world, with a small portrait of Drake superimposed between the two circular depictions of the hemispheres. Ray was momentarily lost in thought as he looked at it. First, he noted that the route depicted along the western shores of North America ended at the latitude of Northern California, as expected.

He was quite impressed with the many sharp ink drawings that depicted various events of the world travels, such as the encounters with the natives in America and the Spice Islands. He also noted that all of the writing was in Latin, something he had not anticipated.

"The books look amazing," he said. "They appear to be in excellent shape. I must admit that I hadn't expected them to be written in Latin; I guess I won't be able to just browse through them at my leisure."

"Mr. Vice President," Simon said quietly, "I have been through each volume in detail and I can assure you that every book is fully intact and the covers are original. I have given my notes to Herb Trawets for his reference. Of course, if this arrangement goes forward, Herb will get the opportunity to closely examine each book himself."

"Thank you, Simon." As this was being said, Ray looked at the dedication on the inside front page, the normally blank page that is inserted before the title page. Inscribed on this page, in a careful handwritten scroll, was the dedication, Presented to Lord Groton, in appreciation for the support in granting the publication of these landmark treatises. T De Bry.

Ray realized that this volume had been presented to a member of Queen Elizabeth's Privy Council, a subordinate to Lord Burghley for sure, but a titled member of that inner circle who would have been involved with the decisions about confiscating Drake's journals. That provenance made the books even more special and valuable. He wondered if all the books had such an inscription; he decided to let Herb investigate that possibility later.

As they sat back down again, Ray said, "Can I ask how you came into possession of these books, Mr. Armstrong?"

"Certainly, Mr. Vice President." Everyone was behaving quite formally.

"I had the opportunity to work on a major multi-million-dollar deal that involved an American company acquiring a British manufacturer over twenty-five years ago. As a result, I spent quite a bit of time in London and I visited many of the large antiquarian map and book dealers in my spare time. I was just beginning to collect books related to early explorers. I encountered this set of books and was fascinated by them, although they were out of my price range at that time.

"I spent a lot of time with the British lawyers who were representing the other party in the deal and we would discuss many different things over the long days we were together. When the deal was signed, I was surprised to receive the set of books as a closing gift from the other side. You must realize that such exchanges are very usual after large deals are culminated and that these books were not valued so highly in those days; tens of thousands of dollars, not hundreds of thousands or more."

"Amazing; you certainly acquired a great asset."

"Yes, I did."

For a moment no one knew what to say next. Then Ray said, "Why don't we get to some of the specifics regarding the books while everyone is present and then perhaps we can ask Herb and Simon to leave us; Herb could examine the books while we talk, although I am absolutely sure everything is in order."

"Fine."

"As I understand it, the current value of the set of books has been appraised at about one-and-a-half million dollars."

This simple statement set off a flurry of comments from some of the others in the room; they had generally deferred to Ray Cartwright and Robert Armstrong until then.

Almost simultaneously, young John Armstrong said, "We haven't actually agreed on a price;" Bob Armstrong said, "Not so fast;" and Simon Katz said, "I never provided a formal appraisal."

Ray Cartwright looked at Robert Sr., who had said nothing, and said, "I didn't mean to stir up a hornets nest; I just wanted to get a reference point for our later discussions and for dealing fairly with Simon and Herb."

That statement got everyone's attention.

Ray continued, "Well, if the market price was one-point-five million, you would realize about one-point-two million, assuming that the brokering book sellers are paid a normal twenty-five percent markup commission. I am going to suggest that we set a starting reference price at one-point-five million for you, the owners; that we add on a twenty percent, or three hundred thousand dollar, fee for Simon Katz; and that I pay Herb Trawets directly for his services."

As this offer was sinking in, everyone stayed silent. The young Armstrongs just saw their realization increase by twenty percent; Simon was more than happy to realize the full commission all for himself; and Herb was fully relaxed, knowing that the Vice President would take care of him generously.

Robert Armstrong Sr. simply said, "Let's use that as our reference point," which settled the issue for the time being.

At this juncture, Simon and Herb left the room, taking the books with them, assisted by some office staff members who were called in with a four-wheeled cart. Before they left, Ray had a brief conversation with Herb in the corner of the room.

Ray was now in the room with the three Armstrongs and the stage was his.

"This is where I make it fly or not," he thought as he launched into his proposal, one that he had created and practiced over the past week, a combination of truths and distractions.

"Gentlemen, let's get to some of the other aspects of our possible arrangement. First, Mr. Armstrong, I understand that you want to make the books available to the Harvard library so that they can be accessed by students and scholars. I understand that desire. I also assume, and here I hope that I am not being too presumptuous or too blunt, that you would like to receive the credit for making the donation. Again, I understand."

The Armstrongs said nothing, waiting to hear more.

"My desire is to acquire the books. They are magnificent and I am a serious collector. However, I can also be patient. Therefore, I propose that we agree on a sale of the books to me but that we defer the actual closing of the deal for ten years. This would allow you to keep physical possession of the books and to loan them to Harvard for a decade. The arrangement also allows me to minimize any political complications. Although everyone knows that I am relatively rich, it is not a good idea for a politician to be seen to be too extravagant; buying some books for over one-and-a-half million dollars might seem excessive to some people."

Again, silence.

"I propose that we sign a binding purchase-sale agreement for the books, with delivery set for May 1st, ten years from now, and the price being two million dollars, which is one-point-five million escalated at three percent, slightly more than recent inflation rates. I will pay Simon Katz and Herb Trawets directly."

After a pause, Robert Armstrong said, "Mr. Vice President, you have made us an intriguing offer. I think we will need to meet in private and discuss it. Although I had hoped to host you for lunch in our executive dining room, I suggest that we break now. If you are going to be staying in Boston for a while, we could perhaps meet again later this afternoon."

"That sounds fine to me. I will actually be staying in the area until tomorrow. So, I will return here when? 5:00?"

"That would be fine. Perhaps we can even have a celebratory drink afterward."

45

As Ray left the meeting room he saw Herb and Simon waiting in the reception area. "I will be meeting with the Armstrongs again later this afternoon," he said. "Simon, I suggest you return then as well to see what develops. Herb, I would like to talk with you a bit; let's go and get some lunch at my hotel."

They rode in silence in the Vice President's limousine, not wanting to be overheard saying anything related to the books. When they arrived at Ray's hotel suite a light lunch of soup and a chef's salad was waiting for them; he had called ahead.

"Well, Herb, what do you think?"

"I had a chance to quickly inspect the books. I am sure they are all complete and in good shape; Simon is very careful about such things and my overview confirmed that impression. Of course, if you do go forward, I will go through them page by page.

"I also did inspect the inscription in the front of the books. You saw the one. They vary somewhat through the series of books, but remember they were published over a period of almost thirty years, first by Theodore De Bry and then by his wife and sons. I suspect that the Lord Groton was a different person by the end of the cycle also; likely the first Lord's eldest son who would inherit the title. In any case, they are all inscribed in a similar manner. That does add to their provenance."

"That's useful. Thanks."

"What happens next?"

"I made them an offer along the lines we discussed. I would purchase the books with a ten year deferral on taking possession and then paying two million dollars for them. Robert Armstrong can publicly loan them to Harvard for the ten year period."

After thinking that over for a moment, Herb asked, "I still don't really understand how you plan to use this deal to free up funds for your other purchase now, but, in any case, doesn't two million dollars fall short of your requirements?"

Ray smiled and said, "Oh, Herb, you have to know that the three Armstrongs are going to have a long discussion about my proposal. First, they will go around about whether they should make the deal at all; remember, that is the big issue between the father and the sons. Then, if they agree that it does work for them, they will discuss the price. I would be amazed if they don't ask for more. That's normal business, even if you are dealing with the Vice President of the United States. You could certainly detect young Robert's attitude when he spoke out about the appraisal.

"And, as far as getting funds freed up; that's where you will need to get involved, my friend. I assure you that you will not be compromised and will be well covered, but we will need to develop a story and some paperwork for the trust. Let's worry about that when we see if there is a deal to be made."

"OK," replied Herb, after a pause and with a bit of hesitation in his voice.

Meanwhile, back at the Armstrong offices, everything was proceeding as Ray had predicted. They were also discussing the proposal over a private lunch. Their menu was much more elaborate: a seafood appetizer followed by a beef filet entrée. After all, they had prepared for the possibility of the Vice President being there with them for lunch.

The discussion about whether to make a deal or not actually progressed relatively easily. Time had helped them all to calm down after the intense debates of a few months earlier. If anything, Ray Cartwright's offer helped them clear the air and put the previous arguments behind them.

The ten year assignment of the books to Harvard satisfied Robert and the sons were willing to wait for the funds; that was certainly better than nothing.

Turning to pricing, they started far apart. Again, as expected, Robert Jr. led the way. "We should get a much higher price," he said. "The one-and-a-half million starting point is untested and might be too low. As well, ten years is a long time and three percent inflation is low. We know inflation can rear up any time and, even if higher levels only last for a few years, it really adds up."

"Bob, I agree we should ask for more," said John, "but we do need to be reasonable. After all, it is the Vice President we are dealing with."

"A very rich Vice President," retorted Bob.

"How much are you suggesting?"

"If we inflate one-point-five million by ten percent for ten years, we get almost four million dollars." Bob had the foresight to get a book of interest accumulation tables before they reconvened to discuss the Vice President's offer.

"What!" exclaimed John. "Are you crazy?"

"Not at all; that's what the numbers add up to."

"You have the book of tables. What do other interest rates add up to?'

After looking in the book Bob replied, "Seven percent would be a multiplier of about two and so the total would be three million dollars."

"That's better, but it still seems high."

At this point, Robert Sr., who had been watching and listening to his sons, spoke up.

"Boys, let's settle down. I have a few things to say.

"First, the Vice President has made us a generous offer in terms of the time deferral and the dealings with Harvard. As a collector, his delayed possession of the books for a decade is significant; collectors are always impatient. Also, the ability to donate the books to Harvard in my name, even if only for ten years, is important to me; he was right.

"Next, the value of the books ten years from now is just a guess. Sure, inflation can be higher, but the value can also go down. Remember that items such as these books are a fragile commodity; it is always a discretionary decision for someone to buy them. In tough times the value can fall dramatically as nobody is buying. Remember what happened as recently as 2009.

"However, I do agree we can ask for something more. In fact, the Vice President would be surprised if we don't; he is a businessman after all. Bob, you can check the numbers, but I suspect that a five percent interest rate would increase the total to something under two-and-a half million dollars, probably about two-point-four. We don't want to be haggling over percentage points of interest or decimal points of value. I suggest two-point-five is fair. I am sure the Vice President is expecting something around that, perhaps a little more, and so we will not surprise him or insult him."

John quickly said, "That sounds OK to me."

Bob, with a little less enthusiasm, said, "OK, I guess. Perhaps we can monetize the promissory note from the Vice President sooner and generate a higher return that way."

On hearing that, Robert said in a firm and determined voice, showing his parental authority and his frustration with Bob, "I will not hear anything like that at all. The Vice President made it clear that he expects confidentiality about our deal for political reasons and I want everything to be confidential so that it does not tarnish my donation to Harvard. Do you understand?"

"Yes, sir," replied Bob.

They adjourned to wait on the Vice President's return at 5:00.

46

The Vice President appeared in the Armstrong reception area promptly on time and was shown into the board room. Simon and Herb were present as well, but they waited outside the meeting room.

After the normal greetings, they all sat down, Ray on one side of the table and the three Armstrongs on the other side.

Robert Armstrong started. "Mr. Vice President, thank you for returning. We appreciate your courtesy in coming to our offices. We have been discussing your proposal at length, as you would imagine. I will say right up front that we are interested but that we do have a few questions and points to clarify."

Ray nodded in encouragement for Armstrong to continue.

"First, we would like to know exactly what type of documents you envision us both signing."

"I actually would want a number of different documents in order to keep the various elements separated and to help with our mutual desire for confidentiality. We would need a binding purchase-sale agreement that specifies that I am buying the documents and therefore will own them, along with the purchase price.

"I would want a physical invoice for the agreed-to amount to be filed with my records for the future settlement.

"We would need an agreement that documents the specific timing of the future payment.

"We would also need an agreement that would give you physical possession of the books for the next ten years, including the right to loan them to other third parties, such as Harvard, but specifically does not allow you to give title of them to anyone else or to impair them financially in any way.

"We would need an agreement on how the books are to be insured. I think you will need coverage for them that handles loss or damage while they are in your possession and control. I will want my insurance to cover them as well, in a subordinate manner to your coverage. Therefore, I would need to have the books for a brief period of time so that they can be inspected by my insurance people.

"There would also be an agreement that stipulates that I will be responsible for the fees payable to Simon Katz and Herb Trawets. They will need to sign that one as well, but not be privy to the other documents.

"Naturally, all the agreements would be binding on our successors and beneficiaries if something were to happen to any of us."

"That seems reasonable," said Robert.

"Oh, one other thing," added Ray. "Since we are all lawyers here, I don't think we need to involve anyone else in the creation of the documents. Perhaps you could draft them for my review before we sign off?"

"Certainly, we can do that," replied Robert, a bit surprised that the Vice President would say this. Often lawyers argued more about who should do which things and how the wording should be drafted than the deal itself. Control of the drafting process was always coveted. This offer showed the Vice President's good faith and professional courtesy. Robert was pleased and, thus, even more inclined to make the deal.

"Is there anything else?" Ray asked in all innocence.

"Yes, there is the matter of the price," Robert answered directly. "We recognize that the starting value you tabled is reasonable, but we believe that the future value should be somewhat higher. You know as well as we do that it is impossible to forecast economic condition ten years forward. However, as sellers, we are committing to a specific sale at a specific time in the future. If we were to just hold on to the books, we would obviously sell them at a chosen time of higher economic activity, not a lower period. We lose that control with this deal. The offset, I am sure you would say, is that we have a bird-in-the-hand in case values decline sharply.

"Nevertheless, we believe the payment ten years from now should be two-and-a-half million dollars, not just two. That represents about a five percent inflation rate rather than three percent."

Ray sat quiet for a moment, pleased that he had anticipated almost exactly what he was hearing. Without comment or discussion he simply said, "That's fine."

The room then went silent. It took a minute for them to realize that they had agreed on a deal; all they had to do was say so.

"So, deal?" asked Ray.

"Deal," replied Robert. "Then, let's have a drink to it," he continued. Everyone agreed. Simon and Herb joined them.

As they chatted over drinks, Robert said that they could draft the documents by the next afternoon and the Vice President could then examine them before he left Boston.

As they were breaking up, Robert said, "Mr. Vice President, I know I will not get past addressing you that way, unless it is as Mr. President, but I would like it if you just called me Robert."

"Sure, Mr. Armstrong," Ray said to the laughter of everyone.

47

Two days later, Ray was back in Washington, signed documents in hand and the De Bry books in his office, carefully stacked on a side table, having been brought from Boston packed in bubble wrap and strong boxes.

Herb Trawets had traveled to Washington as well. He had spent time with the Vice President after the Boston meeting to determine exactly what Ray wanted and had created the necessary paperwork the following day. He was now waiting to join the Vice President in a meeting with his personal staff.

Ray had called ahead the day before to flag to Maria Rodriguez, his personal administrator, that he would need her and the availability of an insurance representative in his office on Wednesday. He just said that he had bought a "big one."

After he had concluded his political meetings with Calvin Begg and Ralph King, he met with Elsie Browning about various office administration items.

At the end of that meeting, she said, "Oh, there is one other item. That FBI agent in Seattle, Efrem Wilson, wants to talk with you again."

Ray's mind froze in shock for a second.

"Did he say what it was about?" he asked.

"Not really. 'Just a follow-up on your earlier discussion'"

"OK. Please get him on the phone for me."

The few minutes that he waited while Elsie placed the call to Agent Wilson seemed to take forever. Ray couldn't imagine what was about to happen. Surely, if it was a big issue, he would have heard from a higher level authority in the F.B.I., even the Director himself.

But, what if it was related to his new deal, on some detail, and then it escalated, he thought. What was he going to say if pressed on his activities?

Finally, his phone rang and he heard Elsie say. "Agent Wilson is on the line."

"Hello, Agent Wilson. What can I do for you today?" asked Ray.

"Hello, Mr. Vice President. I do apologize for bothering you again, but I need to pursue another detail about your purchase of the Hakluyt books last year."

"That's fine," said Ray, breathing slightly easier. "What is your question?"

"It has to do with the method of payment. How did you handle that, if you wouldn't mind telling me?"

"Not at all. As I recall, my instructions were to pay the commissions to Herb Trawets and Colin Mackenzie separately and to send the balance to the seller's bank account."

"Where was that account located; do you remember?"

"Oh, yes. It was in the Grand Cayman Islands, in the Caribbean. Why do you ask? Is that a problem? Those were the instructions."

"No. It's not unusual for people dealing in international business to have banking arrangements in different countries, and it is quite appropriate for you, or any buyer of goods, to pay bills to those locations, as long as the purchase was not for something in the United States."

"Then, what is the issue?"

"We are following up on more details for Scotland Yard. Apparently, the people under investigation are claiming that the higher amount they reported on their tax returns was due to currency gains made in the Caymans. We are helping them trace the money movements."

"Is there anything else that I can help you with?" asked Ray.

"No, that's about it. We are just helping them fill in the details. Police work is really always about details, not the dramatic revelations that you see in the movies."

After they hung up, Ray contemplated what had just happened. Did anything there compromise the deal he had made with the Armstrongs, and, more importantly, the deal he was making with Alan Page and his principals? He knew that the payment to them was also going to be sent to a foreign country.

Thinking it through, he concluded that he was not really buying something from the United States. He was paying Herb and Alan directly for their services in the country, but the seller was not American as far as he knew...the document had come from Canada after all.

He also knew that he could be wrong. What if the sellers were American?

Again, he concluded that he was not responsible for any wrongdoings by the seller. He was just the buyer, following instructions; wasn't he?

Still, he worried about the ramifications if the whole deal became public. He knew the tabloids would have no difficulty in conjuring up headlines about a money-laundering Vice President.

In any case, he must live up to his deal with the Armstrongs. The other matter did not involve them.

He called Elsie and asked her to find Maria.

48

He had a big smile on his face when she entered his office, and just said, "Wait until you see what I have found!"

He led her to the table where the books were assembled. She picked one up and opened it. "It's in Latin," was her first comment. "How are you going to read that?"

He laughed, "I guess I will find a cheap translation and read that. I'll just look at the maps and drawings in these."

Of course, Maria had come to appreciate Ray's collection of books but, even so, she flinched a little when she asked him what the books cost and he said, "Three million dollars."

"Wow, I had better learn to write in Latin! Cogito, ergo sum."

"Carpe diem, ab, modo fac."

"OK, enough! What does that mean?"

"A couple of ways to say, "Just do it! That is my modern translation of the old *Seize the Day* or *Live for Today* versions."

"Now, tell me about the books."

"This is an unbelievable set," Ray began. "They were published in the late 1500s and early 1600s by a fellow named De Bry and his family, documenting all of the significant journeys of exploration to the Americas and the East Indies up to that time. The books are in their original binding and are untrimmed, an amazing preservation after all these years. As well, this set was the property of a Lord Advisor in the court of Queen Elizabeth the First. It's priceless."

Ray's enthusiasm was genuine, although the actual details of his description were carefully designed to support the huge price he had quoted. It was all part of positioning what was to follow.

"Where did they come from?"

"Herb Trawets, who you know, found them through his contacts in the book selling world, a fellow named Simon Katz in New York. They were actually owned by a family in Boston who were looking to liquidate them.

"In order to close the deal, I had to make a concession to the patriarch of the family, a Mr. Robert Armstrong, allowing the books to be loaned to the Harvard University library in his name for ten years. Therefore, I will own the books, but I will not have personal possession for those ten years;

they will be at Harvard. Also, we need to keep my ownership confidential, so we don't take away from Mr. Armstrong's glory with Harvard."

"That's complicated. So, do we need to pay for the books now?"

"Yes, for sure."

"And the insurance? I know you asked me to have the representatives here."

"Actually the Armstrongs will carry the basic insurance for the next ten years. I just need backup coverage. However, since the books will be going away for so long, I think we should have the insurance guys see them now."

"OK, I'll call them in."

"We should invite Herb Trawets in now as well; he can provide added information and he has the relevant documentation."

Maria went to collect the others and then they all gathered in chairs around the Vice President's desk. He wasn't going to sit in the casual area with them; it was important to him that he maintained control of the situation and, if necessary, use the aura of his position to dissuade prolonged discussion.

The Vice President repeated the summary of the book purchase for the sake of the insurance fellows. He showed them the purchase-sale agreement and the agreement to allow Robert Armstrong to loan the books to Harvard.

On cue, Herb reviewed a detailed written description of the books, with many details for each book and an emphasis on their condition, rarity, and special provenance.

Then Herb tabled the invoice. It was on a Herb's Books letterhead and simply read:

Set of De Bry Voyages, 24 Books	$2,500,000
Commission (20%)	$500,000
Total, Payable to *Herb's Books*	$3,000,000

Unknown to everyone but Herb, what was not tabled at this meeting was the separate agreement and invoice from the Armstrongs which showed that the payments were not actually due to them for ten years.

Then the Vice President addressed the two insurance representatives directly. "Actually, all I think that I need right now is a general rider to my basic policy that covers my collection, covering the unlikely situation that something happens to the books and the Armstrong's policy doesn't cover it. Of course, you will receive a copy of their policy. I just wanted you to see the books before they are sent off to Harvard."

The junior insurance representative, Conrad Schneider, spoke up then, "Mr. Vice President, this is all very impressive and quite amazing, actually. I wonder, though, since the amount is so high, whether we should get another opinion on the value of the books, just for the record."

"I guess we could, Mr. Schneider. However, we do have Mr. Trawets' expert opinion and we have the arms-length agreement between me and Robert Armstrong. As I mentioned, Mr. Simon Katz, the renowned book dealer from New York, was involved and advised us all on value; we could perhaps ask him for a formal opinion. I do wonder if all of that is necessary now; we are simply writing a back-up covenant. Ten years from now, when my insurance will be primary, would seem to be the right time for more documentation."

Ray was pushing a bit of a bluff here, but, with the strength of his presentation and the ambience of the Vice President's office all around them, the senior representative, Sascha Ferguson, stepped into the conversation, "That's fine with me, Mr. Vice President. We will process the policy on that basis."

"Thank you all for coming on short notice and accommodating my hobby," Ray said in closing, breaking up the meeting before any further conversation occurred.

After everyone but Maria had left, he casually said, "Thanks, Maria. Please arrange for the payment to Herb Trawets and the shipment of the books back to Robert Armstrong."

"OK, sir." She left with a smile on her face.

Once he was alone, Ray Cartwright let out a huge sigh of relief. "By golly," he thought, "I may have just pulled this off!"

After a short period of contemplation, he called Herb Trawets on his cell phone. Herb was waiting for the call not far away from the Vice President's offices, in a local pub actually, with a pint of Guinness in front of him.

"Herb, thank you so very much; everything worked perfectly. I guess you will be heading back to Seattle now. Maria will be in touch very soon regarding the payment and I will call you in a day or so regarding the disbursements. You have been a great help through all of this."

"You are welcome, Mr. Vice President, anytime. I will wait for your call."

49

Ray sat in silence at his desk. This was his final opportunity to change his mind. He could just tell Alan that the deal was off. Of course, he would need to park the two-and-a-half million dollars somewhere for ten years, but that could be arranged. He would just buy other books and expensive maps from Herb Trawets.

Thinking of the document back in Seattle and the euphoria that he felt when he held it, he knew that he could not go back.

He called Alan Page in Arizona.

Alan was exited and anxious when he heard the Vice President's voice. He hadn't heard anything for almost two weeks and was certainly concerned.

"Alan," began Ray, "I have good news. I have solved the money issue."

"Wonderful," sighed Alan.

"Yes, the money will be available within a week or so. I will need detailed instructions on how to deliver it."

"Fine, I will get the information right away and get back to you. Congratulations, Mr. Vice President, I am sure that you have made a good decision and a great purchase," Alan continued.

When he said that, both Ray and Alan privately broke into smiles on their respective ends of the line. They recognized that Alan just couldn't help being a salesman. They also realized that Alan had just earned a very large fee as the Eagle Scout.

After the calls, Ray again sat in silence. "I sure hope I know what I'm getting into. I could become one of the biggest tragedies in political history."

50

Over two months had passed. It was Labor Day weekend, and Ray Cartwright was back in Seattle. Even though he had been on the campaign trail for months, he would be making the official announcement of his candidacy for President at a rally on Tuesday morning.

Waterfront Park, in the center of the city, with its long open expanse that parallels the Sound and has the city skyline and the nearby mountains as a backdrop, was the ideal location for the event. There was even a bronze statue of Christopher Columbus gazing out over the water, which Ray found symbolic in many ways. Already the campaign workers were assembling the podium and bleachers, draping them with red-white-and-blue bunting, hundreds of American flags, and the now ever-present "ROC Solid" banners.

He was at home in his library, looking at the Drake document. Ten weeks had passed since he had finagled the financial deal that made it all happen.

The follow-up had been straightforward. Herb Trawets had distributed the appropriate funds to himself and Simon Katz, provided Ray with a certified check in the amount of two hundred thousand dollars payable to the bearer (which Ray had sent on to Alan Page,) and then had sent the residual two-point-three million dollars to a numbered bank account in the Bahamas; all as instructed by Alan.

Ray mused that it was interesting how the secrecy had played out: Alan Page apparently had no idea who the actual seller was; Alan and Herb, fellow book dealers in a small market, had no idea about the role each had played in the transaction; Simon Katz had no idea that the deal with the Armstrongs was just a cover for the Drake deal; and essentially everyone, including Jeremy Boucher and Colin Mackenzie, had no inkling about the existence of the Drake document. Even Alan Page's actual knowledge about its content was very limited.

Ray had decided how he was going to handle the Drake document in the long term.

Ten years from now he would have much more direct control over his finances and he would simply undertake another paperwork sleight-of-hand as he issued the funds to pay the two-and-a-half million dollars to the Armstrongs through Herb Trawets while he created a phantom invoice for the Drake document to place in his records.

He planned to continually expand his collection over that same time period; with expensive, rare publications which he would have Herb Trawets source and broker for him. This would provide Herb with an ongoing significant commission, as reward for his assistance, and would enable Ray to continue collecting without attending book fairs and dealing with many sellers – a difficult process for a President to manage.

In his will, he bequeathed his total book and map collection to the University of Washington in Seattle, to further foster information and research about the early exploration of the Pacific Northwest. He also hoped this would increase the reputation of Seattle, which, unknown to many people, had been rated as the most educated and most literate city in the country.

Thus, when the total collection became public, they would find the Drake document in the midst of the very large and valuable collection. Inside the document, he had placed a simple note, saying that he had purchased the document by promising total secrecy about the transaction, but that the need for secrecy ended with his death and he was pleased that its contents would finally become known.

Ray rationalized that this process should protect his legacy.

If the document and the deal were legitimate, he would get credit for bringing it to light, even if some people would criticize him for having held it secret for such a long time.

If it was a legitimate document, but stolen, then it would either be claimed by the rightful owner, a seeming low likelihood, or it would be claimed by some other authority such as the British government. In either case, Ray would look like a bit of a fool, but the document would become public and that would probably override anything else.

If the document was a fake, Ray would look like a dupe, but it would be in the context of a very large and extremely valuable collection that was being donated to the public. It would look like one mistake among many legitimate transactions he would have made over the years.

Besides, as with every other person who had aspired to and achieved the position of the President of the United States of America, he believed that his political achievements and legacy would dwarf any serious discussions about the details of his personal life, including his book collecting hobby.

And, who knows; perhaps after he has retired from the Presidency he will just make it all public. After all, ten or more years from now he may decide that the promise of secrecy has expired.

Meanwhile, he had the document to savor all to himself, a glorious feeling.

EPILOGUE

NOVEMBER (ONE YEAR LATER)

Epilogue

It was election night. He was seated on his patio, looking out at the glowing sunset over the ocean waves. He had a small portable television set up outside and was watching the returns as they were being reported, although there really wasn't much suspense.

The early returns from the eastern and central states showed that President-to-be Cartwright was winning by a huge landslide, a significant contrast even from the presidential election four years earlier. He was pleased with this. The new President was a good man, although now a little flawed in his eyes. He raised his glass of champagne to him in a silent toast of congratulations and thanks.

As the election details continued to come forward he turned his attention to the ledger that was open at his side, as he had often done in the past. The numbers had certainly changed over the past four years and, thus, here he was living his dream.

He thought back over the events of that time:

It hadn't been easy. There had been some close calls and surprises, but, in reality, it had all fallen into place as he had first visualized on that last election night. The ingredients were simple: an irresistible object, even if it was a mirage, and a willing target, even if he was one of the sharpest people in the world.

Actually, he believed that targeting someone as important as the Vice president helped ensure that he would be successful. People in senior positions or ones who are famous seem to come to believe that they are invulnerable. Remember the billions of dollars that Bernie Madoff scammed from celebrities in his Ponzi scheme.

The research and the mechanics of the forgery had been exhaustive but very manageable. The beauty of it all was that all of the actors in the unfolding drama had played their roles perfectly, and they didn't even know they were on the stage. Even more importantly, not a single one of them could ever link it all back to him.

The details were exquisite. "It was a work of art," he thought. "As it should be."

It had taken him over two years of diligent work. The paper, ink, typeset and cover all had to be meticulously researched and created.

Surprisingly, the paper was relatively easy to source. He was able to locate some copies of a publication from the late 1500s that were of little value, due to their limited subject matter, generally poor condition or incompleteness as a result of neglect or scavenging. In any case, all he needed was to find a limited number of sheets of quarto-sized pages from the same paper stock. Endpapers or section separations were the targets as they were blank, except for the one sheet that did have some curling-line designs printed on it, which he had used to add a flourish to the end of a book and a legitimate source of old ink.

The ink required a fair amount of research. There were many sources that described the evolution of ink over the centuries but few that described the composition in any kind of prescriptive detail. Once he had the recipe, it took patience to gather wood soot and walnut oil, among other things, from the far flung corners of the world where modern chemical pollution would not be present. As far as he knew, the Vice President had only tested ink from the last page, but it was a necessary precaution in case some additional simple tests were conducted..

The obtaining of an appropriate typeset was a bigger technical challenge. Again, with some research, he found a network of archivists and hobby book binders who had researched, sourced and maintained antique printing equipment and typesets. Over a number of months he established contact with a local group. As a result, he developed a good rapport with them and an enhanced understanding of the details of ancient printing methods. When he suggested that he would like to print a four-sheet, eight page document in old Elizabethan style, "just for the fun of it," the group fully supported him. After all, that was the kind of thing they did all the time.

Then there was the need to make the whole document look old; bright new ink on the old paper would not be acceptable. After experimenting, he found that some simple smudging and dust blowing techniques sufficed, as long as one didn't look too closely.

Creating glue that would stand up to modern chemical and aging analysis proved too difficult, but the discovery that some documents of the period were simply bound with leather thongs solved the problem. Old leather was easy to obtain.

He knew that the document could not stand up to intensive scrutiny by antiquarian book experts, but he did everything he could to limit the investigations. That was the risk and the challenge. He had sent samples to a European laboratory for analysis to be sure of what the Vice President would be told when he did his own tests. In the end, he had only hoped that his precautions and contingencies would be adequate, and they were.

The recruiting of Alan Page to make the contact and finesse the messages and logistics with Ray Cartwright was the trickiest and most vulnerable part of the whole operation. He had rightly counted on Alan's inherent desire to arrange deals and to make money with little exposure of his own. The voice that he used on the telephone contacts with Alan was easy for him to create; after all as a child he had lived in a household with a father who had been educated in English schools and later adjusted to the American way of talking. In effect, he just talked as his father had.

The Vice President's unexpected money problem did threaten the whole project, but even that, in the end, provided an extra layer of security and additional funds.

The demand for secrecy had been an integral part of the strategy. Of course, it prevented a thorough examination of the document by experts, a scrutiny that it could not withstand. As importantly, it created a plausible context for the private sale, whether it was by an English aristocrat that needed secret money or it was a stolen item from the royal archives.

He regretted that the document was a forgery. In doing his research about Drake he had become convinced that Drake had actually extended his voyage northward along the North American coast. It was quite feasible that such a document detailing the secret journey existed at one time, perhaps still hidden away in some forgotten corner of a castle or manor home.

Now that the deal was done, it really didn't matter to him when the Vice President makes the document public. It would be an embarrassment to the Vice President but, he believed, there was no way to trace the deal back to him.

It was all represented by the numbers in his ledger. The basic book deal and the recycled commissions alone had generated two-and-a-half million dollars.

As he finished perusing his accounts, he picked up the latest issue of *The Economist*. In the back pages, after the expected coverage of the American Presidential election, there was an article about a young, newly-minted billionaire from California who had prospered in the latest technology wave of high-resolution video phones. Near the end of the article was a brief summary of his personal activities, in which he was quoted as saying that, inspired by the new President, he was collecting antique books related to the discovery of western North America.

Looking back at the final glow of the sunset, as he refilled his glass, he thought, "Well, I did make two other copies." He smiled, "No, don't even think about that now; enjoy the moment."

Then he offered a toast, not to the figure being shown on the television but to himself, "Well done old man. That pirate in the Queen's Court, Sir Francis Drake, would be proud of you. "

"Yes, Yrrab, you pulled it off beautifully."

If you would like to buy another copy of this book, you can contact Trafford Publishing via their bookstore, at www.trafford.com, or by phone at 1-888-232-4444. It is also available through the major commercial websites such as Amazon, Chapters, or Barnes and Noble. Your local bookseller can certainly order it for you.

The author would appreciate hearing any comments or to know of any unintentional errors that have occurred. The beauty of on-demand printing is that corrections and modifications can easily be made for future production runs.

If you wish to pursue special events, sales promotions, author's participation, or volume purchases, please contact the author at bstewart@ barizco.com

Barry Stewart is a collector of antiquarian books and maps and avid reader of history related to the early exploration of northwest America and the Arctic. He resides in Calgary & Canmore, Alberta, and Victoria, British Columbia. He spends his winters as a snowbird in Scottsdale, Arizona. He has previously published "Across the Land…a Canadian journey of discovery," which describes Canada's people, places, history, and idiosyncrasies. (Also available from Trafford Publishing.)

From his reading and collecting, he has become a devoted admirer of Sir Francis Drake, a historic legend who was a combination mariner, explorer, military leader, privateer, and pirate.